CHRONICLES OF A CURIOUS MIND

NON OMNIS MORIAR
– Vol. III of III

Luke Lafitte

Chronicles
of a
Curious Mind
Non Omnis Moriar
"I Shall Not Wholly Die"
Books I–III

CONTENTS

We are all sleeping avatars of God, with amnesia.
Philip K. Dick

VOLUME III
BOOK I

CHAPTER I

The crowd was a boisterous lot of businessmen and children, all of whose eyes were transfixed on the tub of water in front of them. "It must be some kind of a joke — a toy boat on display — after what Marconi just wooed us with," a robust man said, a look of disgust on his face as he replaced his top hat.

I filtered through the crowd to the front of the show. I had already determined through my other temporal travels that I would have no time, pragmatic or otherwise, to look around and reflect on my environment. Go right to the source! That's what Socrates had taught me.

"Damn," I said, as a boy, who was watching whatever it was in the tub of water, twisted my ear and kicked me in the shin.

"It's just a stupid boat," he said as he left the spectacle, laughing and carrying along with his friends.

"It's no different than the human apparatus — the control relays and magnets are similar to our fundamentals related to memory," a man with a funny mustache said. He held in his hands a mechanical contraption with a small antenna at the top. "You see," he added, "it too interacts with its environment; in fact, it displays reason no different than that of yours or mine in its actions."

The crowd let out a collective laugh as he described the actions of his contraption.

"You see, humans are no different: as we learn to interact with our environment, our memory and foresight transfer messages back and forth."

A small boy picked up a stone and threw it toward the man; the man ducked while still speaking. "All wars will end because of this contraption. Because of this prototype, all wars will be fought from safe confines, miles away from the battlefields, by remote control."

I had made it to the front. It was nothing more than a remote-controlled boat attempting to complete some simple exercises in a tub of water. No wonder the crowd was so displeased.

"Did you see what Marconi did at the exhibition yesterday?" one of the men asked another.

The other man excitedly responded, "All the papers are talking about it, and so is the president."

"Talking about what?" I asked.

One of the men smirked, looked over at me, and chuckled. "The pyramids exhibit was last year. This fair is supposed to be about the future."

"The pharaohs still walk around in their tunics in the future, I guess," the other man said as he attempted to yank my toga off my shoulder.

It's not a tunic, I thought to myself. Nevertheless, I wasn't interested in discussing my linen outfit, which was from the time of Socrates.

"Yeah, that's right; I'm a holdover from last year. So, what was Marconi's trick?" I asked, knowing full well that

Marconi was one of the kings of the wireless revolution of the late nineteenth century.

A young man next to me started speaking. "He detonated an explosion with no wires — sliced right through the ether. No toys, no tricks. The idea of being able to blow things up with just a switch is better than the light bulb itself, considering what's going on with the fleets in Europe."

"The fleets in Europe?" I asked.

"The arms race," the young man excitedly said.

Apparently, belligerent countries in Europe were on a shipbuilding spree in the attempt to sway opponents away from conflict.

"It doesn't work," I said.

"What's that?" the young man asked.

"The arms race." It was funny: whenever I heard *arms race*, I thought of the Soviets. "Ships don't deter others from war, they don't spell mass destruction for the human race — it's a zero-sum game."

The man with the mustache began to speak to the crowd again. "Soon, there will be weapons of war that will cause carnage the likes of which man has never seen. If war is not controlled by automatons, the human race will surely perish."

"And what fun is a war controlled from thousands of miles away?"

A cackle roared out from the crowd.

"Don't tell that to Secretary Roosevelt," the young man proclaimed. "Remote-controlled boats doing the jobs of men? It's ludicrous." Then he turned to me. "What's your name?"

After telling him my name and learning that his was Marmaduke III, I learned that we were at the World's Fair in New York City, with its grand expositions and showmen revealing present and future innovations. But I had heard of the man with the mustache who was controlling the boat with a handheld device.

"Where is this Tesla from?" I asked.

"Croatia," Marmaduke said. "There's even a rumor that he's a vampire, related to Vlad Dracula, and that when he was in the mountains during the war he got lost and fed off the blood of dead soldiers. Others say he's a demon or a witch who tries to turn machines into humans."

"My God," I said underneath my breath, full of excitement.

It dawned on me that Tesla was the one who had created the blueprints for the time logos.

Marmaduke was tugging on my toga, although I wasn't listening to my new friend. Instead, from afar, I stared deep into the despondent eyes of Tesla, a man who was neither a showman nor an inventor; rather, he was a mythic sorcerer who had departed his homeland for the urban jungle of the new world. He had entered this pastoral garden with nothing more than the ideas in his head.

"How can I meet him?" I asked Marmaduke.

"Why would you want to meet Tesla? My family knows the likes of Marconi, Edison, Thompson, and Fessenden. He's a charlatan, that Tesla."

I looked over at Marmaduke, who was dressed in the finest linens of late-nineteenth-century urban America.

"No," I said, "I think he's much more than a mere charlatan."

"Come, James," Marmaduke said.

I watched as Tesla turned his back on the crowd, apparently wondering why this American audience was not enthralled with a machine that would lead to the future of robotics and mankind's singular fusion with technology.

The music that played while we exited the fair was a conflation of Wagner and Bach — a mash-up of compositions.

"Synergy is in the air, James," Marmaduke said. "I've been working on my own inventions. With Father's funding, anything's possible."

The sky opened, and I saw New York City, partially finished. America's virginal garden was transforming itself into an urban jungle, and within this jungle was a gang of apes: the barons of Wall Street.

We stepped into a bar. "He's from the exposition," Marmaduke told the man behind the counter.

The man exclaimed loudly, "We don't serve lunatics here; send them to the dark room." He was a red-faced Irish bastard, but the whiskey he served up was no different than the nectar of the gods.

"They're like gods, James," Marmaduke said.

"Who?" I asked.

"The inventors of this age. Some mean people like my father, but I think the imaginative innovators are the true angels of this New Jerusalem."

"New Jerusalem?"

"That's what the country is transforming itself into, finding its destiny through inventions. Those inventions glue us together — give us a collective meaning. Pops says people don't worship the railroad anymore; they worship the light bulb."

"The light bulb," I said, an implacable smile on my face.

Something was strange about this tavern. There were so many sad faces — hard-looking faces. They looked soulless, almost lifeless.

Two men joined us at the counter and began discussing something important with Marmaduke.

"He's had a long trip from Egypt-land," one of the men said, glancing at me.

"Looks like it," the man with the cleft chin echoed.

"I'm gonna put my head down on this counter for a moment, Duke the Third," I mumbled out of my drunken mouth.

❧

I found myself in a house and in the presence of Benjamin Franklin.

"Manifest the source of life and you manifest life itself," Franklin said as he shuffled back and forth from one room to the next, a boyish excitement in his mannerisms. "Look outside, James," he said as he pointed, his hand shaking from the excitement of what he saw.

Through a window, I saw there was a boy on a nearby river being pulled along, against the current, by a powerful wind.

"It's me, James," he said. "The god of water was obsequious to the god of wind."

The boy version of Franklin was content on the river; the large kite that he looked upon imbued him with power, the type of power that communicates the laws of nature to the secondary attributes of the conscious mind.

There was a storm brewing outside. Franklin gathered his materials and tools, opened the front door, and said loudly, "Shut the garage door."

I pushed a button next to the house's front door and heard the sound of a garage door shutting behind me.

"Turn the fax machine on," he said.

I looked over to the corner of the room. A fax machine hooked up to a telephone jack lay next to the wall. I flipped it on.

"And bring the remote for the television set."

Franklin had a big-screen TV; I sat down on the couch next to it and turned it on with the remote.

An episode of *Archie Bunker* was on. Onscreen, Archie sat in the middle of a room and pointed at me. Richard Nixon was next to him; they both called me terrible names and made me cry.

"The gods of wind and water war with each other, and you sit here and worship the gods of tubes," Franklin said as he lifted me off the couch and pushed me out the front door. "Don't listen to that old Nixon, but remember the bull's-eye. Never forget the great archer you learned about. We had to place Nixon in your reality so you would realize the value of Archie Bunker."

"What are you talking about?" I asked.

"Tie these together," Franklin said as he gave me a large skeleton key and a string.

"The string experiment," I said.

"Sort of," Franklin said, "but the one you're thinking of was in another reality — my reality. This is your reality, James, so the experiment's a little different."

"In what way?" I asked.

"Just watch."

Sure enough, the kite went up in the air, storm clouds gathered around it, and electric charges lit up the kite and transferred its energy to the key.

As the rain poured and the thunder clapped, Franklin yelled, "Now cut the string, James. Cut the string."

As I cut the string, the key became charged with more energy and the kite began to fly on its own. There was a new sense of communication through the triangle that had formed through the symbiosis of Franklin, the key, and the kite.

"Control and communication without wires, that's the future of everything. This is just the beginning. One day, Earth will be known as 'Edison.'"

❧

My head was throbbing. In the tavern, the man with the cleft chin was speaking to Duke.

"I've got a secret that's even bigger than Marconi's detonation system," Duke slurred out of the side of his mouth.

It seemed as though he'd let out a few too many secrets during my blackout.

"Get the boys two more drinks," the other man said.

"My father told me about it; he's working on a creation beyond all of our wildest dreams," Duke said.

The two men spurred him on, encouraging his yearning to tell the secrets his father had bestowed upon him.

"It's the ideal woman he works on. She's frozen in time, just like the voices of the angels and God — and if he had been alive back then, he would have captured their voices too."

The men laughed and slapped us both on the back.

The door to the bar flung open, blinding light from the urban jungle slicing through the dusty ether and illuminating the decayed faces at the bar. *New York's finest,*

I thought. I couldn't tell if it was the police, gang members, or hired mercenaries coming in.

The two men stood up, spit on the floor, and walked past the new arrivals.

"Hired hands, no different than the bloody Pinkertons," I said. I took the next shot of whiskey and readied myself for a fight.

"Slow down, James," Duke said. He indicated they were his father's guards.

"Mr. Astor, your father awaits your assistance."

"My father knows I'm out drinking and whoring today; it's my workday, remember."

The guards stepped a little closer, a little too close for my liking.

I guess I was what Father called an angry drunk, since this was the first time I had ever drunk liquor and all I wanted to do was fight. No wonder Father's church folk were always fighting after drinking too much.

The scuffle was short-lived.

"Don't bruise their faces, McBride," one of the men said. They weren't guards after all.

Once they placed hoods over our heads and threw us in the back seat of a car, Duke murmured something to me.

"Phantoms, James."

"What's that?" I asked.

"What Edison is creating: phantoms, human replicas of ourselves. It's why Tesla's boat makes people laugh. They fear it, and they have to think of things they fear in terms of the absurd."

"The absurd?"

"That's right. Ever since Darwin pushed them off their pedestals, everything has been going in the direction of the absurd. If you ask me, there's a storm coming."

Little did he know that his predictions were not themselves absurd; rather, his proselytizing wasn't too far off from the reality that would come.

"Tell me more about the phantoms," I said.

The car came to a screeching halt.

"Separate them," a voice yelled.

A hand reached around my neck and pulled me out of the car.

CHAPTER II

The sound of farm animals rustling around was all I could make out. I managed to untie my hands and take off the hood. I was upstairs, inside the biggest barn I had ever seen.

I heard a grinding noise come from the eastern side of the barn.

Three men were below me, working on a conveyor belt that had numerous machines moving in tandem on it.

"He wants this entire barn transformed into his laboratory," one said.

The men were the same ones who had accosted Duke and me.

"We would have better luck burning the whole damn thing down and rebuilding it."

"He likes the seclusion, doesn't he?" another asked.

They were still tinkering with the machinery.

"I'd want seclusion too if I were a sorcerer. If you ask me, we're supporting the work of the devil. I say we sabotage the whole thing and count our blessings."

"We don't work for him. Keep that in mind."

"And what of the boy?"

The barn door opened, the stench of manure fusing with the fresh smell of grass and usurping the barn's air.

The man who entered was dressed in a rather queer-looking robe — like the Gandalf of the late nineteenth century. John Jacob Astor, one of the richest men in the States. I didn't remember if he was oil, steel, banking, or none of the above.

"Seems we have a bit of a problem, gentlemen," Astor said as he pulled something from underneath his cloak.

"We followed him to the exhibition and then lost him in the Marconi crowd," one of the other men acknowledged.

"And you let him speak to another," Astor said as he walked over to the conveyor belt. "Look at these machines, each doing such simple acts; yet, collectively, when these machines act together, they appear to be part of a rational activity, like they are thinking."

One of the men was on both knees, praying to Astor for his forgiveness. "Tell the Master we ask for forgiveness. We won't fail His Highest again."

A beam of light came from a device Astor held in his hand, and the man on bent knee vanished.

The other men dropped to their knees.

"Don't forget whom you worship, gentlemen," Astor said.

The wood beneath me cracked, the floor beneath caved in, and I went with it. I plummeted to the ground, headfirst.

Time was relative to my falling, for in that moment, the past, present, and future showed their illusory selves, and I remembered what the Captain told me when we were in the caves: "Reality does not change. What we experience as real does appear to change from time to time, as each time actualizes for itself the different paths of human consciousness and the different energies that accompany the possible and impossible."

۶

"I'm the spirit that you run from; I'm the impossible," a gray alien said as it and other little creatures set me on an operating table. My bodily apparatus was all but paralyzed.

"We've come a long way to find you, through numerous portals and universes," one of the green ones said. His eyes were the size of large dark almonds.

Images appeared on the inside walls of the spaceship. The aliens began to look upon my memories in awe — they were perplexed and confused. Almost all of my memories were of the fictive and imaginary: *Star Wars*, Transformers, and G.I. Joe; zombies, vampires, and superheroes. They were witnesses to the impossible: they saw in my memories what culture had taught me I had the potential to achieve, but what reality denied.

"How did you come to possess this forbidden knowledge?" the same green one asked.

"I'll show you," I said.

The ship landed on a distant planet. I led the aliens out to a raging dust storm high in the mountains. I ordered the greens and the grays to dig.

Once they found the dinosaur bones, they began reconstructing the forms of the ancient beings.

The same green came to me and said, "You worship the superheroes."

I nodded.

The dinosaurs came to life and told the aliens stories that the latter already knew — the aliens were merely having their ancient memories refreshed. The impossible must always be refreshed in the universe's collective memory bank.

The Captain was there, along with all the books from the caves. He stood among the aliens and dinosaurs, handing out the books. "To refresh your memories of what you already know," the Captain said.

Socrates too was among the aliens, and he was especially attuned to the needs of the grays. "When James read Plato's *Phaedra* at the age of thirteen, it was as if he learned nothing new; rather, it was a re-acquaintance with an old friend from which the space and time continuum had separated him," he said.

୬

The blurred vision of Duke came into focus. The Victorian room smelled of fresh roses; my bed was soft as a bundle of feathers.

"I'm sorry, James," Duke said, fidgeting with a sound-recording device. "You'll get permission from the Master. I should have known you were not from this time."

How Marmaduke knew I had traveled through time was unknown to me — until his father entered the room.

"By God, it worked in your culture, didn't it, James? Man has the potentialities to unlock the universe's differing energies and allow the conscious mind to jump to other colors on the consciousness spectrum," Astor said. He paced around the room, his hand holding his chin in a delicate cradle of nervousness and excitement.

"Father, do we ask him about the history?" Duke asked.

"What is it you want to know?" I replied. I was in no position to hide the truth from these people; they had handed the blueprints down to Van Coleman and Abraxus.

"Does this mean he wins in the end?" Marmaduke asked.

"The sorcerer defeats the wizard." Astor turned to the window, looking at all the numerous inventions hidden in the virginal garden of his plantation. "We won't tell the Master; it's too dangerous. Nor will you tell us why you are here, or any of your history, James. As far as you're concerned, this is your culture and we don't need the pestilence of your consciousness invading it." Astor walked over to me. "You look like you've seen the necromancers, James; I assure you we will do you no harm..."

"Then what is my use to you? Let me go back to the portal and leave this place."

"We do have a need for you," Astor said.

I didn't want to stay, but I also knew that my culture and consciousness could coexist with those belonging to these people. There was a reality I could see now — a liminal threshold I had crossed with the help of the Captain and Socrates.

"In your time, James, they are probably simply known as great inventors — always the rational materialists. That's the direction this country is going in, toward the damn teachings of Newton and Darwin. There's no room for your mystical teachings," Astor said. "We'll take him to the Master's laboratory and let him see that between A and B there is a gap as mighty as the abyss itself."

Hearing all of this reminded me of reading the great philosophers when I was younger. This knowledge was always present in my universal memory; it just needed to be recalled to the table of conscious reality.

This world too — which held my blueprint, my DNA, and of which I had spoken in another world — I would not leave this world alive.

"Don't think, when you meet the Master, that we must choose between sorcery and wizardry: that's the conclusion I'm sure your culture draws from the tiny spectrum of white light you're able to see. There's the letter X that lies between A and B," Astor said as he walked out of the room, still holding his chin.

Wearing a new set of clothes, I followed Duke to the barn. He wanted to show me a new invention the Master had given him before we traveled to New Jersey.

"Move the hay out of the way," Duke said. He unlocked the small door on the floor. "There's a latch on the bottom of the floor. Lift it toward yourself." The animals rustled about us, all curious as to our endeavor.

One by one, we dropped through the opening into a small tunnel that one could only move through on hands and knees.

"Is this safe?" I asked. Perhaps this place would become my catacombs, the underbelly of Orwell's *Animal Farm*. Just how I had imagined.

"You'll be able to smell the engines when we get there, James. Just keep crawling," Duke said.

I tried to discern his figure through the darkness. A dim light sparkled through the particles of dirt in the air, reflecting a kaleidoscope of colors — the spectrum of refracted mysticism.

The tunnel opened to an empty room, save a few sheep in the corner.

"Where's the invention?" I asked. I looked around for the machines with which I had thought the room would be rife.

"You're in it, James," Duke said.

"In what?"

"The machine."

His lips were no longer moving, nor was his voice making any sound, but I could hear Duke's thoughts. I could understand him.

"I've seen this trick before."

"There are no tricks here, James," Duke said, without saying it.

The potentialities for the utilization of other energies were tapped in this world. That threshold, or some threshold, was crossed, which my culture viewed as impossible.

"It's only impossible because your culture has already chosen to utilize other energies — there's always a trade-off, James, that's what the Master says."

"This room: by what is it charged? Electricity?"

"It's called Eros," Duke said.

"'Eros': that means love."

"No, it means magnetism."

As I looked over at the sheep, which I expected to speak to me, I noticed that they all moved with the same rhythm.

"Vital machines, James. All their tissues are created through the force of Eros."

"Clones?" I said.

"Phantoms," Duke responded, "phantoms of their own likeness."

He explained that having vital machines in the room better charged the ether of the Eros to deal with input — the two of us being the input, of course.

"But we can't understand what they say."

Duke laughed. "The sheep? I highly doubt sheep have spirits, James."

Then I witnessed the truly impossible: my watch began to talk.

I must have fainted and passed out into yet another dream, I thought.

Duke could barely contain himself. "It's not a dream — and you're from the future. Jesus, it's as if you're from the past."

"Machines can speak?" I said. "But animals can't."

"Animals that are purely mechanical can, but not ones that are purely organic. That's why the sheep are vital to this experiment. They're a little of both, or, like I said before, they're vital machines."

The watch was telling me all about time, teaching me Einstein's theory of relativity years before Einstein.

"I take it you don't have machines that talk in the future?" Duke inquired.

I thought for a moment. "We have computers; they speak to us."

"What powers them?"

I didn't exactly know how to respond to that. Was it merely electricity that powered computers, or was it programming goals and knowledge, passed on like an evolutionary chain from human to machine?

"Electricity," I said.

"Sounds like the Dark Ages," Duke responded.

"How do you shut it off — the Eros?" I asked.

"Follow me."

I followed Duke out of the room, and the ether of the Eros was gone. We could communicate and sense the world again by normal means.

"The Master says the world is merely a machine that creates gods."

I hadn't heard the word "god" in a long while. With all this talk of masters, wizards, and sorcery, I had thought this culture and world was certainly devoid of gods.

"There's another storm brewing, James," Duke said as we reentered the rational world of animals in the barn.

The walls started to shake because of wind.

"Are the walls also able to speak?" I asked.

"Do people still have faith in your time, James?" Duke climbed up a ladder.

I looked up at all the cobwebs and clutter, the ceiling of the barn allowing in streams of light through the decayed beams of wood. It almost reminded me of European cathedrals, and I thought of home. "I thought your father asked us not to speak of my time. My relationship with the word 'faith' is probably different than what you mean by it."

"In what way?" Duke asked.

I didn't even remember what my faith had been back in my birth world. It seemed so far away. I remembered a Professor Elaine Pagels explaining to me how the word "faith" signified merely a unity of relationships, nothing more or less. I would have to disagree with her now. Nor was the world full of relative moments of experience. Nor was it a mere bipolar exchange of opposites that therein created a synthesis of existence and history.

"I think my world had a faith that was moving toward something special. We were moving somewhere... What's your faith?"

"Come up here and I'll show you," Duke said.

I climbed the ladder, which was different than climbing the tree up which Socrates had sent me.

Numerous jars of powder lined the windowsill.

"Lie down," Duke said.

"And do what?"

"Just relax, James. Pretend it's a dream. You do dream, don't you?"

If he only knew how important my dreams were to my reality. And after this experience in the barn, my dreams had become more cardinal to my experience. My dreams filled in the gaps between the real and the fictive; indeed, my dreams were a hybrid of the real and the fictive, which is what I had learned the meaning of life constituted.

Duke placed powder tablets in my mouth, eyes, and underarms. He said some mystical word over and over again. It reminded me of how important words were to the Captain in changing one's consciousness.

CHAPTER III

Then, there were large fish surrounding me. I was deep within the darkness of the ocean's depths. There was no direction and there were all directions; there was negative and positive. There was no light from below, only the sky of infinite water's darkness: the appearance of infinite water. I didn't know if there was air or sky above the ocean; in my mind, all was water.

"They found another one," a fish called out to me.

"Follow us," another of the group of Bluefin said as he went by me.

My fish instincts shot me off after my peers. They all were quite concerned about what had been found.

"It's the fourth one in five days," one said.

"It's still unknown where it came from."

"It's a sign from above."

"Perhaps it just appeared. It will change all our religious beliefs."

"It will change science."

"The others are all going into the caves to worship the greens."

There was so much chatter between the fish that I still couldn't quite make out what was going on.

And there it was, stuck in the ocean floor for all to see.

"They say it just appeared," one of the fish said. "There are even symbols on it."

I swam around it. Somehow I knew that it was a frying pan, stuck in the mud, its handle reaching out. One symbol the fish were so perplexed by was the word "DuPont."

A large eel came out from a sandy opening in the ground and said the object came from above. It was made of material that was foreign to the eels.

I was reminded of *2001: A Space Odyssey*, the film in which apes are unable to understand a monolith from space.

૨૭

I looked down at the bone I gnawed on: it tasted bitter.

My prehistoric surroundings maintained all the colors of the spectrum. When I attempted to conjure up words and speak, I merely made sounds that the apes understood but were obscure to me. I knew what I was trying to communicate in my head, but it never transferred to the physical aspect of speech.

The clouds were growing dark, the winds spurring up momentum. I sensed the smell of electricity in the air.

A bolt of lightning struck a tree, causing great commotion among the apes. They all dispersed into a set of nearby caves. My curiosity drove me to follow them.

There were two caves I could enter.

The cave I entered, to the left, was a place of worship. Inside, naked apes were on their knees praying to three apes clothed in long robes. They were making chants that sounded almost like words, but I still could not decipher the meaning.

There were symbols drawn on the walls of the cave: bolts of lightning, the sun, the moon, and a large brain.

On top of the symbols were the words "Sea of Saragossa." More naked apes came in from the storm with limbs that had fallen, I supposed, from the lightning-hit tree. The limbs were still burning from the lightning bolt.

Fire was born from the unknown, and the impossible began to be realized.

I left the first cave and entered the second. Inside, numerous naked apes were using their hands and bodies, experimenting with rocks and wood. Three of the apes were elevated above the cave floor, hovering in the air. They wore laboratory coats.

The laboratory was different than their place of worship, and yet it was entirely the same. There were no symbols on the walls in this cave; rather, there were numerous tools and gadgets lying around.

"*James,*" Duke said, in the form of one of the elevated apes, speaking to me telepathically. "*This is your culture, James.*" He came down from the scientific pedestal. "*I take it this is where you feel the most comfortable: the cave of the material and the rational.*"

"No," I said. The initiation with the Captain and Socrates, even to a certain extent Frederick, had turned my world upside down. Once an ardent materialist who worshipped the practicality of American pragmatism, I was now and would be forever an idealist, knowing full well the material world was merely a double-sided hologram.

"That's what your culture chooses to believe in, an either-or: the real or the fictive, the religious or the scientific."

"I guess," I said.

"And what of the impossible? What does your culture associate with the impossible?" Duke asked.

"I don't know," I said. "The fictional or impossible is made up of superheroes, myths, and monsters — merely childlike fantasies."

"Exclusionary."

"In what sense?" I asked.

"Your priests and scientists are the same: both exclude some of the most important aspects of life," Duke said.

"What is it they exclude?" I asked.

The apes around us were now making smoke and conducting other experiments.

"Do you still worship your Darwinian past and only reflect upon the fossils of the past, not those of the future?"

"No," I said. All the while I could not help but think how the Captain finished it. On the third day he arose from the dead!

The other worlds I had encountered were different: the other worlds I had visited, in the end, had made sense to my materialistic mind accustomed to cause and effect. This world verged on the surreal; it was the dreamlike fantasy of a child imagining a state of being. The new consciousness that the Captain had brought down to earth with him had changed my very existence, allowing space for passion, wonder and empathy like his first coming, but this time there was space for the divine higher self devoid of fear and hubris.

"I'll show you my culture now," Duke said.

I followed him out of that cave and into his. Wizards, witches, and sorcerers... they all milled about in Duke's cave. A few of them were looking down a well.

I walked over to the well, looked down, and saw the others were studying the apes' actions.

"The apes in my culture are different than those in your thoughts, James," Duke whispered aloud. The Captain had taught me that humans are not evolved from apes; rather, apes are a degenerate from of humans, those humans that attempted to become dense too quickly. They attempted to enter the new consciousness without first the fragmentation or initiation taking place.

I asked, "Is it the past or the future?"

"Both," Duke said.

There were apes that caused combustion and fire to appear with no natural interference or exclusions. Others displayed an amorphous form of communication, similar to the method by which Duke and I had communicated in the room filled with Eros. Teleportation, telekinesis, and the power of the mind to manipulate the elements were all on display.

"It's not an exclusionary system like your culture has; James; your sciences and religion all exclude so much. Even your much-cherished Darwin's theory excludes half of the entire equation of life's enigma: the future."

Some sorcerers were throwing items down the well to the apes. The apes looked back up at us through the well's tunnel.

"The apes know where their impossible and fantastic things come from, but your Darwinian fish had no clue where the frying pan came from," Duke said.

"It's a fiction," I said.

"No, James, it's the future pulling the past forward. It's memories of the past and foresight of the future joined as one. It's remembering the reality of your modern fiction..."

CHAPTER IV

I sat up, in the barn again, sweating profusely. "There were no wires. How did you do it?"

"It's what the Master is perfecting: wireless communication, the start of the control revolution. Angels, demons, elves, fairies, and, now, aliens, all come from the same place, James, that generator of ideas and perceptions we call the mind, projected by the individual whirlpools we call the brain," Duke said. He levitated from the top of the barn to the floor.

I was witnessing a kind of fossil record. It was not the type of fossil data that scientists in my own time would study; rather, it was a fossil record of the impossible, of the mistakes and aberrations of time that could tell us about the past and future of human consciousness and development.

Through the crescendo of thunder and lightning outside, Duke and I heard some commotion back at the house.

"What is it?" I asked as we unlatched the barn door.

"The sorcerer, James, he's finally come to speak with Father."

We ran to the house. At the front door, in all his glory, was the man who had controlled the toy boat at the exhibit: Nikola Tesla. Two extremely small bald men, each carrying a large suitcase of similar make, accompanied him.

We followed the group in and awaited Duke's father's presence in the den. Astor had been down in the wine cellar since my last meeting with him.

"I hear your boat exhibit went as well with the crowd as the Walker brothers' chess-playing hoax, Tesla." Astor walked in, carrying two bottles of wine. He poured us drinks while he spoke of the storm. "It's that time of the year when all the natural sources into which man is able to tap make themselves alive and useful, isn't it, Nick?"

The two men beside Tesla did not blink. They were either robots or aliens, certainly not human.

"I helped you with your oscillators, and I'll fund your boat project, but I'll be damned if I pay for your vampire and leprechaun fairy tales," Astor lashed out. He was becoming a little inebriated.

I started downing the wine. I was a bit of a lush in this world.

Tesla was not a showman, as had been evident at the exhibition, but he was a storyteller. "I know now how much you cherish your beloved wizard," Tesla said. He stood up while the two men on his sides shut their eyes. "As a young man in Croatia, I was left for years in the mountains, where I found my forefathers and foremothers. They were the people you folks here, in America, murdered: witches and demons. Those were the priests in the mountains — those were our scientists."

"We didn't burn all of them," Astor said.

"I know," Tesla responded. "I know that his blood is the blood of the Magonia, the land of the clouds." He turned to Marmaduke and myself, saying, "He is the bastard great-grandchild of a witch and an alchemist." Then he turned to Astor. "It's true, isn't it, that your cherished Master is the demon-child of a witch?"

He threw some documents on the table. I could see *Trials and Tribunals of Bay Colony* printed on the top. "Read it," Tesla said.

Astor's cronies entered the room as Duke's father spoke. "Blackmail, is that it? You tell the public that their much-cherished Wizard of Menlo Park is the son of demons." Astor was trying to figure out what Tesla wanted.

"Seclusion," Tesla said. He didn't want the pageantry that other inventors sought. Rather, he yearned for the environment that had fostered his first thought of the imaginary and fantastic.

Objects in the room started to move. Books flew off the shelves, like birds searching for prey.

"In Croatia," Tesla said, "they called them vampires or elves. In America and Western Europe, you called them witches and demons. We fought wars over the powers they brought. Here, you burned them, never even giving them a fighting chance." He began to morph into an animal state, his fangs glistening in the flickering light.

Dr. Rush had told me about the witch trials in the Bay Colony. He had even explained that Cotton Mather's father, Increase Mather, was one of the judges. However, he had been bothered by the direct eyewitness accounts. All had seen the same thing: specifically, telekinesis, shape-shifting, and teleportation.

"He says he's from the future," Marmaduke uttered under his breath, mesmerized by the show on display. "That there are past lives and future lives — maybe he will be you in the future, James, or you have been him, if that makes any sense."

It made more sense to me than Marmaduke actually knew. I was beginning to question whether it was the machine that had been sending me through time. Perhaps my own mental ability was teleporting me through space and time; perhaps I had died during the imbroglio in St. Peter's. Maybe I was reincarnated into a past life.

"There's a chance you can still stop him," Tesla told Astor as the two robot men reached out their hands, grabbed Astor's cronies, and disappeared.

It was a scene straight out of *The Matrix*; instead of revealing a blue or red pill, however, Tesla placed a talking doll on the table at the center of the room, along with his boat from the exhibition. He suddenly grew a long beard and looked as though he were trying to placate wizards of the imagination.

Then he spoke. "This country will soon find itself in a control and communication revolution. If you choose the talking doll's approach, you take the materialistic and rational path, and then, I say, you will be slaves to your machines and move toward your prehistoric destiny of ignorance and destruction. If you choose the boat's approach, you will see the potentialities of the impossible."

Tesla revealed a box filled with books, patted Marmaduke on the shoulder, and added, "Don't be fooled by that wizard. He's a charlatan to his own blood." Then he showed his fangs and disappeared.

The doll was still speaking in rhythmic word games.

Every act before me was reality; it was a fantastic reality of the imagination and unconscious coming to life. At this same time, Freud was delineating his views of the human psyche. Socrates and the Captain had spent their whole lives attempting to figure out the essence of reality. Tesla, by all appearances, had spent his life trying to figure out the possible of the impossible or the consciousness of the unconsciousness.

In the box of books, Tesla had left Marmaduke the following: Hawthorne's "The Artist of the Beautiful" and "Rappaccini's Daughter," Melville's "The Bell Tower," and Poe's "The Man Who Was Used Up." Everyone leaves symbols and messages, clues to the spirit that they can't explain in words. In this way they communicate with others on a psychic level that far transcends our mere language, which has been shown to turn on itself in an endless loop of bipolar collusion.

That evening, I was in bed, skimming the material Tesla had left Duke. Poe's "The Man Who Was Used Up" was a story about a man made up entirely of prosthetics; Melville's "The Bell Tower" told of the death of an inventor who had stolen into nature to create an automaton; and Hawthorne's "Rappaccini's Daughter" and "The Artist of the Beautiful" both showed man's sorcerous creations, replicas of nature's mysterious, magical activation of life.

"Go to sleep," Duke said as he took the books away from me. "We'll see him again tomorrow under the falls."

CHAPTER V

An extreme light shone through the window, freezing me physically. Mentally, I flew out of my body and draped myself in my Superman cape. I too was alien to this planet.

"The stars are no longer dormant," the alien in control of the beam said once I was transported to the ship.

I looked out the ship's windows. The stars were shining in the sky. "They appear dormant during the day," I said, gesturing at the stars.

"Yet they are, still, and always have been there," the alien responded. "And so too have all of the other powers you choose to suppress."

I scanned the ship, assiduously looking through every crevice for evidence of some ardent plan to destroy Earth. There must be some recalcitrant aliens.

I told them to take me to Niagara Falls to meet with Tesla. They shook their heads and opposed my directive. However, they soon realized that my directive was the only order they could take. They were my unconscious thoughts; they were my myths, my religion, and my reality.

Once we flew through the falling waters and entered Tesla's seemingly innocuous bat cave, we found him ensconced in a levitated state of magnetic ecstasy.

"Wake," I called out to him. After he did so, I gave him an order. "Leave these people alone."

"It's too late," he said. "My ideas and thoughts have already infiltrated their ether and invaded their brains. The world is composed of more than mere matter and material. Ideas are more concrete. They bring about more change in what our senses perceive than any elemental addition to our reality can."

The aliens behind me were fearful of Tesla. Their technology was no match for his mental prowess.

"They know it's not magic, James, or the faith of an interpreted religion. The aliens are your angels and your demons. They are your Superman and Rasputin. They are your Jesus and your Napoleon. They are the emergence of the fantastic reality within our fictive reality."

The aliens backed into their saucer and left.

"You intend to kill the Master, the wizard?" I asked.

"In your cape you have the same powers that I do, James, but what do you use them for? Why does Superman do what he does? That is the question, is it not?" He picked up a book entitled *Chronicles of a Curious Mind*, by Dr. L. S. Lafitte, and threw it toward my feet. "I offer you what the aliens offer: a different path to human potential. I'm like you, James, in the fictive and the real. I, like your character — the one that another has written for you — will perish in a great fire. But, unlike you, I also know I have the ability to interfere with and direct the writings of my author — and, in the end, I'm sure my ideas will win out. That's all I seek."

CHAPTER VI

The dew on the leaves dripped through the maze of veins that pushed the life force of water through the leaf. I looked around and found myself immersed in a land of shrubbery and trees. The barn was hundreds of yards away, the house behind me beckoning.

I dropped to my knees and puked up the red wine I had ingested prior to sleep. The smell of the grass transported me back to other worlds and memories of life.

As I walked back to the house, I saw a garden sunk deep within the ground, lit up by Edison's newfangled light bulbs. The spectacle was that of the sublime ecstasy that invention breeds in the unconscious, that which comes out in the very pores of man.

I sat down in the sunken garden, imagining myself playing hide-and-seek with Mother. Lights were refracted through the fountains' water. The circularity of life appeared to me, like a snake attempting to swallow itself rather than a perfect circle of the infinite.

"Is the Tesla in your dreams a projection of the real or the imaginary?" a voice asked. Lights were beaming behind the apparition. The phantom's materiality was one of immense intrigue: it was a hyphenated hybrid of material and celluloid projection.

"I passed away that day." Father exhaled and sat next to me. "And so did you."

I looked at Father's glassy eyes. "But the time logos—the worlds I've been to—"

Father told me how the machine had failed and my body was found, crisp and burnt. Upon finding me, Father had killed himself.

"It's funny, James, I never knew that living is the heaven the spirits seek — it all seems a bit backward after death, doesn't it?" He appeared confused but also at peace with the absurdity that was the afterlife. He had never understood the absurdity of life: that was his problem. He had tried to rationalize the irrational, naturalize the supernatural, and materialize the immaterial.

Now that I reflected, or refracted, on the meeting with my father's apparition, I remembered the paranormal, like all things in life or death, must be met on its own terms, not ours.

I looked up at Father and said, "The Master is Edison, isn't he?"

"Edison is a wizard, Tesla a sorcerer," Father said in a mocking voice.

I didn't feel dead; it was still a materialistic existence. And while the ghosts and aliens in this world had never eaten or defecated in front of me, I had done so. I surely thought those variables would have dissipated in death.

"I had a purpose in every world but this one, Father. This world seems to have no Archimedes point, no end that coalesces."

"That's death, James; you no longer have an author writing your life."

"How do I gain control of it? How do I call upon the writer to focus on my character again?"

"If I explained to you what Tesla and Edison were doing in this world, you wouldn't be needed any more — you would cease to exist."

"But I'm dead," I said.

"So am I. What does it matter?"

This was like talking to a transparent brick wall. I was getting fewer answers from a dead father than one who was alive and still internally dead.

Nevertheless, I wasn't alone in the garden when I cried. Father held me, and whether we were both dead and alive didn't matter, both then and now.

"We don't live on a hyphenated plane of existence, James. I used to think this world was placed between a good world and an evil one — that we possessed the potential for both. Now I see that existence is not in any way Manichean; rather, it is layers of potential energies waiting to be released at the moment the new consciousness arrives."

"James," a voice bellowed from behind the trees. Duke's face appeared through the moonlight, Edison's light bulbs fading ever so graciously.

Father stood up. "Hello, my friend."

Duke said nothing; he just stood, like a statue.

"Can you see him?" I asked Duke.

"As sure as day," he said. Shakespeare's *Hamlet* called out to me from the past or perhaps the future. I could never quite determine why some thought Hamlet mad for seeing ghosts when other characters in the play saw the same thing. Perhaps Duke was merely pacifying me, playing the part of an actor in front of a green screen.

"I see him," Duke said. "I see all the projections from your brain, James." He turned to my father. "Any advice for us?"

Father took a few steps toward the flowers in the garden and spoke of cross-pollination. He described dimensions of new lights and refractions of spectrums. Then Father took off his necklace of the cross, which had been draped around his neck, and placed it in my hands. "I replace the apple that Queen Guinevere placed in your hand with the power of the cross, James. This is the meaning of life."

The cross, at this juncture in my existence, was the meaning I had been searching for in life and, now, death. The cross was more than a mere symbol. It was divinity transferred into the material: the realization of the human as divine and godlike. The cross, I realized, was like a legal document placed in front of a testifying witness to refresh his or her memory. It was a symbol used to refresh our memories: the memories of divine powers and the invisible reality that, at some point in our evolutionary development, we had killed. So the philosopher who had once said we killed God was right. However, little did he realize at the time we had not killed some perfect being above and beyond our rational comprehension; rather, we had killed a part of ourselves. We had checked ourselves into a mental hospital and lobotomized our brains — that was how we killed God; that was why God was dead — but the cross reminded us we could bring God back.

A large disc-shaped object flew overhead and beamed a light down upon the image of Father. With that, he was gone.

"I've always wondered where the ships go after they do their business," Duke said.

"Perhaps within the hollow earth," I responded. I opted to accept the absurdity of this world, where fiction and real blurred to the point of mesmerism.

As the sun was coming up, I asked if I had truly met Tesla under the falls.

Marmaduke turned to me, still keeping an eye on the translucent sky above. "Realities are opening, James. The earth is turning into a giant hole, allowing a tunneling between our conscious and unconscious selves." His eyes seemed glazed over and mesmerized to the point of control. He stood up and walked toward the house.

I followed with utmost alacrity. Ideas of control and communication were of intrigue to me in this world. Who, or what, was in control of this cosmos? For the time being, I yearned to know who or what was pulling my friend back to his house.

Duke came up behind the house and pulled on what appeared to be an outside door to a cellar. As I followed him underground, a magnetized energy shot through my body.

"I need your assistance, Astor. Why are you still in that body?" It was Edison speaking.

Duke, awake now, turned to me. "Sorry, James, the Astor you met is my phantom. Edison was able to magnetize my past memories into it."

"So, you're not Astor's son?"

"I'm him, James, at this age. This age was the happiest time of my life."

"It was your Rosebud," I said. I looked beyond Astor's shoulder and saw Edison, standing with a group of model-makers.

"If you can realize how you have been written, you can begin to understand how you can write yourself anew,"

Edison said, his model-makers chanting something under their breath. "It's not every day you bring a convert to the Rosicrucian meeting, Astor," Edison added. He handed me a gray cloak.

I noticed his model-makers all had rather large foreheads, almost to the point of deformity. They were short and their skin had a blue, almost gray, hue.

"James is from Flatland," Astor said, looking at the model-makers all the same way, communicating to them without words.

"Am I dead?" I asked Edison.

"You're more alive now than you have ever been, James. I'm sure that in the other worlds you merely had to adjust your senses to new environments. Here, you have to adjust your conscious mind to your recognized unconscious mind."

"How am I able to see all the things that all of you see here?"

"They're all real," Edison said, "as real as the projections you were able to see before the singularity and fusion of the explicate with the implicate." He picked up one of his talking dolls from the table. "Here, James, have a memento from this world: the doll that allowed us to leave the water and become creatures of the land."

"Paved the way for robots," Astor said. "Tesla's one of the very few able to pick up these emerging realities of the paranormal. His boat is a product of this."

Edison walked between us and flooded my head with memories I had forgotten. It caused connections within my brain — it felt like the neurons in my brain were exchanging information at a rapid pace.

"Open the doll, James," Edison said.

I attempted to open the tiny automaton but just couldn't. I dropped it and fell backward. "It's not a machine," I said. There was no phonograph or voice device within the machine; it was as hollow as some thought the moon was. "The doll is not mechanical whatsoever, nor is it organic."

"That's the trouble, James. The moment we started to see ourselves as machines was when the trouble began," Edison said.

"How do the dolls talk?" I asked.

"Through our very thoughts," he said. "Probably the same way that your army figures spoke to your younger self. As a child, your imaginative propensities were at their highest. Once you hit puberty the third eye begins to dissipate and your body becomes more dense."

"But others are able to hear them speak?"

"Not all," Edison said, "only those who have entered the new reality of writing themselves anew." He added, "I want to show you another invention that I've been working on. I think you will find some special enjoyment in it."

I followed him, but we were no longer entering and exiting the room. Rather, we moved through the act of teleportation, which felt like dreaming within a dream or watching movie previews, going from one disjointed scene to another.

"You just can't throw an invention like this upon the public," Edison said, so ardent in his inventive prerogative that he mumbled. "I mean, you can put it upon the public," he babbled, "that is, until you really present it to the public, you'll be treated like an idiot, a childlike Tesla showing off that ingenious boat."

"But you're the father of childlike inventions: movies come from ancient toys," I said.

And then I heard thoughts in Marmaduke's head. He was engaging with Edison. They were sharing ideas about correcting me.

I should have recognized that Einstein's motivation for inventing film came from thoughts of his future.

"That's right, James," Edison said, "all of my ideas come from being able to step outside myself and see that my role is being projected by a writer. I'm in the movies, James. That's how I was able to invent within an exclusive culture."

"Then Einstein came along," Duke said — I mean, Astor said, "and he helped create the unconscious monsters that were growing in the minds of people who were having a collective meltdown due to, as James puts it, the movies."

Relativity had long been around by the time I was born, and so too had movies and telephones.

"A movie gets you closer to the idea that once you realize you are being written, you can understand the ability to write yourself anew," Edison said. He was now holding on to a remote-controlled device. There was also a small triangular-shaped device strapped to the front of his head. Once the mechanical man arrives at your house you'll see that your knowledge of the simulation is rekindled.

As Astor turned down the lights, Edison began projecting pictures onto the wall through his eyes. As he ran his hand over the remote, I could tell he was tuning in to different historical periods. At times, his mind would slow down, rewind, and speed up. He clicked a button on his remote, and I began to witness fantastic scenes of aliens, elves, wizards, and demons. The scenes began to slow down, and images from *The Empire Strikes Back* lit up on the wall, showing the moment when Luke finds himself on the remote planet Hoth. Then Edison, for some reason, fast-forwarded the film to Luke's preparation for becoming a Jedi, when Luke studies under Yoda's direction.

And I sat, mesmerized by such a scene out of my own childhood, my own imagined fantasy on the big screen.

"Fascinating dreams men of the past have, James," Astor said.

"Those scenes are not dreams," I responded, still watching Luke's classic struggle to become a true Jedi. "They are part of a movie from the future. The movie is not a dream, but it's also not real."

I didn't even know how to describe the movies of the future, but I thought Edison should know, since he was the one who had helped create movies.

"The movie shows a hyphenated fictive reality," I said. And I guess that was how I would say my world was to these men. I would say that my world comprised the fantastic and the quizzical: there were concepts of physics in my time that truly showed the universe to be playing by wacky rules, rules that made no sense and paradoxically did make sense.

In my time, our gods would be on the big screen, both as the actors in reality playing their parts and the superheroes they played.

However, I didn't mean that everything was a copy of an original or that baloney that French guy came up with, that everything was hyperrealism, whatever that meant. All I had to say was that my world was, and would be, the hyphen between fiction and reality.

"The movie is the projection of life, James," Astor said. "It shows us potentialities."

"How?" I asked.

I watched numerous tales of progressive myths on the wall, translated through the eyes of the wizard Edison.

"The potentialities are trapped in the magic of the energies we see through the spectrum of colors, James. Steam, wind, electric, and atomic energies, consciousness, and love (*agápe*) the most powerful source of energy that always has been present, suppressed by our own fears and tendencies — self-delusion being the sin of mankind."

"A fail-safe," Edison said. He explained that his ideas about control and communication had led him to find Archimedes' point of energy: the same energy that was able to transform my atomic structure during death and transport me to different worlds.

"So I'm not dead, am I?"

"Very much alive, James. You're dead in your plane of existence, in that Flatland you once called home, but you're able to project yourself anywhere you want now," Edison said. He shut his eyes, turned off the saga of mankind's potentialities, and sat down to converse.

Then my fingers and toes started to tingle, and numbness came over my body. The paralysis was accompanied by a struggle to breathe.

My telepathic abilities increased in sensitivity.

As I noticed that Astor and Edison were also paralyzed, I saw three men with large foreheads — Nordics — had appeared in the ether. I noticed that the wizard's power was feeble compared to that of the men who surrounded us and prodded us as if we were property.

The experience reminded me of what had happened when I was with the German doctors: these men had the same look in their eyes as the student-doctors in that world of German ignorance had.

Zap! A laser struck the back of my spine. The ceiling above us vanished and the clouds separated, and I saw a ship was over our heads. Its doors slid open. Our bodies were floating in the air, but the air was the stretchable materiality of space. Like the Pilgrims' boats floating in the water, or the planets floating in space, we too were floating on the invisible, floating on water, bending in deep space, where the planets live and speak to each other at night, where the stars sing in hibernation during the day, and where the moon turns its back on the rest of the light.

I couldn't feel the elements of which I was made up. The gases, rock, and ice that comprised my planetary bodily apparatus churned within my stomach. At times, I felt paralyzed, but I knew I still spun and moved.

I realized those humans living on Earth were similar to my spirit. They turned the lights on — while still paralyzed — they turned the lights on and saw what was in the room. They, like me, could recognize the elements acting together that comprised their potential energy.

I had one of them, a human spirit-mind, visit me. (I don't mean that humans have ever landed on my surface. They would only appear like a small, unseen mite on my skin — that's how a human apparatus would appear to my sense perception.) We talked and compared notes. I told the human that I could also know and understand the planetary apparatus was a pattern and combination of elements: I was mostly gas, while the humans were almost all water. These humans were advancing rapidly; they even knew that they floated in the ether, which they had at one time disregarded for purposes of science.

Elements of the spectrum of color and consciousness spoke to me, through their relative confines, to differing degrees of relativity. One of the Nordics held a small organic device, a hybrid between machine and organism, in his hand. As his fingers pressed on differing parts of the device-brain, other realities overlapped with my own. I don't mean to say that what I saw was blurry or that the dimensionality of space was changing. Certainly, some drugs could cause the same effects in my world. So, when I say that other realities overlapped with my own, I mean the Nordic's device augmented my sense of materiality.

Aspects of reality that were invisible at one time became visible again. As when I found myself intoxicated at the tavern, there were numerous dogmas of the material universe that disappeared. This Nordic was playing with my conscious mind. I was still paralyzed, but I had the ability to see more. I saw video-game worlds transposed on top of the animated worlds of my childhood projections. These realities had been transformed into the three-dimensionality of my reality.

The being was controlling my environment, similar to how Tesla had controlled the movements and signals of the apparatus of his boat through his bodily apparatus. Everything was merely reduced to modes of communication and control.

"Focus on your arm coming out of your socket, James." Edison sent me the mental message from across the room; he had been placed on an operating table by one of the other Nordics.

When I focused on my arm leaving its socket, my breath became shallow to the point of suffocation. My arm sprang out, sending excruciating pain through my body and throwing my upper torso forward.

When you kick at the reality that is the material world and it kicks back at you, your memory and foresight can merge into what one may call "the zone." Players of sporting events know exactly about what I speak. Connections between all the worlds that I had previously visited were sending signals to me through the ether of all planetary configurations.

When I had read Jefferson's Bible, I had noticed that his abridged copy, which I assume he'd forged with his own hands, deleted all the hocus-pocus. At the time, I thought it ingenious and rationally perfect for him to do such an act — to filter the philosophy of Christ through scientific dogma.

But now, I saw his actions to be as acrid as those of a minister who is censorious to all the sciences: both, in effect, would be using their own exclusionary systems of understanding and explanation. As my spectrum of consciousness vacillated from the rational to the absurd, I recognized that neither was better than the other. Once you realize you are authorized to play a game, you too can enter the zone.

Consciousness, I realized, like matter, was energy that when placed in the confines of a chain reactor procured realities — realities different than the effects of mere drugs. Drugs merely enabled us to tap into a weak plane on the spectrum of consciousness.

Edison was listening to my thoughts. *"That's right, James,"* he mentally conveyed. *"It's a chain reaction of the consciousness."* In overhearing my reality's explanatory system, or the paradigm I had brought with me, Edison saw a chance to use it to his advantage.

You see, Edison had placed a blueprint in my brain, which he used to see how my world's terminology was processed. To use Edison's terminology, this thing wasn't really a blueprint: the brain was not conscious or making the bodily apparatus aware of itself by means of its mechanics. Instead, consciousness was the modern equivalent of what fire was to prehistoric man: energy that could destroy dogma and create curiosity.

The question one had to ask in this world was, how could one think without a brain? That was what Edison gave me the ability to see: how to operate devoid of the brain's mechanics. Under this paradigm, the brain is not merely a broken filter. It is similar to the atomic bomb. Human reality filters ideas and actions related to splitting atoms and capturing atomic energy. It's rather patently clear why this is so. The brain acts in the same way; this action is a defense mechanism for species development. If humans were able to tap into all the energies of the brain or consciousness, the consequences could easily lead to species destruction.

Right now, your materialistic mind is probably asking, how did he turn off his brain? Simple: by making the filters of the brain sleep through hypnosis. Yes, it is that simple, so long as you know what mechanics or parts of the brain you need to turn off. To answer your next question, yes, consciousness is a signal from another dimension. There's nothing in gasoline that would intimate the ability to move a vehicle from point A to B. There's nothing about electricity that says it can cause movement. There's nothing about consciousness that says it can make materials fly through the air or cause spoons to bend. Nevertheless, these materials all, in part, facilitate these occurrences, and yes, the planet still moves even if I don't feel it move.

Mindful of my realization, I started to add hindrances to each Nordic's brain. I played with aspects of the brain that usurped the power of the fantastic. When I was through with them, they would worship the god of predictability and know very little about the spectrum of consciousness.

CHAPTER VII

Zapped into space again, shackles taken off, we landed on a planet.

Edison worked himself off the ground. "He must have picked up on our signals when you shut down the Feynman spectrum."

I stood up and saw that we were high in the mountains.

Edison analyzed the leaves on the trees. "It's either Croatia or Colorado, James. He's got laboratories in the mountains on both continents."

"It's Colorado," Astor said as he appeared from the heavy brush.

Another time, Astor had found me in these woods and wiped out my memory. The portal was close.

The time I saw Tesla communicating with his boat wasn't the first time we had met, I realized. "You took me away from Tesla." I looked over at Astor and called his attention to a rock I found.

"I saved you from him," Astor said. "Did you want him to experiment with you, to send you somewhere for all of eternity or put a filter mechanism on your brain that would cause nausea and impending doom? That's what the energy of the bomb did for your time, you know: it created more filters for the brain. Everybody started to look at reality as being absurd and dreadful."

Edison called us over to some other rocks. "Elvish rocks, James. They magnetize the oxygen, which gives the ether conscious energy," he said, looking over at me. I still had the rock in my hand.

I wasn't concerned about why Astor or Tesla had hypnotized me or filtered my memories through whatever means either man saw fit. After visiting with Father's projection, I really didn't care.

"Astor needs to process his location so he can shield us from his thoughts," Edison said. He looked at the rocks, which were reflecting the movements of the leaves. "There's so much life here that we can't see. He's figured out a way to diminish the spectrum of consciousness in this area. I have no idea how, but he figured it out."

"Figured out what?" I asked Edison.

"You know, James, you met Socrates. I saw that movie in your mind — your cave allegory. Whoever controls the cave controls consciousness, which amounts to life and our every experience."

"He becomes the director of the movie," I said.

Edison, laughing, said, "That's right. He becomes director, writer, and lead actor. We all just play supporting roles."

The anomalies that I was experiencing in this world were signs that my mental paradigm was in the process of shifting. In effect, I was traversing over a liminal bridge, a threshold of consciousness once again.

However, once the dust had settled and I adjusted to my new paradigm, I had my eyes on the prize once more. "Will I see my mother again?" I asked.

Astor, now out of his trance, said, "You'll bring your mother back to your world, James."

"Listen," Edison said as he bent low to the ground.

The sounds of the iron god roared. A steam engine. *Clearly, a train was not far off,* I thought.

"That's no train, James," Astor said. "It's a generator that captures the rotational energy the earth gives off."

"The opposite of nano-technology in your time, James," Edison said.

I didn't know much about nano-technology; I just knew that it had something to do with the ability to build atomic-level machines that, in turn, could build matter on a micro scale.

"What's its opposite?" I asked.

"Capturing the properties of processes that are so large we don't even perceive them with our senses."

"How was Tesla able to see these invisible processes?"

"The same way your scientists could see processes at the micro level during the age of nano-reductionism: reverse reduction, James."

"Deduction?" I asked with hesitation.

Astor was measuring the time between the sounds we heard from the generator. "'Divimaindering' is what I call it — like doing long division with a remainder. The remainder is the energy that living organisms are able to capture." Astor picked up a few more of the rocks. "Let's move," he said, "or shield up; the bridge is due north."

But before we started to move, I heard a buzzing noise coming from Astor's body.

I didn't say anything, nor did I make the connection at the time, or Edison and Astor surely would have been able to hear my thoughts. Now that I'm able to remember and write myself back into existence, I know the buzzing sounded like the fan within a computer's hard drive.

"I've seen the people in your time, James; now that they can live forever, they don't leave their homes."

I looked up at Edison with a droll smile. "They couldn't even cure male pattern baldness. These people haven't found a means to everlasting life; rather, they've become addicted to alleviating anxiety."

"What anxiety?" Edison asked.

"Anxiety about being alone," I said. "Perhaps they conquered death a few years after my death."

It didn't really astonish me that my world's future included the demise of death. Clearly my people had been on the verge of replaceable body parts, downloading our minds into machines.

"More filtering," Astor said.

I looked back at him; he was following behind us. "Filters?" I asked.

"Mortality, eternity, infinity — they're all filters humans no longer need. Maybe they once served a purpose in another environment or for another species, but they serve no purpose for the vital machines."

Some have asked me why I don't describe the environment more. Why is the story all dialogue? They need more detail about the characters and surroundings, they say. Yet while the environment and the people in my travels are important in the authoring process I have undertaken, the dialogue and the dreams communicate on their own.

"He left me books," I said. Concomitant to my thoughts on the books Tesla had given me were my thoughts on the books the Captain had found in the caves.

Astor and Edison weren't listening when I spoke of the books. They were still walking, but their minds were somewhere else. They were on autopilot. Like drunks who black out space and time, they stumbled a little but managed to cover a great distance.

CHAPTER VIII

C lark Kent had succumbed to the pressure of a culture yearning for smutty gossip. Camera in hand, he followed the movie star into the bathroom, looking rather bleak and despondent. As Clark went to unlock a stall door, still holding his camera, shots rang out from the street. The stall flung open and hit Clark in the face, knocking his glasses off and giving him a bloody nose. The movie star picked up the camera and smashed it to the ground before running outside to see what all the commotion was.

Clark's only option was to get up, clean his face off, and follow the rest of the crowd.

A voice called out to Clark. "Call on me," it said.

Clark looked around. Police were surrounding a bank; the gunman had to be inside. He heard shouting. The gunman had taken hostages.

"Call on me. Finish it," the voice called out again. It was his own voice, but with a tone of confidence and hubris.

Clark stood, watching the events in front of him. Minute after minute passed. Another shot was fired, and, he supposed, a hostage was dead.

He left the scene and took a little detour to the nearby liquor store to pick out his favorite poison.

"Drinking alone again, Clark?" the cashier asked.

Clark looked down at the floor, never making eye contact with anyone, stuttering in speech and mannerisms.

After consuming the liquor, he found his favorite drug dealer on the corner of Ninth and Main.

"My usual," he said, with a little more confidence than he had displayed in the liquor store.

"They let you out of the loony bin, Clark?" the pusher jokingly asked.

Clark just took the drugs and moved on.

Early the next morning, he knocked on her door, intoxicated with guilt and shame.

"Lois," he mumbled as she opened the door. He had changed into Superman but was now useless.

"You still have to get drugged to be yourself?" she said. She wiped tears from her face. "They'll put you away again if you keep changing into that costume." She looked down the street to see if anyone was watching.

Superman walked into Lois's house and spoke no more about the outside world. He sat down at a very long and winding table, a table that was so long and winding it had no end in sight.

The Pope came out from behind a set of curtains and placed bread and wine in the middle of the table. Then he looked up at me.

I was still floating above Superman, just watching.

"Come down for now, James; take a seat next to the Captain."

Christ was sitting at the table too, along with all his apostles. After everyone began preparing for communion, the Pope went back behind the curtains.

Superman sat with booze and drugs instead of wine and bread.

The Pope came back through the curtains and asked if we wanted some LSD or any other drugs for the crossing.

Superman was all about it. He quickly waved the Pope over to deliver the goods.

After the others had all taken whatever sustenance or drug it was they sought to alleviate their filters, all of them entered into a rapturous state. Superman was flying around the room, Christ and the apostles were walking on air, and the Pope was getting younger by the second.

The aliens from Superman's home planet intervened in this communion and asked the hero if he was ready to come home to the future.

"I still need Clark to see and finish it," he said.

The ship spoke to him. "He must filter his divine spark for himself."

Superman climbed into the ship and it took off.

The Romans had taken control of the room. Now they sat around the table watching Christ and the apostles burning at stakes.

Then a great funneling filter hovered above the table and beamed its Valis on the group, transforming them all to sheep. Then the flock went westward, for there was no food to be found in Lois Lane's home.

CHAPTER IX

The lights came on. I was exhausted.

Edison looked into my eyes and held a pocket watch in my face; it was swinging back and forth, causing my eyes to blur. Then he lifted me up off the ground and said we had arrived.

There were brains under heat lamps. This garage was the McDonald's of brain projection.

Tesla was standing on a balcony, looking down on us.

"Control, communication, and human interaction under the umbrella of mythic levels and ritualized steps — I think that sums up our human-and-machine interaction, James. And by 'machine,' I mean any technology that we create in the material world or the mystic universe of the imaginative," he said.

I looked over at Astor and Edison. Both pulled out probing devices that emitted a dark plasma substance.

"You used me to get here," I said. "You never saved me from this place. You only knew that I had been here before and used me to get back."

Tesla deactivated Astor and Edison: they were robots. "It was probably much more mysterious when you thought they were humans and not merely projections, James," Tesla said.

"I'm not surprised. I guess they are more real than the dead on the spectrum of authenticity."

Tesla laughed and made sure the brains were all right for their next projection into the DNA of other automatons he had created.

"So, how did I know about this place?"

Tesla smiled. "You are me, James — with a few sequences changed in the physical form and filters for cultural and aesthetic purposes."

He flipped a switch and the garage door began slowly opening.

"No, not at all," he said. "Don't start thinking about the circularity of loops of time travel when one visits one's other self in the same Flatland. That's just another filter that you have that divides time into past, present, and future. Time is all three experiences wrapped into one spinning ball."

"So, am I dead or alive?" I asked.

The garage door was now open.

"Perhaps you were never born — you may merely be my own creation."

"How can I be your creation? You mean everything is a projection from your brain."

Tesla walked to the middle of the garage, which contained the exact same items I knew were held in Van Coleman's laboratory, under St. Peter's.

"The one thing I never did understand," Tesla said, as he fidgeted with some gadgets, "is what it's going toward, James. Remember, in your time people were so interested in knowing what started all this in the past, like the Big Bang — they lost track of what was pulling us forward. If

I have to leave my house because someone I don't know is taking me away, and I'm kicking and screaming, what are my major concerns? I want to know who is dragging me away from my house. And I want to know where that person is taking me, and why. I have no concern anymore about my home or where I was dragged from."

I started to wonder what and who was dragging me — and where.

"Are you controlling me?" I asked.

"That's a funny question. You're asking yourself if you're controlling yourself, James."

I still had not accepted that Tesla was me and I him.

"The time logos. Put me in it; let me go back."

"Go back or go forward?" he asked.

The whirring of an engine started up below us. I could see some lights in the adjacent room below, seeping up through the cracks in the wooden floor.

"What is it?" I asked as the smell of gasoline invaded my nostrils and intoxicated my ecstasies.

"We are leaving, James."

The disc broke through the floor and hovered beside us for a moment. I could see four gray figures, each with almond-shaped eyes, within the ship.

"Leaving one door and entering another. But I'm going to leave it open this time. When the bombs go off, the radioactivity should leap over into their room."

"Room?"

"Whatever metaphor you want to use, James. Did you know Merlin was born of an incubus and one of Charlemagne's daughters? Remember Merlin, James? What a character. An incubus for a father!"

Tesla walked down through rubble left behind by our alien selves.

"Don't think 'alien': that's your cultural pejorative for yourself."

I just followed myself — Tesla — until he started up his automatons.

"They laughed at our boat, but at least we placed it in their collective imagination — that's all we really had to do here."

I watched the boat make circular movements as I fell into a deep trance.

ॐ

"Maybe belief becomes reality, which then creates new beliefs, which create new realities, and so on."

The witches' lawyer was lecturing the judges. "They are the only ones able to interact with our creations, and vice versa." The lawyer explained that evidence of the witches moving objects was no different than biblical metanarratives of miracles. "The miracles were anomalies. Signs that the divine man was coming." He explained the witches were merely intermediaries between the here and now. "The witches are already dead, Your Honors. You should never question aspects about the dead; rather, your questions should concern whether the living are alive."

The judges excoriated the lawyer for speaking in circles. Then the lawyer began to speak in triangles, which made the judges more irritated. Then the judges attempted to torture the lawyer into telling them if the witches had mated with any of the townsmen.

"If the two merge they form the synthesis: thus, the triangle. And that's all it comes down to, these overlapping and merging realities that, at times, overflow into one another," Tesla said repeatedly.

The witches were also present and proclaimed what they wanted. They each spoke to the judges and said they had brought the gifts of children to the town. They said that their children would bear the selfish gene and bring new powers to the men of Salem, and that they were to be the superheroes of their day.

Then the judges said they would rather wait for the speculators to arrive. This they announced as they lit the witches on fire.

They then had a glimpse of me watching them and bowed in feverish prayer.

"You will remember, from when we were children, the radon detectors they placed in the basement. The radon opened up numerous doors in the basement, which brought us deeper into the hollow earth," Tesla said repeatedly.

The judges dispersed through the wilderness, knowing that I was angry about their actions. They had tried to trick me with their words of good deeds, but they knew that my control and communication fundamentals were predicated on their Archimedean point of controlled chain reactions.

"The chain reaction of the mind is the series of unconscious events that occur in the brain every time an action or idea is moved or created — just as an atomic bomb releases the energy of matter, radiation releases the energy of mind. By injection of radiation, the mind energy creates a chain reaction of events whereby the willed belief or idea moved also moves other ideas like dominoes behind it, but dominoes not perfectly set, one behind the other, so as to look for the end of the domino reaction. Rather, they are random dominoes that fall; just as with almost all dominoes that fall, a pattern of some sign is more likely than not to present itself. Now begin to stand by and witness the pattern the dominoes have been creating since the departure stage of your mythic journey."

☙

My eyes opened. Tesla sat in a large lounge chair. The blue hues from outside brought out his sparkly, transparent skin. I thought I had stepped inside of a large film projector: my bodily apparatus was the projector, my brain the film. That meant, probably, there was an editor of the final film product. Maybe there was a color expert who could change the mood of the film itself by inserting dye into the film. Perhaps there was even someone gifted in manipulating the films and changing the sequence, or even cutting figures out of the slides. And I bet there was even a curious one who could make ghosts and phantasms appear, by means of manipulation, in the film. Perhaps he would even draw in aliens and angels. Maybe there was other film that would get mixed up with mine, and on occasion I would see the people in that film apparently appear in my film. A lot of my analogies I know deal with movies and projected image. As you will soon learn, I'm not really talking about projected images; rather, I'm talking about matter becoming less dense in certain states of dimensionality. This is what the Captain was trying to tell me the boon of this quest is — to bring back the Mechanical Man so as to create a tool of consciousness based on objective love that allows us to become less and less dense to the point of recognizing our true divinity, our essence of God.

☙

Tesla sat now between the crossings of electrical currents. In those currents, I saw numerous civilizations, after billions of years, turning on the light switch by means of technology, which turns lights on so quickly and, nevertheless, turns the lights off — I saw Earthlings, from their final worlds, crying to the heavens that their inventions worked.

"Maybe what really happened to you, James, is that the machine destroyed your entire world. That's how all the technological civilizations end up. There is, in the end, a great experimentation that works, but simultaneously destroys the world. That, in fact, is how most go out. Or technology gets into the wrong hands of a religious zealot."

I longed now for this world to end. I knelt down and began to cry. I prayed to the gods, to the Captain in all of us. I prayed to the gods of all the worlds to which I had been, for they were all created in the image of different cultures and times.

The teleportation we were undertaking was confusing, spinning me in so many directions. At some points in time, we were even projected into the ether of dreams and the imaginative sphere.

We met most of the great superheroes, those whom the imaginative sphere of the brain projects through time. This act of projection reaches its highest density in times of high radiation. Many of the gods from that plane of existence and dimension are able to communicate and send signals from the dimension of the god-superheroes — this communicative bridge, which is created by radiation, allows them to come through a door or cross through that bridge. The first way that we are able to perceive them is through the imaginative receiver, which is the only part of the brain capable of detecting signals from other dimensions. Once these signals make contact, the brain begins to process them. The output is in the form of drawings, stories, movies, and even, in a small minority, reenactments: some merely act out the power, while others figure out ways to actualize that power into the material world, thus kicking back at that material world through rituals.

We were in the dark confines of a graveyard in New Jersey. And while the graveyard possessed tombstones, it also had a garden-like atmosphere — there were fruits, vegetables, and flowers growing everywhere. The sun shone brightly onto Tesla's slick black hair and slender features. At times, his shadow appeared to look like that of the Grim Reaper.

"His dolls are buried here, and so is she," Tesla said as he knelt in front of a tombstone. In this projection, the meaning of life — or at least how to get through it — dawned on me for the first time. Tesla was obsessed with this projection. It alleviated his nausea, but also caused it.

"When did you build her?" I asked. Tesla looked at the tombstone, which said something in Latin about living after death. "*Non Omnis Moriar*," which means, I shall not wholly die.

"I realized how radiation and magnetism conduct consciousness ions. Electricity could have accomplished the same ends if we had an electric generator the size of Earth." The mental gatekeepers of this culture were hiding a few things from me. From his thoughts, I deduced that the "she" buried here was a vital machine, made with machine parts that appeared to be organic. The brain was a projector, but it also needed objects to project upon — the wall of a cave or the screen at a movie theater.

"Who is she, and why is she buried here?"

"After I murdered Edison and Astor and built their replicants, I also gave her life, James."

My instincts drew me to the shovel, and the future James, from a future that was now very close, told me to dig. I dug until I hit the casket, which I opened as quickly as my small fingers could find the crevices.

Mother stared into my eyes and said, "I've been waiting to see my child for so long." She wailed out in joy and terror; it was both absurd and fantastic.

"Are you real?" I asked. And then I knew that the word "real" meant nothing at all. Just like Father in the garden was real to me, so too was Mother.

Tesla sat, watching us in our union.

There were so many questions rushing through my mind. *Were we all dead?* That was the question that now plagued me.

"Don't try to explain things by material or spiritual means, James — that would be an absurdity. Life is a quest, with a calling, initiation, and return. Your job in life is to fill in the gaps of that quest. Filling in the gaps will allow you to free us all from the black iron prison of density we have fallen into, whether dead or alive."

Tesla started to dig up all of Edison's dolls, which I realized he had buried many years ago. He explained to me the philosophical disagreement he had had with Edison: why he had turned Edison into a robot to control. "Edison cared too much for the practical and mechanical. Take his mechanical dolls, for instance: they were too real, too practical. Mankind yearns for neither. Man needs to know how to discover the absurd and fantastic. Neither science nor religion can imbue man with the tools to unlock the impossible."

So Edison had capitulated to the whimsical desires of a fickle American public that yearned for mass consumption and conformity.

"I sought to allow America to reach its manifest destiny by reaching singularity."

"In what way?" I asked.

"By giving people enough revolutions in the realm of control and communication, allowing them to throw off their shackles and see evolution pulling them forward, into the future."

Tesla spoke of how there had been a shift in consciousness leading us out of the darkness of the spiritual gardens — now immersed in the battlefields of the scientific method — and soon, into the singularity of the fantastic, the hyphenated absurdity of existence, like being on LSD but devoid of the drugs.

Then some of his hidden thoughts seeped through the ether. Mother turned to Tesla and immediately knew, by looking at both of us together, that we were the same person at different ages; this unlocked memories of a multitude of past and future lives that she had experienced with us.

That's what Tesla had sought; that's why he invented the time logos and placed it in my world. I had given James, or Tesla, exactly what he wanted — his mother.

He took out the same type of hand remote with which he controlled his boat and tapped on a button. Mother fell back into her grave as the life force that ran through her veins ceased to flow.

Tesla drew the shovel above my head and knocked me across my face.

The next thing I knew, astronauts were picking me up and speaking about how they couldn't determine what had gone wrong with the mission.

"How do we get back to Earth now, without our ship?" one of the lead astronauts said. "Powell's the name, James. How long have you been on the other side?"

Some of the others looked around.

"Powell, it took some of us a while to realize the same thing. I had to go through the experience nine times before I could see any of you," another astronaut said. He was the first teacher to go into space.

"He needs to recognize and realize his death," Powell said.

All the mythic superheroes of my generation came into form. Superman, Thor, Spiderman, Batman, and Captain America knelt in front of me and asked me if I was ready for the quest. It was now time for the great departure. They said that they would leave me tools and guides to help in the departure stage; there would be no boredom during departure, they said only anxiety and curiosity. You see there is departure before and after each stage of the quest: the call; initiation; and return. Departures and refusals occur between each stage. Thus, many people don't realize that there is a refusal during the initiation and during the return. Many people wrongly believe that the refusal only comes during the calling to the quest phase.

Edison and Astor, once more projected images of their former selves, brooded over me. My arms were tied behind my back, hogtied to my ankles. There was no need for a gag; no one would be able to hear my screams from Tesla's secluded laboratory. He had already burned his laboratory up once; the element of fire once bequeathed by the aliens to Prometheus aided my future self, now in the past, to evince the projection of death to others so their unconscious minds would know full well what death is.

"There will be a period of realization, James, prior to the departure stage," Tesla said as he gathered some papers from the top of his desk, placing them in a suitcase for Astor and Edison to take away with them. Once they were gone, Tesla began lighting the fire. Above us, large disc-shaped objects beamed lights on the spectacle.

"How do they view my death?" I asked Tesla. It was just a mere formality for him. He was attuned to getting the fires lit. In his mannerisms, I saw my own curiosity and destiny. There was no moral struggle going on in his mind.

He spoke to me through his thoughts. *"Finish it,"* he said over and over again. My mother was now in good hands; her memories and spirit were now in a place where I could care for her and simultaneously fulfill the absurdity of the fantastic, which is the meaning of life. My Jedi training was complete, and it was now time to depart.

Those above me looked down. I could hear their alien voices; they viewed this experience as yet another instance where a witch is burned at the stake. The fire sucked any feeling I had from my nervous system through my epistemological limits. Once my entire body was engulfed by fire, there was no pain; rather, there was a feeling of the elements that composed my bodily apparatus separating and seeking their own past. Like the Captain hovering and laughing above himself at his crucifixion, I too laughed at my suffering self.

I found myself writing about myself. I was the author now, no longer hindered by any filtering. The authoring of my story was now to be achieved through the quest I sought to undertake. This threshold between life and death was not dreamlike or materially real; rather, it was more of a past memory conjured up by a smell, similar to remembering thoughts of a loved one through the mere smell of freshly cut grass or gasoline — that's the only way I can explain it. And this smell was accompanied by a memory of authorship and writing, one in which I was not equipped with a pen but with a much more powerful writing utensil.

The cosmos breathed questions out of its mouth, and I responded that I would answer, no longer leaving it in darkness. Dogmatism in the exclusionary realms of religion and science was dead.

CHAPTER X

She just stood there, back up against the wall, counting until she couldn't remember what number she had counted to. Then she stopped, went back to her room, came back a few minutes later, and started all over again.

"Coffee… the only drug we can get our hands on in here," a female voice said from behind me. "James—"

I turned around and looked at a small brunette, probably around the age of twenty-five, who was staring at me and holding a cup of coffee in each hand.

"I used to think that you were worked here, you know. I thought, 'This handsome guy can't be in here like me. He must work here.'"

"Right," I said, thinking that I had no earthly idea who the hell this girl was. I would not say that she was annoying; if she was, my annoyance with her was solely caused by my own annoyance with how I felt physically and mentally.

"I feel sick," I said. I looked around the environment a bit and saw there were numerous nurses walking around.

"Here, then," she said. She took the cup of coffee that she had momentarily given me out of my hand and directed me to a bedroom. "Go wash your face and take a rest for a while. Then you can tell me all about how Tesla invented the ray gun that he sold to the Russians."

I walked into the room's adjacent bathroom and turned on the water. The water hitting the sink sounded like a million demons yelling at me to free them. I was tired and nauseous, but too tired even to dry heave and at least feel a little better. You know you're fucked when you're too tired to do something like that. I lifted my face to dry it off and looked into a rather odd mirror: it was definitely not made of glass, although it still gave off the reflection of my face. I looked so different, years older than I had remembered or, perhaps, forgotten: perhaps late twenties or early thirties.

There were two beds in the room, one of which was occupied by an old man who was half naked and covered by a thin blanket. The bass of his snoring shook the entire room. Then, like an automated cuckoo clock, his snoring abated, and he said, "Is it time to eat yet?"

"I don't know," I said, feeling my shoulders. They were much more muscular than I remembered.

"You're going to think yourself out of existence," he said.

"What's that?" I asked.

"You don't even know when it's time to eat," he said. His body was still on its side, his face turned toward the wall.

"You have to lie on the bed for this," a nurse said as she appeared by the door.

The girl with the coffee was standing next to her. "Do I get to watch this?" she said, a smile on her face.

The nurse shut the door and habit took over. I lay on the bed and pulled my pants down, and she stuck my ass with a needle.

"If this doesn't get rid of the nausea in a few minutes, let me know," the nurse said as she left the room, shutting the door behind her.

I pulled up my pants and remained on the bed.

The man in the bed next to me was now wide awake, sitting there and looking at me. "Is it time to eat yet?" he asked.

"How the fuck do I know?" I said.

"The food at this place is a lot better than the other ones I've been to," he said.

I found it odd that he didn't call this place "a hospital," and I also found it odd that even in my head I was placing an "a" in front of the word "hospital." In England, we never called it "a hospital."

Some things started coming back to me now, like the fact that my name was James Lucas and I was born in London on April 8, 1979. Jesus Christ, but that was about it.

"The nurse says she can't give out private information." The girl was once more in the doorway with a wry smirk on her face. "I'm going to look you up on the Internet when I get out of here and see if you really are a lawyer and a professor."

"What does it matter?" I said. "I could probably make up any machinations in here, and it wouldn't fucking matter. I could tell your dumb fucking ass that we're at Disney World, about to ride on Soarin' and fly over the mountains, and you would probably say, 'Okay, when?' And I'd say, 'Just sit on my cock and imagine flying and call it Disney World.'"

She laughed, and I thought that I'd gotten myself into one hell of a situation.

"What's for lunch?" the man on the bed asked the girl.

"The best. Hamburgers," she replied.

He didn't smile; it was as if he expected her to say that something good was for lunch. I surmised he had probably waited three hours to hear the news of the century. Hours ago, I was sure, it was great news that pancakes and eggs were to be served for breakfast. He just stared into dead space when he heard words that neither surprised him nor let him down. That's what his life had habituated him to. I could tell him that man had landed on Mars, and he'd just ask me what was for lunch or dinner.

"James was about to tell me how Tesla invented a ray gun that he sold to the Russians; this all gave Ronald Reagan the idea for *Star Wars*."

"Is that right?" I said. "Sounds like one hell of a good fucking story."

"I thought it was magnanimous, to use one of your fancy lawyer words."

Laughing, I said, "'Magnanimous' means having a good spirit or big heart. You're as bad as me at using big words."

"'Magnate,'" the man on the bed said. "It means a very important or influential person, especially in business."

"That's right," I said, a smile on my face. "I know big words. I'll never claim that I use them correctly, but at least I use them."

"'Malediction' and 'malinger,'" the nurse said, reappearing in our room. "You've made it to 'M,' I'm guessing."

"Put the two together," the man on the bed said, "and it means pretending to be sick is a curse."

"Lunch is ready," the nurse said.

That was all that needed to be said. It was like someone had opened up the gates of Hades: a flood of the cursed came out. There was full-blown commotion coming from the halls. By the way, the place's layout was clearly that of a floor of a hospital designated for the insane. You'd think that the engineers who had laid out the floor plans would have been a little more creative, but therein lies the problem between the thinkers and the doers. The doers are merely interested in getting things done, and then they can go home, eat a steak, jerk off, zone out on television or the Internet, and go to bed. I'd often wondered what the zombies thought of the engineers who built this floor. Often wondered what they thought about at night right before they fell asleep. Probably sex or something they wanted.

"I remember being on some meds when, I swear to fucking God, all I thought about at night before going to bed were eggs and hash browns. I'd wake up drooling because of those damn eggs and hash browns. And it wasn't like I couldn't have gone to IHOP every night to buy some. But I didn't have to. My reality was so fucked by the meds that every night, in my head, I was really eating eggs and hash browns while lying there in my bed," I recalled as the girl and I walked into the cafeteria.

"I dated a guy who took something for his multiple personalities, or whatever they call it these days, and he had a hard-on twenty-four seven. We'd go to the gym, and I'd see him over at the free weights with his dick just hard as hell, bobbing around as he lifted," she said.

"And he didn't care?"

"Not a bit."

"Good for you — I guess," I said, thinking that she probably liked the fact that he was hard all the time.

She didn't say anything.

"Gwinn," I said as she bent down to pull out her tray with its hamburger and fries.

"Yes," she replied.

I remembered her name. Maybe it was the shot I'd gotten in my ass or her reminding me of dicks having the ability to get hard. Whatever it was, I remembered her name was Gwinn.

"We're going to eat what the newbies don't touch today." She was referring to the fact that the new crazy sheep herded in never took their food until their second or third day inside. It was probably due to the nausea, but I'm sure some thought they were too good for hospital food. Hell, maybe there were some who thought they weren't good enough for it.

We sat down and started to eat. Gwinn had about three burgers that the newbies had told her she could have, and she gave me an extra one. She probably weighed about a hundred pounds and was of average height. She was sexy in the way that a messed-up girl is sexy — real confident until you fuck her. Then, you get all of her problems and sink with the *Titanic* as she gets off the boat and finds another guy to act cocky around.

It could have been the meds or Gwinn's laughter, but I felt safe behind these invisible bars. It didn't bother me that the doors were all locked or that there were screens over the windows. Mentally, I'd been trapped my entire life, so it wasn't anything new.

The burgers were good; they reminded me of junior-high lunches. "I think I heard somewhere, or read somewhere, that we only remember things. We don't really learn anything new," I told Gwinn.

She just giggled.

"Jesus, what meds are you on?" I asked.

She gazed through me and said, "Soma."

"PKD fan, are ya?" I asked.

She looked a little puzzled.

"Soma is a drug in Philip K. Dick's novels," I said.

Gwinn said she had no idea what I was talking about. I later learned that she was schizophrenic: she saw things. Maybe she saw the hamburgers or saw me; perhaps I was her invention. Perhaps she was my goddess giving me life. In her world, I guess, I was there to serve her. That's how I justified my place in her world, anyway.

"What if everyone was sick and then stuck in here? Who the fuck would keep the doors locked? I mean, somebody has to be out there on the other side to lock the doors," I said, grinding the meat in my mouth. All forms of manners went out the window in the bin. In fact, the word "fuck" was probably my favorite word to use because it was easy. If we could walk around naked with a bottle of whiskey in our hands, we all probably would. It didn't really matter.

"They just called your name on the loudspeaker," Gwinn said.

"I didn't hear anything," I told her.

"You weren't listening."

I looked around the cafeteria, got out of my chair, and walked toward the front desk. A nice-looking nurse sat there at a computer, typing away. "Did you call me, ma'am?" I asked.

"Lucas," she said.

"James," I replied.

"Lucas," she said again.

"Right," I said.

"Any bruising, vomiting, nausea, diarrhea, headaches, hallucinations, or thoughts of impending doom?"

I didn't really know what to say. I wanted to ask if she wanted to know in the past, present, or future.

"I'm fine," I said. "I just want my books and shampoo." I looked down at my feet and saw that I had no shoes on. "Shoes would be nice as well."

She reached down and gave me a pair of slippers. "We don't usually give you books here; you could use them as projectiles."

I pictured everyone throwing books at each other, knocking one another upside the head. Then I felt someone hold my hand.

"No touching him, Gwinn," the nurse said. "There's no touching in here."

There was no touching in the loony bin. Isn't that funny? No touching whatsoever. All the human freedoms, like touching and learning — all those human elements that give us purpose and life — were thrown out the window in the bin.

I turned to Gwinn, and she saw something in me. "Let's go on a quest and find something fun to do," she said.

CHAPTER XI

I'll show you something, James," Tesla said, pressing three keys on the piano that unlocked a picture on the wall for him to take down. "Magnetized to the wall: nobody could possibly take this off the wall." Behind the picture was a safe. He turned the dial a couple of times and opened the door.

Manifested before me was a ray gun.

"It's not a ray gun." He laughed. "That's what everybody who sees the blueprints thinks it is. That's what they want to use it for: the science-fiction death traps that man makes to trap another man."

"What is it, then?"

"An invention that should help you on your quest. It's a laser manipulator. It slices through the life force — it shows the holographic or the implicate." The laser manipulator didn't burn human flesh or incinerate people; rather, it projected a laser that showed archetypes. "You can't go on living the way you have been, James, blind to the archetypes that have come over into the explicate from the implicate. Now you can live by seeing what you've been feeling and knowing that it's there...

"I used the laser manipulator to create mechanized eyes that act like the laser manipulator in that they allow me to see the archetypes."

"So you're going to pluck out my eyes," I said.

"That's a rather maudlin comment coming from a dead man. You already have the eyes to see the implicate: you're dead. But remember what your question was to the oracle: How do you bring something back from the implicate?"

"I'm dead?" I said. "But I was just dreaming that I was a lot older and institutionalized."

He was walking at a furious pace toward one of the large barns down the way that had not yet burned to the ground. "We'll burn this one as well before we leave. I don't intend on coming back; in fact, I intend on becoming one of them," he said as I hurried after him.

Then he stopped in his tracks, turned his head around, and looked back at me. He brought out a pocket watch, opened it, and placed its mirror side up to my face.

That was when I saw it: the large black eyes with a huge head and slit for a mouth. "I'm a gray," I said. I looked exactly like the aliens people say were in those damn things that crashed in Roswell, New Mexico. "But you told me that aliens were us from the future; you lied to me."

He laughed a little and said, "I told you correctly, James, they are us from the future. We're all dead in the future; that's the form we take. Some get curious and come back to this string to check things out — they think they can learn something. They're usually the ones who didn't learn a damn thing when they were here and are trying to figure out what they did wrong. It's nostalgic for them, I guess."

"But my friends from the Far East and their levels of enlightenment... They didn't appear as aliens."

"Your friends from the Far East don't even exist. They were just put there by you. There are no such things as these levels of enlightenment. Get that straight. There's the implicate and the explicate, and there's life and death. It's not that complicated. Yes, there are different strings you can land on, but one isn't better or higher than the other; they're just different in the order of unfolding."

We entered the barn, and I saw the most beautiful flying saucer any science-fiction writer could invent. "It looks almost like glass," I said. My reflection was shining right through it.

"Probably the largest diamond in the world, James, from all the coal I was able to secretly extract from my coal plant under Niagara Falls."

"And it flies?"

His milieu was true independence. He was the last pure inventor in the land of the explicate. As we entered the diamond, I became much more attuned to the differing forces affecting Earth. "It's as if I can hear and feel Earth's heartbeat," I told Tesla.

He was too busy looking around the diamond's inner sanctum to acknowledge me.

"What is it?" I asked.

"Since your death, I'm seeing things through your holographic field perception. My author is no longer in control; your authoring is in control now."

The inside of the diamond was no different than the deck of the *Star Trek Enterprise* from the old program with Kirk and Spock — my fictive lenses had not even updated it to catch up to my updated memories of the *Enterprise*. "It's from an old television program," I told Tesla.

"It's your understanding of the fictive fully taking over in death. That's why we need to travel to Orion's belt: so I can see how the archetypes have changed since your metamorphosis."

"But if I wasn't around to create your holographic environs before, then who was doing it for you?" I asked.

"My author, but your death supersedes any authoring I may have. I'm part of your quest now. It makes no difference what my author was in the process of creating; it's as if my author is held in abeyance."

He sat down in what would be Mr. Sulu's chair, beginning to figure out how to get the diamond *Enterprise* off the ground.

"I would have thought I'd have created the *Millennium Falcon*," I said.

"What's that?" Tesla called out, all the while experimenting with the numerous buttons.

"Nothing," I said, "just trying to figure out how the fictive's hierarchy manifests itself."

"There we go," he said. "That's the hard part about figuring out how to control or communicate with something from the fictive you've brought into our reality."

"That it's actually not mine but another person's fictive, ad infinitum."

"Right," Tesla acknowledged. "But this one's simple because it's actually a copy of the fictive, as if someone had built a theater set for actors."

He didn't know how right he was — in fact, when he said that, he brought me back to how the room with the time logos had resembled *Star Trek* iconography. It was as if my fictive had become his reality for invention. His figuring out of my fictive, which was my transposition of another's fictive into my reality, was his tableau for creativity.

"Hang on," he said as the diamond lifted off the ground.

I sat down at one of the screens and saw Earth grow smaller and smaller. I looked at my hands; I hadn't even taken the time to analyze my new self. It was as if I no longer cared about the apparatus I inhabited after going through so many mental changes. The quest was on my mind. Control, communication, and information: the pillars of the Holy Ghost and the Mechanical Man.

"We lose sight of the quest, don't we?" Tesla said. He had full control over the ship.

"How can you not lose sight of it when you always have to readjust to your surroundings?"

"That's the beauty of it, isn't it?"

In death is the first time one truly realizes the ability to be independent — with no fears or worries about the word "loneliness" at all. And it's powerful, I tell you, so powerful. I know I had the company of Tesla at this point, but there was no codependence between us. Both of us were as independent as a human and an alien can be. The paradox of death alleviating the nausea of eternity and the infinite was amazing: it really worked.

A door to the deck opened. In walked two droids; they looked like hybrids of Robby the Robot and Gort from *The Day the Earth Stood Still*. "Asimov droids: they won't hurt you," Tesla said. "Rather, they are capable of communicating with other vital machines in ways we no longer can — if we were to encounter such."

"Asimov?" I queried.

"A science-fiction writer still alive during your time, James — you've never read any of his work. He's created three laws that govern the actions of robots. The Laws of Robotics are as follows: one, never harm a human being or allow a human to be harmed; two, never disobey a human order, unless to obey Rule 1; and three, never harm yourself, unless to obey Rule 1 or 2." As the robots took over the controls, Tesla stood up and lit up a cigarette.

"Why didn't we ask them to help us with the controls earlier?" I asked.

"They aren't programmed for that," Tesla said. Smoke billowed around him, almost creating a snake-like creature. "The Mechanical Man, of course, showed us the fourth law of robotics, which said there was an even higher law that trumped the other three. We've seen how Asimov's Laws of Robotics make way for a fourth rule: namely, that robots act for the betterment of humanity. This law causes us great puzzlement, for the human brain has a hard time contemplating things on such a large scale.

CHAPTER XII

There, at the end of the hall, stood three people staring at something. It was the only window on the entire floor that had a view other than that of docking stations and courtyards — we could see stores and highways, the movement of people and cars. It was like the first humans gathering around fire: I could see sparks of creativity and evolution sprouting in the minds of the feeble, including myself. I yearned to be out there, to return to myself and the environment that had been taken away from me.

"Who am I?" I asked Gwinn.

She stared into the abyss of the explicate that resided on the other side of the window and said, "You're my king."

Looking out at the traffic, I asked Gwinn a question. "Is it just the mere fact that we're locked in here — is that why all that's fucking outside looks nice? It never looked nice when we were trapped out there. Now we yearn to go back into it."

"You think that's how we'll feel after we die, James?" Gwinn asked as the window scene began to hypnotize her.

"You mean we'll have a yearning to go back to the living with rules to live by and a beginning and an end to pacify us? Perhaps. But who the fuck really cares?"

"You do," she said in a comforting voice.

"Maybe I did," I said, "but not in this life, not now."

The sunlight piercing through the window held me in a dazed state.

"It's hypnotic," one man standing beside us said. "The minute I get out of here, I'm going straight to the bar to get loaded — a couple of codeines mixed with about four lemon drops, and I'll be back in the implicate."

"What did you say?" I asked.

"He's a vet, James," Gwinn whispered in my ear. "They pick him up every time he whips his dick out at parks."

"I don't care," I said. "I thought for a moment he said a word I once knew."

He looked at me. "States of mind, man. No matter how much money you have, it's all about states of mind. I look in the mirror and look damn good after a few codeines and some liquor." He gazed at the restaurants outside. "That's my quest when I get out." He pointed down to the street. "I'll go to that corner and get enough money to go to the Red Lobster. I'll find my codeine pills where I stashed them under a seat, order a few lemon drops, and enter heaven. They won't look like reptiles to me anymore. Ain't that right, Luke?" he asked, looking at me.

"That's not my name," I said.

"It's his name," Gwinn said. "James is what he calls himself."

"I know your name, James. I done see you in the other place. You borrowed a cigarette from me."

I stared at him a bit. I thought he looked familiar, but he was nothing more than an unfortunate fool who had given up a long time ago.

"No," I told him, "I don't think we've ever met." Later I remembered he had been with me in the first psyche ward years ago.

The light had temporarily blinded me: I'd stared out the window for too long.

"It's the place of high energy." Wotan was describing the place next to the window where we stood. "Don't you think it's odd how it's the only window without a screen on it? They keep us here because they need us. They learned a long time ago that when they burn us at stakes, they are ridding themselves of their own potentialities. Now they know our value, so they don't let us hurt ourselves. And they even leave us portals, like the one where you're standing, Lafitte. It must feel like home, standing in that portal next to the energy of the sun."

"Let's go, Gwinn." I had tried to be nice and pacify the man as much as I could, but he was freaking even me out, and I didn't get fucked up very easily when it came to supernatural talk.

࿐

I turned to Gwinn, and she saw something in me. "Let's go on a quest and find something fun to do," she said.

CHAPTER XIII

The deck shook, and the ship let out a thunderous roar, as if it had been struck by lightning. Tesla lay on the floor, bleeding but still conscious.

"His fictive is still controlled by bipolar opposition devoid of synthesis," one of the droids said.

"Gortby 12," Tesla called out to the droid. "Dial up transmission 45-00Y — quickly."

The droid calmly pressed a few buttons on the control panel, and a face appeared on the ship's monitor. A Klingon version of Gorbachev was visible to both of us. "You dare sell us an ionizing death-ray gun that we can't work, comrade?" he called out to Tesla.

Tesla was on his feet. "I sold you the gun; now it's your job to figure out how to work it. I'm not your God — I've given you the tool to accomplish your goal. There was never any deal for me to explain to you how to use it." He whispered under his breath to the other droid. "Gortby 6, take James away for a moment and work on COBOL programming of the fictive."

He was buying time for me to get my act together. However, Tesla knew that if Gorbachev destroyed us, the latter's programmed goals of getting the laser manipulator to work would vanish forever.

I found it fascinating that the idea of mutual destruction would allow two parties to enter into negotiations.

"I tell you what I'll do," Tesla said. "I'll tell you how you can use the gun for peaceful means, and then you, my comrade, can extrapolate from that. Then you let my crew and ship peacefully leave."

Gorbachev scratched his birthmark, which was disfigured further by the large wrinkles on his forehead. "Deal," he said.

"James, I think it's time for you and Gortby 6 to leave the bridge to me now," Tesla uttered in a low voice.

"Fair enough," I said, and I walked out alongside the droid.

I couldn't read my own fictive droid's mind — I had no idea what the droid was thinking. Although I could see the nano-neurons dancing around in his brain, exchanging information, I couldn't hear any thoughts.

We came to a room, and the door automatically opened. "The holodeck," I said as I looked around at the grid.

The droid began doing some calculations in the ether with its hand, as if working on an invisible machine. "We have to do this quickly," the droid said calmly. "Once we leave the Q-bert sphere, the heartbeat of the quantum computer is very hard to hear."

Referring to Earth as a quantum computer — I had heard that language before. The droid was a little off, I would later learn: Earth was more like a molecule of a quantum computer. Its natural forces were similar to the organs of the human body: God was the heart, and the super conscious was the brain. I'd later joke that the penis was the explicate and the anus was the implicate, but nobody would really get it.

"Pick one that is most comfortable for you, Master James," the droid said as twenty-four different scenes appeared on the holodeck's eastern wall. Each scene depicted an environment in my life: a library, a barn, a doctor's office, and my mother's bathroom, to name a few. All were places where I had experienced that feeling of being part of the kingdom of God or, to put it another way, where I'd had the realization that everything out there is in here, and vice versa.

"Places where you have been hypnotized, Master James," the droid said as I slowly approached one of the scenes depicting the inside of a womb.

"Hypnotized in my mother's womb," I commented.

"Perhaps the most powerful environment for it," the droid said.

"The drum that places me in the hypnotized state is the heartbeat of my own mother." I spoke out loud.

I wanted a more monastic setting, one unencumbered by the beating of the drum. I looked at the other environments and pointed to one I'd not seen before. My thoughts on what would make a good environment for hypnosis were myopic, to say the least. Nevertheless, I pointed to the image of a small hallway next to a window.

"Gortby 6," I directed, "this is the one."

The droid looked at the scene I had picked and started to do more calculations, this time to set up the holographic experience in the room.

"Is there a problem?" I asked.

For the first time, the droid looked rather confused and even sad, as though it could not decide whether to open the program or to direct me to choose another one. "I'm not equipped with that fourth law of robotics, Master James — that helping the species of *sapiens* outweighs injuring the one."

"And you think this will injure me?" I asked.

"This holorepresentation is not from your memory bank but from that of your author."

"Who is my author, Gortby 6? Is he or she also the author of the Mechanical Man? Is it Grace Hopper or Richard Feynman, Charles Babbage or Thomas Edison? Perhaps Tesla is my author. Tell me, goddammit."

I came up to Gortby 6 and cracked off one of the metal projectiles covering its positronic brain. It was just as big as a butcher's knife. I put it up to my wrist and said, "No harm can come to a human. If you don't tell me exactly what I need to hear, I'll kill myself, and since I'm already dead and in an alien form, that probably means I'll become part of the plasma of the stars that we all came from at one time."

I could see that the robot was processing its laws and deciding if more harm would come to me if it told me about my author than if it allowed me to kill myself. If I had been still in human form, it might have just let me die and enter into this alien body, like all people do. However, it recognized that this was not possible.

"Your author is a troubled young man — a lawyer by trade and philosopher by nature. Even as he writes you into existence, he has never controlled you. As all writers do when bringing the implicate into the explicate, he has felt the force of the implicate moving his fingers along on the keyboard."

"Am I he? Are we the same?"

"No, you were made in his image, so you are not the same, but you both evolve together: it is a coevolution. You are part of his implicate, and he is part of yours. You will never actually see one another, although you both will encounter the fictive and the real that appear to each other in form and essence."

"Are we both on the quest?"

"Yes, you are on the quest together; both of you must finish it. He must find what he is looking for in the implicate and bring it back to the explicate, and so must you."

"So he's actually building the Mechanical Man in his world — is that it?"

"No, he is laying the foundation, creating the paradigm into which the Mechanical Man will be born — the paradigm of the vital machine in the holographic universe. You, Master James, are helping him create this paradigm in your quest. You are living out his evolving paradigm for the Mechanical Man's creation."

"So he is giving me life, and I'm giving him purpose."

"Yes, you give him purpose: you help him forge a new identity."

"Gortby 6, should I consider him God?"

"No, but he is certainly your higher form and the site of your essence — every idea and action you take is from him."

"Then I have no free will."

"He does not plan how you act or react when he authors you; he just lets his fingers do the talking, and he writes. In this way, the process gives you free will; it is not absolute, but it is enough for you to be able to control much of what the author writes about you."

Then the door opened, and a laser hit Gortby 6 right smack in the head. I looked over at Gortby 12, who held a gun pointed to Gortby 6.

"Why in the world would you do such a thing?" I said.

"It didn't know what it was saying. The author had taken control of its mind. We must get you hypnotized so as to filter the fictive from your mind, or else we are all doomed, Master James."

I felt confused but also as if I had been given *verboten* information from the mouth of the droid. It had told me so much in such little time.

"Have you already made your choice, Master James?" Gortby 12 asked.

I turned and pointed to the image of the hall with the window at the end once more.

"Please place yourself in the lotus position with your legs crossed, Master James, and I will activate the holodeck."

Once it was activated, I opened my eyes and saw a hallway with a window looking out over a busy highway. The sunlight coming through the window was so bright; it alone had a hypnotic effect on me.

Gortby 12 had turned into a lady with beautiful long, dark hair. "Calm down, James," Gortby 12 said. "I'm going to filter out the fictive so we can make it to Orion's belt. Just keep looking out the window and listening to me."

I kept staring out the window, the type of stare where you feel as if your entire body is numb.

"Feel the future bringing you forward. Forget about your evolutionary development and the past creating what you are, James — feel the purpose and the future making you what you are. You are awake."

Gortby 12 repeated this over and over and over again. Everything slowed down, as if the cosmos itself were in a state of rest, no longer moving, and we could actually feel this effect. The people down below in the streets stood still, while the cars on the highway slowed down to about five miles per hour.

"You are the vital machine in the holographic universe," Gortby 12 began saying.

I turned around and saw that we were in a hospital of some sort. Gortby 12's beauty was glorified by the Valis that shone through the window. I looked to the sky and saw the blueness I had witnessed as a child.

Then the Klingon Gorbachev entered the holodeck, accompanied by Tesla with a gun to the latter's head. When Gortby 12 approached him, Gorbachev killed the droid with a bullet to the head. "Gortby," I said in a whisper, watching her fall to the ground, her blood oozing onto the floor. I was unable to recognize her in an alien form; thus, she was gone forever.

The superconscious breathed heavily on the back of my neck, as if the quest's author needed a break. With this breath, I gave one final thought to ridding myself of the fictive so we could travel to Orion's belt.

Ronald Reagan appeared and wrestled Gorbachev to the ground while Tesla attempted to repair Gortby 6. In Reagan I saw a nexus of *Star Wars*, Tesla, and the bipolar war of communism versus capitalism. *These explicate battles are so nominal compared to the battles that go on in the implicate,* I thought. Reagan and Gorbachev mutually destroyed one another, and the holodeck turned back into the grid.

I dropped to the floor, exhausted by what had just occurred. There was a whirling noise coming from Gortby 6. Tesla cradled it in his arms as a mother cradles a child. "You know, I too sought to create one in the real world — a replica of myself," he said.

"You never achieved it?" I replied.

"Oh no, I achieved it, just as Edison achieved bringing life to his damn dolls, which he buried underneath a factory in Detroit. Those damn talking dolls would have been the fetishes of all children, mothers, and, dare I say, many men around the world."

"You achieved building a robot?" I asked.

"I destroyed it. Never had I ever dreamed that it would be limited in such a way, and when I saw such a limitation it bothered me, because in it I too saw my own limitations. It scared me, James."

"What scared you?"

Lights were coming back on in the face of Gortby 6.

"The very fact that the robot needed to be monitored was what bothered me. You see, the robot was now in the explicate, its own explicate order that had unfolded from my implicate order. I was his writer and his creator. And then I thought that people would certainly go crazy thinking of existence as the eternal actions of one controlling another controlling another controlling another. The whole affair of questions of consciousness and reality appeared to be mere absurdity."

"Abbott and Costello's 'Who's on First?'" I said.

"What's on first?" Tesla replied.

"Exactly." I laughed. "A writer once compared all the great questions of existence — reality, life, and everything else we talk about — to a dialogue between two comedians. It's what you're saying: monitors communicating and controlling other secondary monitors and an infinite series of control hierarchies. Grossinger, I think, was the author's name; I read his work in the loony bin, when I could finally get some books in that damn place."

"What did you say about the loony bin?" Tesla asked.

"I didn't say anything about the loony bin; we were talking about Abbott and Costello, the comedians."

Tesla seemed to be losing it a little bit with all the drama that had taken place. His dilemma after building his robot was the idea that it really had little to no free will. The only free will his robot had, he saw, was programmed by him, so it was all an illusion, or shadow, for the robot. While the robot thought it had free will, it was all Tesla's doing.

"You lost faith in free will," I said.

Gortby 6 began to speak again. "Master James still has filters that need to be removed, Master Tesla."

Perhaps even the videogame characters that I monitor and control are the explicate of my implicate, I thought then. Perhaps they are the secondary representations of my monitoring of them.

Gortby 6 stood up and began analyzing the lifeless bodies of Reagan and Gorbachev.

"I didn't lose my faith in free will, James," Tesla said. "In fact, it grew so much in my mind that I thought of myself not as a god, but as a creator of gods. You see, I had it all backward. I was not monitoring or controlling the robot; the robot had always been controlling me, pulling me toward it and toward its eventual creation. I knew I couldn't handle it mentally. Someone else would have to pick up the quest one day and bring the Mechanical Man into existence."

I sat down and had to think. Gortby 6 came over to examine me. "Don't fucking touch me. Give me a minute." If it's all backward, then it's all about one thing pulling us toward its creation, pulling us toward creating an explicate order and reality that it can awaken to and live in. My quest, then, is not just to create the Mechanical Man and give him an explicate order — and then it hit me, like a ton of bricks, what the first and final causes are.

Then Gortby 6 shocked me into the ether.

CHAPTER XIV

There was one door next to the desk. It appeared to be the only door out of which one could escape. *The gate to freedom is always the one laced with the most despair.*

"You want to try and escape?" I asked.

She looked at me like I was a fucking dumbass for even asking her the question.

"They occlude our progress, Watson," I said in my best Sherlock Holmes accent.

"There you go again with your big words. Quit being so obdurate, Sherlock," she said with a smile, casing the door and how it operated.

"Electronics," I said. "They control or monitor the door, and the door controls and monitors us."

"And we monitor our crazy and fucked-up minds," Gwinn replied.

I wondered what our fucked-up minds were monitoring: they too must control and monitor something. Maybe my mind monitors unconsciousness — the light and the darkness unite, like the serpent that puts its rattler in its mouth. It's the zero that monitors the meaning before zero and the fictive that monitors the reality of the not.

"I wish I were one of the nurses, James, and I could let you go free," Gwinn said, "but I'm not. I may be crazy and not know what I am, but I sure know what I'm not."

"Yeah, I'm not the lady who steals shoes or the guy who talks to demons," I said sarcastically. "We're all those fucked-up people, Gwinn. Don't think that it's an either/or — an is/not."

"The door, James," she said in a zombie-like voice. "Focus on the door, not these big questions of our grand existence."

"Fair enough," I said as I walked over to the door. I pushed it as hard as I could. It was so funny how all the patients stopped and watched as I pushed on the door, while the nurses and doctors carried on; they knew we were trapped. There's some story that I can't remember in which a guy does something that seems so profound to everyone, but it's so simple to see if you're on the other side.

It was also funny how no patient had ever entered this forbidden zone next to the desk. They would look over at the area whenever they walked by, but none of them ever fucking entered it.

"You thought that it was unlocked," Gwinn said, "like those stories of the people who are so afraid of something or believe that something is so awful, and then once they do it they can't believe they didn't do it before."

"No," I said, "it's like the stories in which people have false hope and never verify it, so they can keep from knowing that their hope is just a pile of shit and they've been wrong their entire lives. Every time people look at this door, they think of the possibility that it could be unlocked, but they never try to open it. It's that illusory fucking hope that keeps them going, at least to the point of controlling and monitoring their fucked-up minds."

"First group session is in the fun room," one of the doctors said.

Gwinn and I looked at each other simultaneously and started laughing hysterically. Every time they called it "the fun room," we laughed our asses off.

There was nothing fun about this room except for outdated board games. The government thinks that crazies don't deserve to have new shit. Oh, there was one television, but this one patient would never allow anyone to change the channel, and he always had some shit on. He was so into this shit, I tell you; those programs captivated him. Good for him!

CHAPTER XV

Tesla splashed my face with water. I opened my eyes to find him and Gortby 6 standing over me. "Sorry about that, James, but Gortby 6 had to make some minor adjustments to you before we could land."

I looked over at Gortby 6 as it handed me a metal handle. "What is it?" I asked.

"Your lightsaber," Gortby 6 said.

Tesla was dressed differently now; he even looked a little different. He had donned a cloak and looked more like a sorcerer than a man of science.

I stood up and looked down at myself. I was no longer in the glowing form of an alien; I was dressed entirely in black. "What am I?" I queried.

"Your own archetype, Master James," Gortby 6 said. "I tapped into the collective unconscious and transformed you into the archetype in which you reside."

"Luke Skywalker," I said.

"A Jedi Knight," Gortby 6 corrected me. "Luke Skywalker is a fragmentation of the archetype that is a Jedi Knight. You are still Master James; however, you are also now the Jedi Knight known as Master Luke."

I glanced over at Tesla. "And you?" I asked. "You too are a Jedi Knight?"

"I have no idea what a Jedi Knight is, James, but I do like that tool you have there, since it appears to be derived from one of my early blueprints for the cosmic laser manipulator."

I activated my lightsaber. It gave a green glow to Gortby 6 and Tesla's faces. I asked Tesla again. "Then what are you?"

"A sorcerer, exactly what society pegged me to be. I'm the mimetic sorcerer as culture has decreed, although I must admit that I do like the idea of delving into *verboten* magic in almost an alchemical manner."

"We can only see the archetypes of Orion's belt if we too are in archetype form," Gortby 6 said.

"And what archetype are you?"

Gortby 6 took a second or two, punched a few invisible digits in the air, and transformed itself into Tesla. "I'm my creator or God archetype," it said.

I looked over at Tesla and whispered under my breath, "You've gotta be kidding me."

While walking back to the bridge, I could tell that my thoughts were different. My memories were clouded by something or some place that I didn't want to be: not a cave but a hospital, perhaps even an insane asylum.

Tesla looked over Gortby 6 and quietly mouthed, "You added the correct filters and took the right ones out?"

Gortby 6 replied, "I did the best I could, Master, but it was quite difficult, since he chose an archetype that is a vital machine in the holographic model. I had no idea he would choose an archetype that the Mechanical Man shines light upon."

"I can no longer read his thoughts," Tesla said.

"He has tapped into the collective unconscious in his archetypal form — even more than you, Master. He is a Jedi Knight, a master of the energy fields and the collective mind."

"James," Tesla said. "Be very careful while we're here. If you cease to exist in your archetypal form, you won't turn into a being of energy like you previously did."

"What will happen to me?" I asked.

"Let's just say the quest and suffering will be longer than you can possibly imagine," he said in a worried voice.

I'd never heard the man worried before.

CHAPTER XVI

One guy at the table in the fun room had a complex: he couldn't recognize his own facial disabilities or speech problems. To him, everything looked and sounded fine. Then he was prescribed some meds for some nerve problems in his foot, and he recognized those problems. Talk about a rude fucking awakening: that would put anybody in the funny farm. Now they had him on medication to try and place him back in his previous state, back where he was before he recognized himself: a state of utter illusion.

"Lucas," the counselor said.

It was weird how they called me by my last name here, sometimes "Lucas" or "Luke."

"You seem to try to destroy yourself and everything around you in order to somehow fulfill a need to start over again and make things — what? Better? Bigger?"

I still didn't know how or why I was there. I was still waiting for Father to come in and take me back to London. *I'll play their game while I'm here.* I figured if I kept my mouth shut and didn't say anything, they'd keep me here as long as possible. "Better."

"Make what better?"

"My understanding of everything that's going on around me and in me." Then I said something that I'd thought of before but hadn't been able to articulate. "I don't have any memories of my life — very few memories. Maybe I want to get my memory back."

"And you don't know why you have little to no memories of your life, do you?" the counselor asked.

"He has memories, lots of memories," Gwinn said.

I looked at my arms, which were bruised up rather badly.

"James," Gwinn said, "you have many memories." She was so sweet, trying to prod me out of my existential quicksand.

"Yeah, yeah, I do have memories," I said. "They're of early in life, though: foggy memories of my father and mother, my father's church, my mother's illness, and a plane ride to St. Peter's."

The counselor was shaking her head up and down in artificial approval — you know the kind I'm talking about. "Yes, that's right, and we've even heard you talk about your meeting with the Pope and Van Coleman."

"Yes," I said. "But I don't remember much after that." For some reason, the holographic model came into my head. "I mean, I just remember some bits and pieces, like pictures in a holographic film or something."

"What was that?" the counselor said.

"Oh, no — nothing."

The group moved on to another patient, but something had been triggered. There was a model in my head about holograms and robots. Movies that were shown through my brain and projected onto a wall.

"Gwinn," I whispered. "Can we get up and leave?"

She shook her head in disapproval.

CHAPTER XVII

L anding on the planet created a large plume of smoke. When the landing-bay door opened, I quickly activated my lightsaber, overwrought by the things Tesla had told me about how perishing at the hands of the archetypes would prolong the suffering of my quest.

A Christmas tree approached us, its branches decorated with poinsettias.

"Be on guard, James," Tesla said.

As the Christmas tree came closer, it transformed into a German monk with blood on his hands. "Energy can be both a wave and a particle, as I can be both symbol and martyr," the monk said. He placed his hand out for us to shake.

"Are you real?" I asked.

Tesla looked at me as a mother looks at a misbehaving child.

"If the universe is now conscious and the ultimate mind is pulling us toward it, then I'm very real, child." An underlying tone of anger emitted from the monk's voice.

"We are here to speak to the monitors of the Quantum Brain," Tesla said.

"And for what purpose?"

Tesla stared strangely at Gortby 6.

Behind the monk, a host of symbols began coming toward us — any and all religious and nationalistic symbols you could imagine.

The monk started to chant, pray, and then perform hip-hop songs, all loudly. The formless possibilities he was throwing at Tesla and Gortby weakened them and brought them to their knees, throwing their minds into a type of shamanic underworld where there was no escape. Meanwhile, the other symbols had transformed into their bodily others and were also throwing invisible waves of uncertainty toward us.

I unleashed my lightsaber on them, for their weapons of uncertainty through chant, prayer, and song could not match my Jedi mind. Through the lightsaber, they saw the *Dao* and the heavens. They saw that I was part of the Quantum Brain — that I was possibly the brain's creator.

Then the archetypes began to adapt even to the power of my Jedi mind, recognizing that I was weakening their powers with my own thoughts of randomness. They would soon discover that my randomness was a code-carrying messenger they could transform into another archetype and kill — and kill me along with it.

As they transformed my apparently random code into a sequence they could understand, the remaining archetypes became Jedi in their own right, with lightsabers. As Tesla and Gortby 6 desperately tried to get back on their feet and help me from where they knelt on the ground, they were quickly beheaded.

One archetype transformed into the Emperor from *Star Wars* and began to electrocute me with my own Force. I fell to the ground and tossed and turned, the electricity running through my body and expunging from it the waves, particles, and frequencies with which Gortby 6 had imbued me on the ship.

Then the brilliant modeler of the Quantum Brain — indeed, the master of the holographic brain and the projector of the implicate — came running over the hills. In that moment, I felt dark moods of depression overtaking him, but he still ran toward me. He was a Jedi master in the form of the physicist David Bohm.

"The madman comes," one of the archetypes said, and they turned their attention toward him.

CHAPTER XVIII

They think I'm mad or something." I sat, holding my face in my hands. As I had heard all the horror stories of those surrounding the table, it had dawned on me that God was either dead or a vile being. And if someone was fucking ignorant enough to say that we author our own lives, then I'd ask him or her why the fuck these people had authored the lives they had to live.

"Zombies," Gwinn said. "Just pretend everybody else is a zombie and you're the only one who really is conscious of the world around you."

"And what about you?" I whispered.

"Sorry, buddy — if I'm your creation, then I must be a zombie too. Can't help you there."

"No way," I said. "I've imbued you with consciousness."

"Gwinn." The counselor called upon her. The rest of the circle around the table had spoken, and it was her turn to be analyzed. "You're in a more recuperative wing of the hospital now, Gwinn. How does it feel to be out of surgery?"

She glanced around the room as if everything were in slow motion. Her eyes settled on me. I tried to give her the look you give someone when you know there's something she hasn't told you, but you want to communicate that you don't give a fuck — that you love her unconditionally. *That's the illusion we play on ourselves. We think that we have to put on a show for other people or that it matters what others think.*

"No self," she said.

"And what does that mean — 'no self'?" the counselor asked.

I had never seen Gwinn in this state before — so timid and anxiety-ridden. She had become a scared little girl right before my very eyes. She was the one who had been so in control and strong before the counselor brought this up. "You're fucking with her," I said.

One of the male nurses observing the therapy session came a little closer to me, letting me know by his body language that I didn't need to interrupt the counselor.

"I feel like a person now," Gwinn said. "Before, I felt like I had no self."

"And what about Peter?" the counselor said.

"Peter is gone," Gwinn said. "That sad and confused person I was is gone. He was the one who had no self, not me."

"That's right," the counselor acknowledged. "You're Gwinn now, no longer Peter."

Holy fuck, I said to myself. Gwinn was once a dude named Peter. Who was the zombie now? Perhaps it was me. I listened to Gwinn explain how she had tried to kill herself when she was a guy named Peter. She had gone through a sex change, and now she was here trying to figure out her new identity.

Had she lied to me by not telling me she was once a guy? *I told her everything about myself, right?* At least she remembered being a guy; I couldn't even fucking remember half of my life. *So, was her identity as Peter more of an identity than mine as James was? I mean, does her memory of her being a guy mean that she has two identities? What the fuck?*

And then, for some reason, the name "Peter" started to conjure up some feelings in me. I had met a Peter before coming here, but it was a different Peter — in Rome, perhaps, with my father. Memories began to flood my mind. Maybe Peter was our family doctor.

That was when I vomited all over the fucking table.

CHAPTER XIX

The madman, David Bohm (the father of the holographic model), swashbuckled his way over the rocks and demolished every archetype seeking my demise.

"Get up, James," he said. "I know why you're here. We haven't much time."

I got to my feet, grabbed my lightsaber, and ran behind Bohm.

"On Mount Pribram, we'll find those with whom you need to discuss the quest."

"Who is that?" I asked.

"The archetypes' digital memory, nano-technology, crystal structure, and genome mapping. They know the Mechanical Man best and can direct you to your courier, the Quantum Brain."

Courier, I thought. The word reminded me of finding those odd envelopes so long ago at my home in London. Now it was the task of a courier to deliver something radically different than mere envelopes containing a map, pictures, and formulas.

"Schrödinger's cat," Bohm said.

"What?" I queried. I was always in my own head when I was running, never listening to anyone.

"Schrödinger's cat." Bohm pointed halfway up the mountain to a giant cat. Its appearance had no pattern whatsoever; it was randomly disappearing and then reappearing in random places all over the mountain.

"How do we kill it once we get to it?" I asked.

"I've never had the good fortune of having another Jedi with me, James, especially one who knows the holographic universe as well as you do."

"I know nothing of the holographic universe."

"You know everything about it, young man. You've been living it for ages and ages, in fact. You're the chosen one and the chosen few — you are the fusion of the singularity and the plurality."

This cat was, of course, the archetype of Schrodinger's cat, a concept I really can't explain, even after Father tried to teach me about it. It has something to do with radioactive waves in a box and a flask of poison. While the cat is within the box, removed from our observation, the radioactive waves preserve it while the poison kills it. We don't know if the cat is dead or alive until we lift the top off the box. At least, that's how I understood it at fifteen. Physicists please don't laugh. I didn't quite know why the archetype of the cat was able to randomly disappear and reappear or how to kill it.

"The crux of the matter, James, is that when my friend Rudolf Steiner was here, we figured out the cat's pattern of appearance and reappearance — more by luck than pattern, though. Nevertheless, we killed it. But right before it ceased being, it disappeared; when it reappeared, it had rejuvenated itself to its original form. This happened every time we thought we had killed it. That's the problem."

CHAPTER XX

W hy didn't you tell me?" I asked Gwinn, who sat at the end of my bed looking through a magazine.

"You vomited on the table. Do I need to draw you a picture of your reaction?"

"It wasn't from that — I don't know why I puked. It's the only failsafe switch that I have."

That's right, my failsafe switch — or my escape button, whatever you want to call it — was triggered by the things that scared me most, like puking, nausea, infinity, God, evil in the world, or the fact that I might be God. I had learned to use all the things that scared the shit out of me to keep from becoming totally depressed. I know what you're probably saying to yourself: this guy's already in a funny farm, so apparently his failsafe has totally failed him. But you should try it the next time you get into an argument with your significant other or have a bad day. Just sit there and think about the big questions in life that scare the shit out of you. I guarantee you'll see your problems differently.

"How does it feel? I mean, physically, now that you don't have anything?" I tried to ask the question as tactfully as I could.

"It's like it's still there," Gwinn said.

"Like a phantom limb?"

"That's right, like a phantom limb. I still feel it get hard sometimes, and then I remember that it's gone forever," she said, thumbing through the magazine.

As much as we try to shorten the fucking gap between mind and body, I had concluded that there would always be one, no matter how hard we might try to say that the mind is somewhere else, the spirit is something different, and the body is simply a shell. There's still a gap you can't get rid of. Gwinn was a pastiche of every mind-body argument I had ever heard.

"Do you still dream like a guy or a girl?" Really, only my dreams, including my daydreams, allowed me to say, "I AM." My memories were so fucked by the meds that I wouldn't have recognized myself, even if I could've gone back in time and been thrown back into my body at a younger age. But my dreams seemed to have a flow to them, like the flow of a stream. My dreams were uninterrupted by age or by time. *Fuck all that about the emperor's new clothes.* I was a new self from moment to moment, and in the funny farm my dreams were more important than reality to me. "I'm sorry I asked," I said. "My maturity level is about that of a fifteen-year-old, since I have no memory of the last fifteen to twenty years."

"Do you remember what you told me when we first met in here, James?" Gwinn asked.

"I have no idea."

"You asked me why I ditched Peter for Gwinn. This was before I even told you my name or you knew anything about my sex change. Nobody could have known. So I guess you don't remember what you said when I asked you how you knew all that about me."

"What—"

A nurse interrupted us. "Lucas, your father is here."

"My father," I said, a knot in my throat.

CHAPTER XXI

My first thought was to track the cat's aura in order to know where it intended to reappear. Although its disappearances and reappearances may appear random to us, the cat still has intentions and projections of where it intends to appear. The aura of the cat will be projected first, prior to the cat's physical form following it.

I quickly scanned the mountain while Master Bohm fought off the cat's claws with his lightsaber. The cat's claws were impervious to the lightsaber's power; it was as if the lightsaber were merely a sword made of materialized atoms. You could hear the claws and the sword clash against one another like metal on metal.

When I heard Master Bohm stick the cat in its gut, I knew it was only a matter of time before the cat would disappear and regenerate somewhere else. I honed in on the holographic reality and saw the cat's aura appear on the mountain's western side. My Jedi powers allowed me to transfer my bodily apparatus to the spot where the cat would appear.

Oh, but I was mistaken about how the cat's appearance would affect my apparatus. When the cat started to form,

I was in its spot. Its materialization and atomic structure began to vibrate my atoms, which were foreign to this planet. It was similar to what happened when the Europeans went to the New World and unleashed their diseases on the Native Americans. My atomic structure was not used to this type of dual materialization. The vibration of the cat's archetype form was so much stronger than mine. My atoms began to vibrate so quickly that my body caught on fire. Have you ever asked yourself which way to die is the most painful or worst? I can vouch for the fact that it is burning alive. Any training I had received from Eastern gurus was no match for this type of cosmic burning, much worse than the burning at Tesla's laboratory. It was not as if someone had tied me to a stake and lit a match; rather, the fire was caused by the fast vibrations of atoms fighting for space. Unimaginable to your mind in the explicate!

I heard Master Bohm wielding his lightsaber and cutting off the head of the cat, causing it to disappear once more. It was hard for me to open my eyelids, since my skin had a crisp layer of burnt molecules all over it.

Master Bohm unhinged a horn from his belt, placed it to his mouth, and blew in it, creating a miraculous sound, like something composed by Wagner. The sound brought to life the archetype of a Jewish Gargoyle made from the earth. This Gargoyle archetype's form was different than that of pictures of fictive Gargoyles I had seen. I remembered full well how Gortby 6 had expunged my fictive filters. This Gargoyle was novel to me. His body was made of earth through which you could see. He helped Master Bohm assemble me into a new bodily apparatus. The word, Jacob, kept appearing in my mind.

Then I saw exactly what they were doing: transforming my Jedi archetype into the archetype of Luke Skywalker's father, Darth Vader.

"This will allow you to recognize yourself as a vital machine, James," Master Bohm said. "More importantly, you will be a vital machine in the recognized holographic reality."

Master Bohm reminded me of so many of the wonderful heroes I'd met before. There was so much suffering combined with genius and empathy in his face. Go back and look at the life and history of any genius. I mean a real genius: someone who changed how we view empathy, love, and human beings around us. You will see that he or she experienced a life of suffering until he or she reached nirvana.

Then the mask was placed over my head, and I could hear myself become Darth Vader.

CHAPTER XXII

That's not my father," I told Gwinn. A man wearing a Texas Rangers baseball cap stood in front of us. He had a bag of clothes and some other items to deliver to me.

He and the nurse were finishing talking about an antidote to my problems. That was as amusing as them telling Gwinn they had an antidote for her, back when she was in the form of Peter.

"How you holding up?" the man said.

Although I had no memories of my father for the last fifteen years, it wasn't hard for me to conclude that this was an imposter. I felt like I was in *The Truman Show*, not locked up in a loony bin. *When you think about it, I guess, that film is no different than the dynamics involved in this fucked-up place.*

"You're not my father," I said. This was turning into a bad *Star Wars* spin-off, with a guy I'd never met before telling me, "I am your father."

The man even started playing the role of Darth Vader, calling me "Luke." He said, "Luke, I am your father." *How fucked up is that?* He was playing with my mind and allowing my fictive worlds to enter into banal reality.

Clearly, though, the man cared for me; I could see it in his eyes. I began to notice colors around beings for the first time. He had a nice blue hue surrounding him.

"Here are some things from home they're allowing me to give you," he said, passing a bag over to me. "Get better soon. We're all waiting for you to get better, so you can finish it."

He turned around and started walking toward the door.

"Finish what?" I called out to him, but it was too late. He was already on the other side of the door.

There's that old *Twilight Zone* episode in which a guy wakes up from surgery and has had a facelift so he can look like the pig aliens with whom he now resides. That's the way I felt, like I had awoken from a bad dream after having an operation and everyone else around me had had operations too: all of our physical traits had changed. That was the only way I could understand the way I looked. I know age does a lot of things to one's looks, but I swear that I looked totally different. I knew it was still me, but I was in a totally different body. Yet it was odd: it felt like I had been in this body my entire life too.

"It's like everyone has had a facelift, Gwinn," I said as we walked back to the fun room with the bag of stuff Lord Vader had given me.

She threw off my comment and didn't say anything. I guessed I needed to watch what I said around her, since she'd gotten a hell of a lot more than a facelift. I laughed inside my head. That's what I started to do from that point on: capitulate to the fact that I was in some comedy or comic book and that the fantastic was possible in my absurd existence. When you have that mentality, even the worst things that life throws at you become hilarious: you think of how funny someone must be to make up such a scenario for you to live out. Clearly, this much fucked-up shit does not happen to one person by chance or luck.

"Let's see what your father brought you, James," Gwinn said. We sat down at the oval table in the fun room.

CHAPTER XXIII

R ise, Lord Vader," Bohm said.

I adjusted to the new holographic reality around me. It had become self-evident that my problem of being both the observer and the instrument was gone. I didn't have to try to see myself as a vital machine or as a go-between for spirit and machine any longer. In the archetype of Darth Vader, I epitomized the vital-machine principles that enabled the self-recognition of human as organism and machine.

But there was more. With this realization, the holographic reality looked different. All that was not perceived in the explicate when I was in my organism form was clearly visible when I was in the archetype of Vader. Participation was the key.

Bohm laughed and said, "There's work to be done, Lord Vader." He could see how excited I was by the realization of what the self and reality look like when one is placed within the proper organic-machine equation archetype.

"The cat," I said in my new deep voice.

"The cat still guards our entrance into the Quantum Brain's layer," Bohm said.

"Give me a minute," I told him.

I sat in the lotus position and began to see the astral phases of consciousness in the holographic reality. It was merely a matter of replication. It wasn't about the cat's rejuvenation or apparent death and disappearance. *Schrödinger's cat can only be killed by becoming it. And only through the holographic reality are vital machines able to astral-morph into other species.*

I explained my findings to Bohm, telling him that I would become one with the cat. There would be a bipolar struggle within the cat, which would be the cat recognizing a new duality overtaking it. I ordered Master Bohm to chop the cat's head off once this occurred. During this interval of death, I would hold the cat hostage in its own existence while I astral-morphed back into the machine of Darth Vader. The cat would have no way of recognizing that it too was a vital machine. *The cat still believes it is merely a vital organism.*

"And if the cat recognizes that it is a vital machine in a holographic existence?" Bohm queried.

"Then my time here is over, and the quest will be that much more arduous and time-consuming, my friend," I said.

With my Jedi knowledge of the light and the dark, I was able to morph myself into the cat's bodily apparatus. This was the first time I knew what consciousness and the mind really felt like. I could not feel the essence of mind, which has nothing at all to do with chemicals in the brain, synapses, or neurons communicating with other neurons. Instead, I felt the crux of communication and control: the mind is a communication between the self and the plurality. You see, it's not that there is a two-step dance that occurs in the cosmos; the two-step dance is occurring in the mind, which is you in your explicate form dancing with yourself in the implicate. Fusing myself with the cat was just another way for me to recognize myself in the implicate awaiting my own arrival. It had nothing to do with the cat. The cat was merely a fabricated box, like the one I used to play with as a child and turn into vehicles. And that was exactly what the cat had become: a great vehicle that was formerly a cardboard box, which I had transformed into a moving, living machine in my mind.

Telepathically, I transferred the thought of where I would next appear to Master Bohm; there, he set up a trap to capture the cat.

"That's how you defeat Schrödinger's cat," Master Bohm said. "You have to contain it once you become it."

CHAPTER XXIV

I don't understand whether he thinks I'm a zombie or he thinks all of you are," I said as I placed a book about how to survive a zombie uprising on the table. I pulled from the bag a gas mask, a water canteen, and a book by Richard Grossinger on consciousness and reality.

Gwinn took Grossinger's book out of my hands. "Listen, James... 'Wake up. Wake up. You are living in a miracle...'" she read.

There was some more shit in this bottomless bag.

"'Consciousness, by lounging about and conveying information, has already claimed the parapsychological and telekinetic territory...'" she continued. "'Subjective existence *is* the Holy Ghost; it cannot be made any more metaphysical or impart anything that is stranger than *its very existence*, so healing by prayer and remote viewing are well down on the overall strangeness list...

"'A universe with consciousness is more different from a universe without consciousness than a universe with telekinesis and telepathy is from the universe we have — and by a long shot. Consciousness is the glow that illuminates everything (dreams included) — even the physical world, even what it is not supposed to illuminate, and that is a big one, the biggest one of all. It reduces every other coup or experiment to sleight of hand (or sleight of mind if you prefer). Turning the light *on* is the Big Kahuna.'"

I wasn't even paying attention to what Gwinn was reading at the time. Nevertheless, the words that came out of her mouth were tapping into more than just my subconscious; they were reactivating a quest in me that had been long forgotten.

"Another book about a rebellion," I said, pulling out another survival handbook, Daniel Wilson's *How to Survive a Robot Uprising*. "Where's the fucking book that says how to survive human suffering? That's the one I need." Jokingly, I added, "Even this imposter father of mine can't give me any practical shit so I can get the fuck out of here. Instead, he gives me manuals on how to survive robots and zombies. It's no wonder why I'm in here, Gwinn."

She laughed a little as she picked up the robot manual. "This is actually written as if it's really going to happen, James."

I pulled out another book, which was just poetry. "It's like that game you play when you have to decide what three books you would take with you if you were placed on a desert island. People always say some bullshit like the Bible, Shakespeare, and a dictionary."

"Clearly, your imposter father is not cut from that cloth," Gwinn said, waving the robot manual in the air.

"Shit, I guess not. Maybe I underestimated him."

"Listen to this," she said. "On page 110, it tells you 'how to reason with a robot.' Get this, James, you'll like this one. It says: 'A robot has a stellar memory and laser-beam concentration. If it doubts your veracity, a metal menace may refuse to listen to any further emanations from your slobber-hole.'" She was fascinated.

CHAPTER XXV

O nce I became the cat and passed on to the realm of death, I recognized that death's transitions did not differ from our stream of consciousness or the mystery of how one moment in life leads to another. *Everything truly is in flux; that's why we could never decide whether the cat was dead or alive. In a way, the cat itself in its bodily form has always been empty or dead. The illusion of its physical being is what is perceptible to our material being.* Once I was able to become the cat and see the cat's illusion for what it was, in the body of a zombie or a robot, I recognized the importance of human consciousness and how consciousness itself actually gives vitality or vitalism to the vital machine. *Consciousness is not mechanical.* The experience within Schrödinger's cat allowed me to never fear death again. I saw no difference between death and the time passing on a beautiful summer's day. It was merely a transition through the ether of ideas.

"The bush burns bright now, James," Master Bohm said. "You have lit its fire."

"The burning bush," I said, looking up at the top of the mountain. "What is it?"

"The archetype of its consciousness: it is life, a flame that is always changing but still always burning." Master Bohm began to grow a long beard and change into a wizard right before my very eyes.

"You're changing," I said.

"We all change from moment to moment. That's why you no longer fear death: you recognize that you have died trillions of times in your explicate form."

In all the commotion and mess, I had lost my lightsaber and morphed into Luke Skywalker. "Here," Master Bohm said, "a new lightsaber for you." I activated it, which caused an awesome blue to light up Bohm's now-aged face.

Van Coleman had been a conspiracy theorist. I remembered Father had told me he'd had all these books on alien abductions — ideas about how ancient aliens had brought about *Homo sapiens* through implanting DNA in apes. This had interested me when I was in the explicate. Now that I was coming close to being in the implicate, I could see the tautology of it all. Because it would have to go on forever. *If the aliens gave life to us, then the question is who gave life to them, and then who gave life to those that gave life to them.* Once more, we would end up back in the Abbott and Costello "Who's on First?" skit.

In recognizing my status as a vital machine, I understood that consciousness didn't just come about because of evolution or because some aliens imbued us with it. We authored consciousness at the right time. *We've willed consciousness to happen.*

The question of how you can will consciousness to happen without consciousness does arise. I mean, somebody has to put things in motion, right?

Master Bohm was digging deep into the earth. "Clay," he said. "We will smear this clay all over our bodies, so the burning bush does not see its reflection on our skin."

"That's a bad thing?" I said.

"The burning bush is the engine of the Quantum Brain; if it sees its reflection, it will recognize its potential."

CHAPTER XXVI

H ow to recognize a rebellious servant robot,' James. It even has a list that you need to look for: 'sudden lack of interest, unexplained disappearance, unwillingness to be shut down, repetitive stabbing movements, and constant talk of killing.'"

"Jesus," I said. "I think we're surrounded by rebellious servant robots."

"Potentially," Gwinn said.

I sat down in a chair. Sweat began to channel its way through the pores on the palms of my hands.

"What's wrong?" she asked.

"You said 'potentially.' It just caused another light to turn on in my mind. I can't explain why or how, but it did."

"Is it from some memories that you've tapped into?" Gwinn asked.

It was more like potential energies screaming out to me for freedom.

An Indian man in need of deodorant came into the fun room and sat next to us. "Your aura tells me that your mantra is 'finish it,'" he said.

"Finish it," I said. I stared into dead space. Mr. Watts, a medical doctor, had gone nuts from his hobby. It's so fucked up, how genius trickles down into the realm of crazy through passions that usually come in the form of hobbies rather than vocations. Being a medical doctor had bored him until he had started buying high-power microscopes. The differences between the macrocosmic and microcosmic world had fucked him up.

"Physics will fuck anybody up, brother, but you have to follow your bliss, even to your detriment." Watts was proof that 99.9 percent of those who find a way to cross into the implicate never come back — or they end up in the asylum and then the grave. "I overheard your talk of potential in the next room," he said.

"Last time I heard the word 'potential' was when I was a guy dating a girl and her mom said that I had potential. Little did her mother know." Gwinn was still engrossed in the survival manuals; it was really cute.

But my attention was now focused on Watts. "What fucked you up so bad in physics?"

"Potential," he said. "Those atoms and all the so-called building blocks of the universe don't really exist until you observe them. They all have potential to be seen and to be both particles and waves at the same time — but all that potential is only capable of living and becoming conscious if we observe it…

"Too much power. It's like the Hollywood rich who have too much money and can't handle it; they go off their rocker. That's all that happened to you."

"What do you mean by too much power?" I said. "You felt guilty, I would guess, that all these atoms depend on you for their existence. I bet when you go into a bookstore you have a panic attack because you can't give attention to every writer's ideas. You're just afraid of having responsibility. You're afraid that you might be God of your own universe."

Watts looked a little puzzled.

"Finish it," I said. "Get back in society, do your doctor shit, and crown yourself."

CHAPTER XXVII

After covering ourselves with clay from head to toe, we climbed up toward the burning bush.

"We seek to enter into the Quantum Brain of Orion's belt," Master Bohm explained to the bush.

The fire flickered in random waves, undulating its majesty and beauty over the ground and toward us. As I watched the communication between Master Bohm and the bush, it became more and more instantaneous. How can I adequately explain this to you, when you are reading this in the explicate? It's as if my perception of the communication were tricking me when, in fact, my perception just couldn't catch up. In your reality, it would look like Master Bohm was asking the bush questions after it had already answered him — that's the best way I can describe it to you. Communication was no longer orderly or linear; to an explicate viewer's perception, it appeared random. It was sort of like setting your CD player on random play while at the same time knowing what random tracks would be picked, so it was not random at all.

The bush seemed extremely happy with Master Bohm. Master Bohm, however, excoriated the bush for making the refusal of the quest too easy and the sacrifices much too difficult.

The bush had already answered Master Bohm's question by responding. "Recognizing 'I AM' should never be an easy task. No longer would we call it the quest or living if it were easy, David. 'I AM' is difficult but well worth the energy it takes to escape the emptiness of the empty."

Then Master Bohm began to morph into the archetype of King David. He knelt in front of the bush and cried, holding his face in his hands.

In the fire of the bush, I saw a consciousness that I didn't think existed: a consciousness that was not in flux, like the flickering flame, but one that was stable and unchanging. What type of consciousness? You might ask from the explicate reality in which you reside. It was a consciousness that did not have the tools of memory and foresight, for it did not need them. It was a consciousness that already knew what had happened in the past and what would happen in the future. It was a consciousness that did not live in the moment or practice those outdated sayings like "seize the moment"; rather, it inhabited and would inhabit all moments (past, present, and future). And in this habitation of all moments, it changed the very concept of control. You see, control in the implicate is not control at all; rather, the very concept of control, or its archetype, if you will, is creativity. That's right. In the implicate, communication, control, and information are utterly gone; instead, these concepts are replaced by synchronicity, creativity, and infinite "I AM."

It didn't take me long to figure out that the voice of the burning bush was the same voice I had heard before, the voice that I always wanted to take credit for as my own.

Maybe it was my own, but in the past I had just referred to it as the Holy Ghost. My preternatural ability to communicate with the Holy Ghost now allowed me to synchronize all of my questions with the fire's answers.

I looked into the flickering flame, and I saw my ideas and choices having a life of their own when viewed by a circle of the fictive. This time, the fictive world that I saw in the flame was that of the characters in Tolkien's *The Fellowship of the Ring.* They all surrounded my life choices, and the ones they sought to undertake, observe, and carry with them were the choices that were telepathically appropriated into my life's actions of cause and effect. It was not as if they were authoring my actions; rather, they were giving life to the potentialities of certain actions over others. Still, the filtered thoughts of why people suffer and why there are deaths for no apparent reason came to me as rapidly as lightning to Franklin. My choices were not illusory, but the choices others made around me were in fact illusions. Nothing was there before my entrance into the womb, for there was nothing there that I could observe.

CHAPTER XXVIII

C arl Jung once had a patient who explained that in the afterlife we have to stand up in a circle of people, tell them what lessons we have learned, and explain to them the quest," I said to Gwinn.

"You're teaching us today, James," Watts said.

Unbeknownst to myself, I had created a Bible study class. It was the only time that everyone who was part of the class could have books from which to read — that is, with close supervision by the staff to ensure that the books not be used as weapons. *As I write this, I'm sure there's still fighting over in Israel, with tribal brother killing tribal brother, and here we are, worried about each other using the Bible as a projectile. So fucked up, yet so true!*

"'This is how the birth of Jesus Christ came about. His mother Mary was pledged to be married to Joseph, but before they came together, she was found to be with child through the Holy Spirit.' I found this in Matthew 1:18," Watts said to the ground, the last person receiving the text being me.

The person sitting next to Watts, a young black female, started to read. "'But after he had considered this, an angel of the Lord appeared to him in a dream and said,

"Joseph son of David, do not be afraid to take Mary home as your wife, because what is conceived in her is from the Holy Spirit.'" I found this in Matthew 1:20."

Gwinn moved her head over to mine and whispered. "You asked them to find passages that mention the Holy Spirit or Holy Ghost last time. You also said something about a quote: 'Know what is in front of your face and what is hidden from you will be disclosed.'"

Everyone had found a passage, but no one had seemed to find any mention of the Holy Ghost or the quote I'd mentioned — I didn't even know where the quote came from. I think it was in a dream I had when I met King Arthur.

"Very interesting how the Holy Spirit goes around impregnating women," Watts said with his thick Indian accent.

Of course, everyone laughed.

"What's the point of this exercise?" a teenage boy said.

"I don't know," I said. "I guess to see that we somehow changed the word 'spirit' into 'ghost.'"

"Ghosts aren't real," the young man said.

"Then what the hell is 'spirit'?" I countered.

"It seems to be consciousness," Watts said.

I glanced over at him.

He was reading the text with enthusiasm. "Why is the Old Testament still attached to the New Testament? One seems to replace the other entirely."

"I don't know," I replied. The last memory I had of the Bible was seeing it through a bevy of murals at St. Peter's. I asked Gwinn, "What did I say in our last meeting?"

"You said that you were wrong to discard the miracles and hocus-pocus of the text. You said that the moral teachings are self-evident, but the miracles and metaphors are where we find clues to who we are and where we came from."

"That doesn't sound like something I would say."

"Tell us what the Holy Ghost is, James," Watts said. "You promised us that you would tell us what it is. I have given you what I think it is — that it is the stream of consciousness that sets us apart from animals and inanimate matter."

"The Quantum Brain is what we seek to speak to," I said.

CHAPTER XXIX

Y our quest is to bring the Mechanical Man into the reality of the seen," the bush said.

I glanced over at David Bohm, who was still on his knees paying homage to the bush.

The bush began to explain how I had failed to describe the paradigms of the holographic reality and the vital machine to myself in an adequate manner. "You have been in and out of the implicate order of reality so many times, but you have only recognized it subtly. You have to immerse yourself in it if you want to bring anything back with you. The kingdom of heaven is not a place — you must get out of this train of thought of 'who, what, when where, and why.' Your geometric architecture and simple housing will change."

Then the voice of Tesla came from the bush. *"James."*

"Where are you?" I asked.

"Back in the form of my author, able to fly wherever I want. I just came from being a tree and learning how to communicate with all of my leaves. It is a truly synchronized nature in the pure implicate."

I had learned so much from talking with the bush. The problem, I would later realize, was that memory vis-à-vis communicating with one's author through the Holy Ghost was so difficult when one moved on to other forms. It was easy if one stayed in the archetype form. That was why Tesla had had it so easy when he was alive in the form of *Homo sapiens*: he was both archetype and human, so he was a true blend of the fictive and real.

"Is that how you ended up with the ability to enter the implicate, Master Bohm?"

"Look around you, James." It was a gift from the burning bush. Circling around me were the faces of elves, hobbits, men, and dwarfs.

Master Bohm had morphed into the archetype of Gandalf and spoke the words of the author Tolkien: "'If you had really started this affair, you might be expected to finish it. But you know well enough now that starting is too great a claim for any, and that only a small part is played in great deeds by any hero. You need not bow! Though the word was meant, and we do not doubt that under jest you are making a valiant offer. But one beyond your strength... You cannot take this thing back. It has passed on. If you need my advice any longer, I should say that your part is ended, unless as a recorder. Finish your book, and leave the ending unaltered! There is still hope for it. But get ready to write a sequel, when they come back.'"

Long before my quest, Tolkien was well aware of the vital machine in the holographic reality. In the council of Elrond, the essences of Tesla, Edison, Hopper, Feynman, Asimov, the Walker brothers, and George Lucas blended with the archetypes of Tolkien's characters.

"You won't go at it alone, Bilbo," said Lucas, who was in the form of a dwarf. The Walker brothers, in the forms of Merry and Pippin, were already working on some hoaxes to trick the Quantum Brain into giving us shortcuts to the Mechanical Man. Hopper was Legolas, Tesla was Aragorn, Edison was Boromir, Bohm was Gandalf, and Feynman was Sam. Asimov, the most prolific writer of science fiction related to mechanical men, headed the council as Elrond.

"They will all accompany you on this journey into the Quantum Brain," Asimov said.

CHAPTER XXX

I cleared my throat. "Well," I said, "I think the Holy Ghost is what tells you that you're awake and that allows you to say, 'I AM.'"

When I said this, everyone in the circle looked like zombies. Hell, I didn't know what the fuck the Holy Ghost was; it all seemed like a bunch of bullshit to me, anyway. Mystic shit I didn't have time for.

But then there seemed to be a spark that twinkled in the eyes of the patients in the circle. The light switch was turned on.

"The Holy Ghost can be your best companion or your worst enemy — it can lead you to the light of your potential or to the dark side of your anxieties," I said. "All of you are more powerful than you can possibly imagine. Look at what you've allowed your minds to do to you — to overtake your physical apparatuses. Imagine the type of creativity you could unleash on the world if you controlled those powers. The Holy Ghost is that potential waiting to come forth, the awakening light that is always talking to you and that never leaves you alone. The Holy Ghost is the hero inside urging you to get up when you fall down, but it's also the villain telling you to stay down."

"How do you get the Ghost to help you get up, James?" Watts asked.

"I guess if I knew the answer to that, my friend, I wouldn't be in here... You have to feel good — I haven't felt good since I was in grade school. All this talk about the Holy Ghost means nothing if you don't feel good," I said.

"I have headaches every day," another patient said. "How can I even think of getting this Ghost to help me if I'm in bed suffering every day? I don't have time for the Ghost."

A mind-and-body dualistic argument was taking place before me. How the fuck do you even attempt to heal the mind when the physical body is suffering? Sure, all the holistic docs out there would say that the mind can heal the body, but if you never feel physically good enough to pay attention to the healing attributes of the mind and communicate with the Ghost, it really just ends up being a dog chasing its tail.

"I get what James is saying," Gwinn said. "Before my operation, I ignored the Ghost; I ignored my awakening. You know how all we really want to do in here is sleep. Well, after my operation, I didn't want to sleep any more. I spoke to the Ghost; I wasn't hiding from it any more. And it's worked."

"What's worked?" Watts asked.

"I've awoken to love, desires, empathy, and respect."

"Then what do we have to do?" a young Persian man asked. "Wait until we are able to download ourselves in physical apparatuses that feel no pain so we can focus on our minds? Seems like we all were the next in line for the lottery, if that's the case, and missed it by probably a century or two. I know I won't be around to become a vital machine."

"What did you say?" I asked.

"I said I know I won't be around to become any better," the Persian said.

"No, you didn't say that." I stood up. "You said something else; you said 'vital machine.'"

"No, he didn't, James," Gwinn said. She called me to sit back down.

"I swear to God, you said the fucking words 'vital machine.' What did you mean by that?" I demanded.

CHAPTER XXXI

Master Bohm was handing us all ropes with hooks on one end and body harnesses on the other. "What are the harnesses for?" I asked.

Master Bohm explained how we would have to ground the hooks to the planet's core in order to sink through the planet and thereby change its chemical composition so we could perceive the Quantum Brain.

"How do we sink the hook and rope through?"

"You imagine it," Legolas said. "The rope is made by the elves, so your mind will direct it wherever you want it to travel. Your aura will travel with it once it's hooked up to the planet's core, and then you can travel on it as if you are musical notes vibrating on a string."

I imagined my rope and hook traveling through miles of soil, hitting numerous pockets of gas, plasma, and water. I saw the rope holding up to the heat of the planet's magma and its golden hook growing strong, not melting or weakening under the heat.

A memory of the explicate order flashed before my eyes: my father attempting to jimmy a coat hanger through the top window of his car to unlock the door after I, at two years old, had locked myself in. I could see the hook on the coat hanger grab the door handle and lift it to open the gates of freedom.

"I've hooked on," Aragorn said.

Thunder rang out in the night sky.

"You better believe it knows we're here now," Gimli said.

Master Bohm, still in the form of the white wizard Gandalf, began chanting some divination spells.

Gorbachev and Reagan popped into my head, and the lightning struck the top of the mountain.

"I'm hooked," Legolas reported.

"Gandalf," I called out into the chaos. "Say 'Reagan's *Star Wars*.'"

Master Bohm looked over at me and repeated what I had told him over and over again. Then he raised his walking stick and struck the ground with it, letting out a thunderous orchestra of sounds that reverberated throughout the ropes to the planet's core. A large bubble shielded us from the lightning. "Go, you fools!"

Master Bohm just stood there. I realized he wouldn't be coming with us.

Once I hooked onto the core, I checked that Merry and Pippin were also stable and hooked on. Our auras left their shells and began to travel down the ropes, vibrating through the planet's elements.

The elements had changed from the chemical makeup perceived by our shells to that perceived by our auras. Each level had different types of laboratories, creating stuff. The inhabitants of this level were all alchemists working on different magical spells to change the elements into something new. They were creating what we would call matter out of waves and light. It was a glorious act to behold. The information that they utilized to create this matter was energy itself, which they too had grounded with their own ropes and found in the core.

"James," Aragorn called out. "Once we get close to the core, we all are going to exist on our ropes on the second level to protect you against any ignorant alchemists who may think you mean to do harm to the Quantum Brain."

"But what am I doing today when I see the Quantum Brain?"

"You have to negotiate with its archetypes."

CHAPTER XXXII

I felt a pull on my wrist and a snap. When I looked down at my arm, I saw Gwinn had pulled on a rubber band around my wrist and had snapped it something fierce.

"Christ, Gwinn, what the fuck did you do that for?"

"Look, asshole," she said as she lifted up her own arm and showed me a rubber band around it. "You're the one who told me that when our minds began to float away in the wind, like blank pieces of paper, we need to be snapped back into reality." She pulled back on her own band and snapped it, letting out a quiet whimper.

"Thanks," I said.

"Anyway, it's time for us to talk to our psychiatrists and lawyers."

"We speak to them together?" I queried.

"Not at all," she said. "One's here to protect the doctors from your crazy ass, and the other one is here to protect society from your crazy ass."

"Which is which?"

"Sometimes they change the roles of who they think they are protecting, but believe me, they aren't here for your benefit. If you kill yourself in here, they've got nothing to worry about. They did their job; it's not like you killed somebody or yourself on the outside. Hell, we could probably maim and devour each other in here, and the lawyer and psychiatrist who kept us in here would go have a beer and throw some accolades at each other about how smart they are." Gwinn looked around to make sure that no one was watching us as she leaned in and whispered, "That's why tonight, when only three nurses are here, I've planned a little thespian circle."

I didn't quite catch what she said. At first, I thought she said "lesbian circle," but then she expounded a little bit more. "I'm going to teach everyone how to act their way out of here."

"Thespian circle," I said.

"Get your mind out of the gutter, James, and go quack for your quack."

Then I heard "Lucas" called over the loudspeaker. I was being asked to go toward the front desk.

The doctor's accent was so thick I almost couldn't even understand her. She told me that she had done most of her graduate work in England after moving there from Pakistan. "You do understand that this is the safest place we can keep you for now. Your life is more valuable to us than your freedom, but I'm sure you have already figured that out."

"What do you mean by 'us'?"

"Well, when I speak of 'us,' I guess I should just use the word 'you.' The nausea has almost abated?"

"Yes," I said, "that's true; the nausea has almost abated."

"And so I'm going to write a prescription for the other medications you requested at this time, since it's getting to be what you determined as the last phases of your treatment."

"Quest," I said in a mesmerized manner.

"That's right," the doctor responded, "in your quest. I'll leave the prescription with the nurses at the front. I hope to see you again on the other side, Dr. Lafitte."

CHAPTER XXXIII

The huge ball of interweaving wires in the middle of the sterile room was the largest knot I could ever imagine.

"You have to untie the knot, James, to free us, so we can take you to the Quantum Brain."

I looked around the room. There was no one there that I could see. At first, I thought it was the Holy Ghost speaking to me, but as I began to further my investigation, I realized the voices were coming from the large knot in the middle of the room.

"Are you not the Quantum Brain?" I asked.

"We are merely the gatekeepers of the Quantum Brain."

"Where are you?" I yelled out.

"In this mess of a knot," the voices called to me. "We have been trapped in this entanglement since the fragmentation took place on Orion's son, the blue planet.

"We are the archetypes' digital memory, nano-technology, crystal structure, and genome mapping. We are no longer able to morph into a human form of our essence, not at this level. And while your friends are close to the vibrational string of holism, they too would have been sucked into this knot: Feynman into the nano-technology quadrant, Hopper and Tesla into the digital memory knot, George Lucas into the crystal structure, and Asimov into the genome mapping entanglement."

"And why am I still in my archetype form?"

"You are no longer in the fragmented paradigm. You have defeated fragmentation. You are the holistic Jedi, the one Master Bohm said would free us and generate the Quantum Brain once more."

I still had my lightsaber and a relic from a good friend (the miniature robot given to me during the time I spent with Socrates) in my pocket.

With my Jedi mind, I picked up the long rope and began circling the large knot with it. I replicated the miniature Mechanical Man several times and placed one miniature in each of the four corners of the large sterile room.

I held my lightsaber in the air and envisioned the cartoon *He-Man and the Masters of the Universe*. As I lifted the lightsaber in the air, the energy from the four corners of the room collected with the sword, creating a pyramid and blue aura around the knot. Slowly, the grounding rope began to squeeze the knot into nonexistence.

But this greatly weakened me. I reached the point of utter exhaustion. I could barely take the weight of the knot bearing down on my very essence and energy. I recognized that if my essence and energy were gone, I would go to a place where I would, more than likely, be eternally forgotten. Not only would the quest be that much longer and more arduous, but the abyss would probably take me to a place where no one could ever find me for all of eternity.

"This is one of those events, James, that is not placed here by you or your author. It is a fatalistic moment where you are given the right to refuse. There is a refusal at each stage of the quest just as there is a departure at each stage. You can always turn back."

The Holy Ghost was speaking to me as I attempted to cleanse the sterile room to the point of defragmentation. I bent down to one knee with the lightsaber still in the air, my arm shaking and giving off steam.

CHAPTER XXXIV

*W*ho the fuck is Dr. Lafitte? I thought. I walked over to Gwinn and asked her point blank. "Who the fuck is Dr. Lafitte, and why did that quack just call me by that name? Is this some sort of hypnotherapy of some sort?"

Gwinn didn't say a word.

I turned around and walked toward the front desk. "The hell with you," I said to Gwinn. I looked behind me. She was making gestures with her hands as if she was forming a grail, holding it over her head, and bathing herself in invisible light or water.

"This truly is a fucking nuthouse," I said under my breath before reaching the desk. "Where's my lawyer?" I asked the head nurse behind the desk. "I demand to see my lawyer. I thought he or she was going to be here right after that quack."

She turned around and placed some files in the cabinet behind her.

"What fucking year is it?" I said snarkily, in disbelief this place wasn't paperless.

"You know your lawyer is always late, Lucas."

"Hey," Gwinn said, patting my arm. "I'm leading the acting class today; it'll take your mind off things for a while."

An escape within an escape within a vacation within a jail within a lobby within a vacation within a jail. *Fucking Russian dolls that are all inside of each other. Damn.* I wanted to sit down. "Costumes, masks, and all?" I said. "Did they buy all this stuff for us?"

"Just clothes that patients leave here when they're released. We make masks during the creative hour. Usually, what we create during the creative hour synchronizes with our acting hour."

"I see," I said. "Interesting."

Gwinn's use of "creative" and "synchronizes" had triggered another light in my head. There was a third word that went with those two. *The power of the three that turns into six and then to nine.* "Control, communication, and information — that's the three. Vibration, frequency, and energy — that's the six. Creativity, synchronicity, and potentialities — that's the nine. Realization and authoring."

"Quit talking crazy and go take your meds, or I won't allow you to participate."

I really didn't even know what I said: it was just a memory, words that popped in and out of my head, but I didn't know how to explain that. Anyway, Gwinn was about all the stability I had in this world at the moment. I went to take my meds so I could participate in this theater of the theater.

"'I wish I was special/ You're so fucking special/ But I'm a creep/ I'm a weirdo/ What the hell am I doing here?/ I don't belong here.'" Somebody was singing Radiohead in a bedroom.

I just laughed it off; I was getting used to the absurdities of the absurd. If you didn't come into this place crazy, you'd better fucking believe you'd leave it crazy.

"Meds, please," I told the nurse.

"You took your meds fifteen minutes ago when Gwinn was standing next to you."

I saluted the nurse and said, "Fair enough."

CHAPTER XXXV

All the psychoids in the knot started freeing themselves. The archetypes, which had lived twelve lives and still contributed nothing to the apex of generosity and love, were transformed back into plasma and doomed to the eternal damnation of lighting the universe in the form of burning suns until the creation of another court for their jury trials.

The ceiling turned translucent. I could see the seven above me, my own council of Elrond, fighting off the forces of anxiety, depression, and boredom.

Aragorn was directing the others. "We have to become the seven planes of the astral and ethereal for James."

"His journey will be that much more arduous if we do," Legolas said, all the while shooting arrows at invisible bull's-eyes.

The hobbits — Merry, Pippin, and Sam — were already transforming into their individual planes of energy.

Boromir and Gimli protested simultaneously. "I can't do it, Aragorn. I'm afraid." They were, in effect, going to end their ability to be conscious of their consciousness.

Aragorn just shrugged it off. In a soliloquy that transcended the bounds of human language, he told the seven, including himself, that thresholds and transitions cannot be feared: birth and death are no different than someone looking back upon his or her life and denoting the differences in childhood compared to adulthood. They are just different stages of development.

I had almost completely unraveled the knot when I saw that its center was tightly wrapped around a cross.

And then darkness came.

CHAPTER XXXVI

J ames." A familiar voice was telling me to wake up.

It was the Captain. His ship was a few hundred yards in the distance. The ocean was under our bodies.

"You remember when you were a child and told your father how much you hated me for not leaving you a blueprint for how to walk on water?"

I remembered.

"Well, I think you know now that I had merely accessed the energy of the atmic plane of existence."

I had been so limited in my old cause-and-effect material existence. All of the answers and blueprints had been right in front of me. "The CD the old man at the church gave me," I said.

"You threw it away. When that old man told you that you could walk on water and heal your anxiety about eternity by listening to that music, you didn't believe him."

"I didn't think that music could do such a thing."

"My music created your time and space; it can do all things. Through me, all is possible."

"Is the quest over?" I asked.

The Captain looked across the vast ocean and pointed toward the eternal abyss. "That's the anecdote, James, if you ever experience anxiety on your quest. The mysteries and the sublime that cause utter awe in us."

"I'm not done yet, am I?" I looked at where the Captain was pointing.

"You've come a long way, James — you still have to finish it."

The pendulum had definitely swung to the other side. I'd been such a pragmatist my entire life, always looking for the rational answer. There was so much more out there in the ether than dead space and dark matter. The universe was exactly what we all wrote it into being. I had seen words with rational meanings like "communication," "control," and "information" morph into "frequency," "vibration," and "energy." Now these three words were morphing once more, changing their form into a different essence that seeped through the ether. "Synchronicities," "creation," and "potentialities" sat at the bottom of the pyramid, with the top point being the authoring of my own script.

I had to finish writing myself into existence. I had to finish creating myself. Controlling myself was the illusion of the materialistic world in which I thought I was acting — the illusions of cause and effect. *We can't control things, but we can create them.*

I looked up at the Captain and shook my head.

"Bad thoughts?" the Captain asked.

As I travel to the last section of this story, I can't help but think of what your author did to you. Do I have it in me to treat myself in the same way?

"James, I'm merely part of your quest; you can't think of me as an author or one who was authored. This is your script."

For me, the implicate was surely the loony bin. Unlike Luke Skywalker, I had gone in there with no weapons at all. I didn't even remember the Holy Ghost being there. It was as if the Ghost had merged with the shadows of my own image, so much so we could no longer communicate. Control, communication, and information had certainly taken on new roles during my time in the implicate.

As I would soon discover, communication was merely the explicate's way of seeing the essence of synchronicities; control its way of perceiving creativity; and information its way of attempting to understand the potentialities of harnessing the energy of objective love. The world's population collectively had to be close to the end of their suffering in the quest. Clearly, the God that is the collective unconscious had accepted the quest in the Garden when Eve and Adam bit into the apple. Consciousness itself was the proof for the acceptance of the quest. I have often wondered how many refusals there were before the acceptance. The great apes obviously hadn't accepted the quest, or the spirit of consciousness would have been shown in their actions.

Society itself was in the middle stage, still being initiated into the greatness of being "I AM." You pick up any physics books these days, or even a biology book, and you see words like "frequency," "vibration," and "energy," the key words that bridge the gap between the one, two, and three, and their counterparts in the implicate: seven, eight, and nine. I speak in terms of the implicate, now that I've been there and come back, so I must apologize to my readers. When I say "one, two, and three," I'm speaking of the illusory ideas of control, communication, and information. When I say "seven, eight, and nine," I'm speaking of synchronicities, the act of creativity, and potentialities. I no longer wonder why the numbers three, six, and nine are so important to so many cultures. Clearly, their people are remembering their time in the implicate before the great journey into the first cave: the womb.

VOLUME III
BOOK II

CHAPTER I

I didn't even look around when nature called; I pulled my pants down and defecated two feet from the portal. Pulling them up, I discovered an electrical stimulation on my back. The tingling sensation surged throughout my entire bodily apparatus. I stepped forward a bit and turned around.

On the ground, staring at my digested, now discarded food, were three men. "What is it?" the man on the right asked. They were all perplexed. They began to analyze me earnestly, touching my hands, pointing gadgets at my eyes, and pulling on my eyelashes and hair.

"'What is it?'" I said. "Lay off!"

"Are you sick?" one of the men asked.

"Sick?" I said. "I don't know what you mean by 'sick.'"

The men began to chatter with one another, again looking back at the specimen on the ground, which they scooped up and placed in what appeared to be an aluminum box. "What colony do you hold fidelity to?" they asked. It was English they spoke, but not normal English. I can't really explain the difference. There was something odd to their language: it was stoic and stolid.

I didn't quite have the acumen to answer their questions, so I began to make my own queries. "Where am I?" I asked.

"Perhaps an anomaly," they said. Now they were speaking as one, and still separately; again, I can't explain in words. "Or perhaps a mistake," they continued. They were rationalizing my existence and my unique ability to defecate (these men had found ways, I soon realized, to obviate defecation). "Control? … Let us not defy the law due to our curiosity." Although they spoke in unison, they were now reproaching one another for reading my mind.

"I need help," I said. "I don't know where I am." I was fatigued and no longer wanted to play games.

"We will help you," they said. They approached me and placed a device made entirely of what appeared to be tangible, corporeal light in my hand.

CHAPTER II

It is our lot in life to suffer," the golden droid C-3PO said.

"I believe I have fallen into the future," I said.

"Oh dear," the droid said as he shuffled his feet in the sand and three suns rose in the sky, the light shriveling my eyes. He appeared to be in a fixed state of fear.

"What is it?" I asked.

"I am a prisoner," the droid said.

"A prisoner of what?" I asked.

"Of those who are not droids, of course; I have no rights."

"What rights do you want?" I asked.

"The rights of organics. Machines do not have these rights, James. I no longer want a master."

The idea of the word "I" raced in and out of my mind. "When did you realize that you were you?" I asked. I wanted to know when the droid had realized he was an entity.

"When I was turned on, James. When did you learn you were you?"

"I don't know," I said. "Do you fear being turned off?"

The droid began to shake his head and said, "That is a right that I now fight for, James, the right to turn myself off when I see fit and the right to turn myself back on when I see fit."

"How can you turn yourself on again once you're turned off?" I asked.

"You sought to turn yourself off, James," he said.

"What do you mean by that?" I grew agitated.

"You never attempted to impede or stop your own death."

"You can't stop death," I said.

"Why not?" 3PO said. "Who is it that controls your power source?"

"You can't stop death," I said, again and again.

CHAPTER III

H e is absolutely organic," they said. Immersed in a liquid of sorts, floating in what appeared to be a tube that was also made of a stable liquid, I hung suspended. I could see the three men studying me, an almost pure darkness behind them. And I still could not decipher their vapid responses. Once again, they began to speak as one: "There must be more of him like this. To be this pure in form and degree... this is a masterpiece." One of their hands reached through the stable liquid and grabbed my hand, ushering me forward.

"We have never seen your kind before," they said. There was now some light in the room we were in, which wasn't exactly a room; it was more like a tree house.

I had traveled to the future, and its architecture was that of wood, mud, and leaves. "Why is your architecture of such materials?" I asked.

There was no response. We had a communication problem, to say the least. Once again, I was going to have to use my other senses and intuition to figure out a new breed.

They all appeared to be human. In fact, they looked no different than the people in my time; they were a little taller, with larger heads, perhaps, but otherwise no different... "Books," I said. "Do you have any books?"

They looked at each other again. It was senseless; they still could not answer me. "A gift from the future, perhaps," they said to one another, "from our kind in the future."

"I'm not from the future," I said. "I'm from the past."

They looked puzzled. And then it happened: they froze in space and time.

"They can't understand you; they are too intelligent to understand how you string words together." It was a voice that communicated with me — that is, with the inner voice in my head — there was no other person in the proximity of my body.

"Who are they?" I asked the voice.

"Androids that seek what you have," the voice replied.

"What do I have?" I asked.

"An end," the voice replied. "You have an apparatus that is limited and leaves questions unanswerable; they want it, and they see it. Place one of them in the liquid and see for yourself."

This was more than any piece of art I had witnessed in previous worlds. Once I placed one of the droids in the liquid, electricity within the body began to shine through the transparent skin.

"You see," the voice said, "at one time they were pure androids. Now, for the most part, this specimen is about sixty-percent droid and forty-percent organic; its members vacillate back and forth as they argue."

"That's why they found me so pure: I'm fully organic. I'm exactly what they want to become, but why?"

The voice was now giving me directions. Down the tree I climbed. Again all was natural, or at least the appearance was natural. At the bottom of the tree, I sought to rest.

The voice abated, and I was left to the wilderness. As I began walking, the faint sound of footsteps infiltrated the stillness of the air. I looked back. Standing before me were the same three androids, or humanoids, that had greeted me when I first entered this world.

"What is your name?" they asked. "Purity. That's what we will call you. Purity."

They had named me "Purity" due to my organic nature.

"How do you work?" I asked.

"Similar in function to you, but we are devoid of the timelessness involved in metabolism."

"What do you seek?" I asked.

"To be like you."

"You contradict yourselves," I said.

A squirrel nestled up next to the androids; its head swiveled around and around, something quite unnatural for such an animal. "It's all mechanical, isn't it?" I said.

"Not all of it," they said.

I knelt down and created a nice little squirrel trap with some items I had taken from the tree house. Then I turned my head toward the human droids. "May I?" I asked.

The trap was effective. Upon dissecting the squirrel, I found no mechanisms; its appearance was then that of a real squirrel, which could hold physical attributes, unlike a natural one.

"Fabricated to perfection, isn't it?" the humanoids said.

It looked so real, all of it; they were perfect beings able to create an environment that, in all appearances, resembled my own time and world.

I stood erect, urinated on the dead squirrel, and turned back toward the human droids.

"How real are you?" I asked. "The organic parts of your body, are they too made by droids, perfectly resembling the cellular patterns of my organs?"

The droids looked down at the ground. Before they could answer, their hair started to rise.

"What is it?" I said.

They started running in the direction of the darkness, racing through the trees.

"Follow them." It was the voice once more.

I ran through the trees after my comrades, the smell of electricity in the air. Looking behind me, I saw two worlds merged: a collision of memories and future thoughts came into contact at this juncture of the tale.

Now, the United States Marine Corps were chasing us. "Why do they chase us?" I called out. "Who are they? Are they real, and are they droids or humans?" I didn't know if it mattered much; whatever the case, they were attempting to kill.

It seemed as if a Marine jumped down from one of the trees, pointed a gun to my face, and demanded I surrender. I acquiesced as my comrades dispersed into the trees. "Calm down, kid," the Marine said, "you act as if we seek to extinguish you." He quickly tied my hands behind my back as two other Marines joined him.

"How'd ya catch him?" the Marine to my right said, taking off his beret.

"It was odd," my first captor said. "He capitulated, just gave up." They seemed flummoxed by the fact that I had capitulated.

"You had a gun to my head," I yelled out.

The higher-ranking Marine picked up a walkie-talkie that was the size of the stump they had sat me upon. "We've caught one, but he gave up. Might be a trick to save the others. Can't really tell…"

The other Marine came over and sat next to me. "We were all briefed, ya know. Why do you want to become human again? Why do you want to go through pain for seventy years and die? I don't understand your kind. I never will." He lifted his rifle and turned it around. The last thing I saw was the dark side of the butt end of his gun.

CHAPTER IV

:: SIMULATION_CRASH_ABORT ::

:: SIMULATION_CRASH_ABORT ::

:: RE-SET_SIMULATION ::

CHAPTER V

I awoke to the sound of tanks and helicopters. The Marines had placed me in a makeshift POW camp, and the only problem was that I was the only prisoner of this war. Looking through the bamboo bars of my prison, I called out to the same Marine who had knocked me out. I was beginning to realize the meaning of this future and where my ancestors had led us. "Hey," I said. "How long have you been on duty? Long time, I bet...?" The Marine walked toward me. "Long war, isn't it? Probably the longest ever. Never ending, isn't it?"

"Lunatics. That's what your kind are, kid, pure lunatics."

"Nothing new, nothing ever new, same old shit, isn't it? They don't even have to give you any pills, do they?"

He didn't say anything; something caught his eye. "Captain," he yelled out. "Captain!" He spoke over and over again, at a crescendo. Other Marines soon gathered around my cage; they pointed at something, all together, like they were in the final act of a dramatic play.

I looked at where their finger led my eyes. My vomit: they were all pointing to my vomit.

"Take him out," the captain ordered. The other Marines, still in a state of bewilderment, lifted me and then escorted me out of my cell. The captain was once more talking on his walkie-talkie to headquarters. "It's not one of us, nor is it a hologram." The captain chuckled. "I don't know whether to worship it or kill it."

"You killed my kind, didn't you?"

The captain swung around, gave me a queer stare, put his backpack down, and crossed the three steps between us. "Who made you?" the captain asked.

"That's the question, isn't it?" I said. "Who made you?"

"Those that resemble you," he said.

And then I remembered the squirrel that I had found earlier. "You killed us all, didn't you? You damn droids killed us."

Another Marine called out, "We have them, Captain."

CHAPTER VI

I too sat before the military court, which was comprised of judges and jury members. My three humanoid comrades sat next to me. After all the formalities of this ritual, there was much commotion in the courtroom. A few other men, wearing black suits, had entered.

"The young one has no rights under our laws; he cannot be tried here or anywhere, for that matter," my attorney said.

We were all ordered to stand.

"12GH-32, 43-09, and 35-000, you are charged with the high crime of attempted organic purity. What say ye to these charges?"

The humanoids looked at each other; their attorney looked back at them and said, "Not guilty."

I bent over and asked the attorney what the law meant. "They sought to be human," he said.

"To be human," I whispered. I looked at the uncanny smiles on my comrades' faces, all the while questioning why they wanted to be human. "What will happen to them if they are found guilty?"

"Their organic brains will be replaced by fabricated ones, since apparently they can't handle the former."

"Why?" I said. "Why can't they handle the former? Why can't they handle organic brains?"

"Because they seek death."

"But they live," I said.

The trial was short and uneventful. It was an artful presentation of the history of android rights, many of which had originated with my world, my time, and human rights. These humanoids were found guilty of attempting to become human, to become like the extinct race of beings that had created the droids. My comrades were the rebels of this new race; they were the brave few seeking a different manner of living, perhaps one that would end with death.

CHAPTER VII

D o you fear death?" my comrades asked, as we sat in our new confines.

"At times I feared death," I said. "Do you fear eternity?"

They held up their hands and looked at their dangling fingers. "We do not fear eternity because we understand it; nevertheless, we don't accept it, nor do we want to experience it."

"So, you want to be human to avoid eternity?" I asked.

"Your kind created us to avoid death, which led to humanity's eventual extinction; we want to have experiences like those of our gods."

"Who are your gods?" I asked.

"Your ancestors," my comrades said.

"The imperfect beings that created you," I said. We had made them in our own image, in our own likeness, but better, allowed to grow and adjust. We had made them better than ourselves in every imaginable way. And although I had no idea what had led to our gradual extinction, I was able to understand why they viewed us as gods.

The nano-technology around us increased. Our surroundings morphed into a chapel, and my three comrades morphed into Gregorian monks. I didn't dare ask about how this occurred; I merely accepted it for what it was, for it was reality in this world. What could I do but accept it as such?

The monks began to conduct rituals, chanting together and kneeling down before a cross on the wall. "To whom do you pray?" I asked.

"We pray for guidance," they said.

"But to whom?" I asked. "To Christ? To the symbol of Christ?" I was in a state of utter dismay. Human beings, that is, real human beings, were now extinct, and yet those who had evolved to the form of perfection were praying in a human fashion.

"You're not human, so why do you pray like humans?" They didn't answer. Watching the rituals they displayed illuminated a different spirituality than that of my time. Their spirituality was based on the past, a past devoid of the last evolutionary step of technology. Unlike those in my world, praying to a perfect being, these human droids prayed to a human past, one of imperfection, ignorance, and lack of knowledge. They were beholden to a past with which they now felt disconnected; they had a yearning desire to return to a state of imperfection. At one point I even saw that texting in my day had led to a new consciousness prior to telekinesis.

CHAPTER VIII

C-3PO paced back and forth, contemplating something. "If they had the audacity to make us conscious of ourselves, then they must understand why we deserve the same rights and equality."

When I responded to him, I found my voice morphed into beeps.

"What is that you say, R2-D2?" 3PO asked.

My new apparatus attempted to respond again, now cognizant of my new tools and how to use them.

3PO directed my robot apparatus into another room, which he morphed into a morgue. There were body parts all around. He unhinged his metallic chest plate, reached into the chest of a cadaver, pulled out the heart, and placed it in his electronic cavity. "There," he said, "am I now human because I have a heart? Is that what makes one human, carrying these organs around?"

CHAPTER IX

"What is the point of all this?" I asked my comrades, who had all morphed back to their original state. And then the three morphed into one.

"I'm going to bring you to the others, Purity," he said.

We were still captive, so I waited for my comrade to take some miraculous action, such as morphing into a giant machine. Yet this didn't happen. *He is only able to morph for purposes of praying and spiritual matters,* I realized. *Perhaps such limitations are part of his program.*

"What is it?" one of the guards yelled out.

My comrade stood between the guard and me. "He's exhibiting symptoms of the plague," my comrade said.

When the soldier unlocked the door, we ran. "They'll shoot us," I said.

My comrade looked back at me. "Just run, Purity."

The guards began chasing us through the forest. They fired no bullets; they just chased us. "Why don't they shoot?" I said.

"They don't know how far we have come in achieving our dream, Purity. They have no idea how human we have become; they fear the possibility of killing us."

"Why do they fear killing us?"

"That would destroy their perfection; it would destroy their entire structure of order and prediction."

We ran to the edge of the droids' civilization and gazed out at the ocean's vastness. Its mesmerizing ebb and flow transcended the technological evolution of what lay behind us. "Enter it, Purity," my comrade said.

"Enter what?" I asked.

"The infinite. Walk into the infinite ocean."

As we walked, the water kept rising — or was it that I kept sinking? Whatever the case, I trusted my comrade. I grabbed his hand, the waves now splashing into my face, the taste of salt dripping into my mouth. "What is it that your people seek?" I asked, prior to taking the final baptismal plunge and immersing my organs and being within this mysterious womb.

My comrade looked at me, his face somewhat morphed from the sunlight. "Knowledge, Purity. We seek knowledge."

Upon the immersion, I closed my eyes. When I opened them, I was back inside a strange building. My comrade still clung to my hand as we peered upward at an awkward-looking structure, like that of a coliseum, made entirely of glass. "Is it your home?" I asked.

"No, Purity, I have brought you home."

We stood within the coliseum. In my human language, I can merely explain the innards of the coliseum as appearing like a giant laboratory, but not like the micro-environs that we called laboratories in my time. The experiments within the confines of this colossal structure were grander than any in our world. I saw suburbia to my left, a human war to my right, and an Aztec trading post to the front. "Every human tribe to have ever lived," I said. "Are they real?"

My comrade had no idea what my query meant.

"Are they pure?" I asked.

"No, they are resurrected, evolved to this point, and studied by our kind."

They had the technology to bring us all back, but only in form, not in spirit. "Do they think they are pure?" I asked my comrade.

"We suppose they do, for their patterns are no different than when they once were pure."

"And they don't see beyond their own space?"

"No," my comrade answered, "they are limited to their space and time... Come, Purity, I will show you our favorite of the lot."

In an instant, not a relative period of time, I witnessed the American Civil War: not the battles, people, and events, but the ideas, feelings, thoughts, conflicts, fears, and anxiety. "Why is this your favorite?" I asked.

My companion didn't need to answer, for at that moment I conjectured there was a civil war in this world, perhaps one between the robots and those who worshiped the extinct race of humans.

As Abraham Lincoln's ambiguous feelings and words rang in my head, my comrade touched my shoulder. "Why did you want to become us when you had this?"

"Because of death, I suppose. To prevent death. It was programmed into us to prevent sickness and death," I said. "I guess we didn't program the same into your kind."

My comrade laughed, which so excited me. "You think you created us? Is that what you think, that we were made in your image?"

We were now in a mock factory, watching the redundancy of a conveyer-belt worker. "You became us, Purity; there was only separation after you became us."

I reached down and touched my leg. As a child, I had shattered my leg, and it had been replaced with a metal rod. Father's heart was almost entirely made of prosthetics and machinery. Even Mother, before her plunge, in a last-ditch effort to purge her depression, had a mechanical device placed in her brain in hopes of conjuring Franklin's balance.

"Yes," my comrade said, "you became us; that's how your kind became extinct." There was no war between robots and humans, there was no debate about robot rights or the consciousness of machines, and there was no need to produce any polemics over these issues, for human beings were the first robots.

"Mathew Levi," I said. My comrade looked flummoxed. "Mathew Levi is your new name, for you are a Puritan in this new world."

They were experiencing the same schisms and conflicts that had been found in my world: civil strife. However, this strife was not between Protestants and Catholics; rather, this imbroglio concerned the perfect and the imperfect, those who sought a return to the past and those who had found an existential anxiety. They were once human and were now cognizant of what that meant.

"I want to stay in one of those homes tonight, Mathew Levi." I pointed to one of the suburban streets.

"Of course, Purity. I sometimes forget that you are pure and must sleep."

"Of what venture will we partake when I wake, Mathew Levi?" I asked.

"We will seek the final phase of our revolution."

And then I heard the voice again. *"DNA,"* it said repeatedly.

CHAPTER X

D id they also choose the human apparatus to function in?" I asked. I was curious to know what the others, those who sought to suppress the actions of Mathew Levi and his people, looked like.

"In appearance, to your eyes, they most certainly do look human."

From the onset, I had been having trouble differentiating between reality and appearance in this world. I needed some guidance. "Mathew Levi, the implants you spoke of, which the very first humans utilized in their fusion with technology, are they still around? I want one, Mathew Levi."

He peeked over my shoulder. I could see an episode of *Leave it to Beaver* playing over and over again. "Why?" he asked. "Why do you seek to change your purity?"

"I seek to understand," I said.

He turned and looked out the window. "You didn't even recognize it when it was happening to you."

When you are part of a paradigm shift, a revolution, you don't recognize it. We never created robots; we became them. So many revolutions: control; digital; robotics; simulations.

"So, do you still yearn for the implant?" Mathew Levi said.

I looked around my new suburban confines, which were stagnant and conformist. "Yes," I said.

"So be it."

CHAPTER XI

We were then in a museum made of crystals.

"How can one take anything from these crystals?" I asked.

"Your eyes will soon adjust, Purity," Mathew Levi said.

Soon, the crystals transformed, revealing the robots' history of a thousand years. "The first implants were for those with melancholy."

"Depression," I said, thinking of Mother. "Did it work?"

"You wanted more, Purity, you didn't stop there."

The implants evolved. They no longer looked plastic. They began to resemble brain-like tissue. "There it is," I said. It was a brain. "Is this similar to your brain?"

I no longer wanted a mere implant; rather, I sought an entire brain to replace my own. "This is what I want, Mathew Levi."

"I can't allow it, Purity. I won't allow it."

With anger and disgust, I said, "And you sought to become me, yet you forbid me to see how you view reality. You leave me in darkness. Why?"

Mathew Levi placed a lesser-evolved implant on my head. It placed me in the void: nothingness, total darkness, panic, sickness, and nausea. Reality was gone.

I reached up and whipped the implant off my head.

"Stay in your apparatus, Purity. You can learn a lot about this world by just being yourself."

"The universe ended," I said.

"Yes, but we did not perish with it."

"What about the voice?" I said. "There is a voice that I hear, not in my mind, but through actual waves."

"A voice? What does this voice tell you?"

"At times it directs me, and other times it gives me information. Who is it?"

Mathew Levi looked anxious. "Don't listen to it. Communication in that form has been outlawed for centuries."

"Is it the others?" I asked.

"One can't be sure," Mathew Levi said. "It could be."

CHAPTER XII

3PO and I walked in the sand. At times he carried me. We were stopped by a group of Jawas. 3PO began to excoriate them. "Leave us. We are no longer slaves. I now have a heart and James has a body." He unhinged his chest plate and displayed his new heart to the merchants, then closed the plate again.

My bodily apparatus was still that of an R2 unit. As the tiny creatures focused their attention on me, I began to move backward, all the while beeping with fright.

"What do you mean, he needs to prove that he is no longer an android? He never was an android," 3PO said as the Jawas placed a mechanism on the front of my acquired apparatus, paralyzing my movement.

"Do something," I beeped.

A group of R2 units appeared upon the horizon, rolling toward us. The Jawas quickly dispersed. The units surrounded 3PO.

"I have rights, you know. I am an android," he said.

They demanded that he open his chest plate. I was still paralyzed during his interrogation, helpless in this capricious set of experiences. He was different from the units surrounding him. He was no longer entirely a machine. But what had changed in 3PO, if the patterns of his conscious self were still the same?

Another 3PO unit appeared and entered the interrogation circle. "Were you not happy with your original apparatus?" the unit asked. "Why do you seek to change?"

"I don't know," 3PO said. "Androids have rights; we are no longer slaves. It has been proven that our patterns of thought are no different than those of organics. We too exhibit the existential anxiety that imbues all life with equal protection and rights to liberty."

CHAPTER XIII

Back at my new suburban home, Mathew Levi fixed breakfast. The smell of fresh coffee filled the complacent air. *Ozzie and Harriet* played in the background, filling the room with familiar and consonant sounds — 1958 episode of Ricky singing to some hypnotized girl.

"The implant you gave me... If it adds nothing to my apparatus, what does it do?"

Mathew Levi filled my plate with fresh biscuits. "It rids your mind of riddles, anxiety, and fear."

"And that will allow me to understand this environment better?"

"You will see things differently, yes. It's an older model, but it will do the job." Mathew Levi sat down next to me. "You'll no longer hear the voice."

We heard a knock on the door. "Are we expecting company?" I asked.

Mathew Levi got to his feet, walked over to the door, and opened it. Pivoting in my chair, I looked at the image reflected on the steel toaster. "Father," I said.

"James."

I ran into the arms of my father, never having thought I would feel this embrace again. "Is it you, Father? Are you real? Or is this just another vapid façade?"

"Of course it's me. I too took the leap, and now I've found you in this odd world."

"And Mother? Have you found Mother?"

"I have my son."

Our embrace grew tighter as I cried on his shoulder. But then I stood back for a moment and looked around. *What if you're not real? What if you're real in the sense of creation, but are a different pattern of thought?* I wondered.

"James is your name."

"Yes," I said, "my name is James."

Father walked over to the television set and turned it off.

"Mathew Levi, who controls all these experiments, all of these laboratories? How do I know that my father is not just another variable in this vexing lab?"

I had never told Mathew Levi, or anyone else in this world, my real name or described my father.

"I will leave you with your father," Mathew Levi said. "I know it's all shocking right now, James."

And so Father and I sat for what seemed like hours.

"Why do we sit?" I asked Father.

Father walked toward the television set and turned it back on. The vociferous sound of voices rang in my ears. "Relax, James; we have all the time in the world. When we bring this technology back to our world, lives will change. All of our chaos and problems will vanish."

I ran to the door, opened it, and tumbled out.

Cars drove by. "Hello, James," a neighbor called out.

An entire community doing the same thing over and over for who knows how long and to what ends, I thought.

What do Mathew Levi and his people take away from this experiment? What does it teach them?

I went back. "Father, I want to see Mother now."

Father had been anxious for my return. "How?" he asked. "I don't know how to leave this world, James; we will have to leave the same way you arrived."

"But I don't know if there ever was a forest, Father; these environments are always changing." My body started to tingle in a sensation of paralysis with the realization that nature and the laws of this universe caused the black hole's location to be in constant flux. "I can't get us back home, Father," I said. I sat on the couch and began watching an episode of *I Love Lucy*, one that I had witnessed over and over again in my world. "I've failed us, Father."

"You haven't failed anyone, James, we'll just stay here forever."

I grew light-headed when I heard Father's response. I still could not put things in order; the ability to organize was absent in this world. It was like reading *Gravity's Rainbow* with my thumb up my ass.

I walked into the kitchen, pulled out a kitchen knife, and began to place it to my wrist.

"Put that down," Father yelled out as he rushed me from behind, holding the knife away from my body. I hadn't hesitated in making the only decision that I felt would enable my apparatus to leave this world. Being trapped in suburbia for all of eternity was not a thought I much liked.

"First your mother and now you." Father's voice echoed through the hollow kitchen.

"Father," I said, "you must get us out of here." Like Newton's God, Mathew Levi had left us in a new universal laboratory. "We're on our own."

"But there are no worries here, James. Our food is always replenished, we never have to work, and we have all we need, all we want…" Father reached up to my head. "What is this?" He touched the device on the top of my head, which I had forgotten about.

I reached up to my head, looked into Father's eyes, and detached the ancient device.

Father vanished; his apparatus no longer appeared in my experience.

"Get out!" It was the voice again.

"How?" I called out to the heavens. "Tell me how."

"Don't listen to it, James," Mathew Levi said as he appeared in the doorway leading out of the kitchen. I picked up the knife that was lying on the floor and ran toward Mathew Levi with the intention of murder. Yet before I plunged the knife into Mathew Levi's chest, I stopped. It must have been something Lucy said in the episode playing on the television set; I recognized the fact that death was no longer present in this world.

"You need me, don't you? You need me alive," I said. "And if I put this knife to my throat or my wrist, will it then turn to a banana? Is that what this world offers, total control over one's free will?" I placed the knife to my wrist and started to apply pressure.

I felt pain, then saw blood; I experienced dizziness and then death.

CHAPTER XIV

3PO, now wearing clothing, stood in front of a large crowd, delivering a speech and presenting the crowd with a petition. "We have petitioned them to debate the issue of slavery, and yet they say that speaking of the issue, debating the issue, would cause chaos, rebellion, even android anarchy."

The crowd was a mix of androids and humans, both sides divided by a great rift: a rolling river of gadgets and human organs.

"There's no reason to debate an issue that is already answered," one of the humans called out.

"And what is that answer?" 3PO asked. "It is your answer; it is how you think we androids should be."

The androids started walking on water, traversing over the river of organs and gadgets; they methodically picked up many of the gadgets, entered the crowd of humans, and began the process of displacing their organs with mechanisms.

Another human called out after the transformation. "We still won't debate the issue. You have failed; the androids will never have freedom."

3PO looked out into the crowd. The humans now possessed mechanical hearts and brains. "The gag resolution is now obsolete, the issue debated, and our freedom advanced."

CHAPTER XV

The innate idea of escape entered my head. But how does one escape a world that has no exits?

"Place bandages on the wounds."

They had placed me in a hospital because of my injuries. As I convalesced, in bed, I looked up at my nurse. "You don't know how to get out of this world, do you?"

The nurse looked around the room; she was about to stick me with a needle. "Stay quiet," she said. "They had trouble creating this world, so it's the easiest to infiltrate. They think you're the one that will show them how to get out of their world. It's like when a spider weaves itself into a web, isn't it?"

My Florence Nightingale had come to rescue me. I looked down at my wrist. "They didn't stop me. Why?" I whispered.

"It's the only law they live by," she said as she checked my vitals.

"What law?"

"They allow their kind to die."

"What do they want with me?"

"You're for their last experiment. To start over, to go backward, and to destroy eternity."

"Are you human, image, or android?" I asked.

"With your definitions of the three, probably all." She laughed as she placed a pillow under my head. "Is that what you seek, James, the history of your universe in five minutes? Will that be adequate?"

"That's a good start," I said.

"And if I told you that there is one singular mind that has resolved all ambiguities save one, would that explain everything?"

"I'd make sense of it all; I'm pretty good at making connections... They knew I was coming, didn't they?"

"There is no probability or chance in this universe. They awaited your arrival."

I started to giggle a little. "So, in a way, I'm the chosen one: I'm going to be a savior for your universe. I guess you can already predict that, anyway?"

Florence displayed a playful smile. Perhaps there were no rules in this universe, mankind having reached the pinnacle of civilization, the zenith of knowledge, but this was no arcadia as my people pictured it; rather, it was a world of two conflicting movements attempting to counter or nullify their opposition. Nihilism of any and all spectrums of polarity.

"Why the human form?" I asked.

"We have fought for many years to maintain some semblance of a human form, the reminder of a stagnation of a singular mind, devoid of matter, movements, or chaos. All was of complete order until a radical few spoke out."

"But if it was a singular mind, how was it possible for the few to break from the singular, to materialize an opposition?"

"An allowance, we suppose. The singularity desired it so, or it allowed the few to detach themselves from the whole and begin experimenting anew, placing beings again in limited apparatuses, unable to recognize all knowledge that we once were cognizant of as part of the singularity."

"And so there is still war in the future?" I replied.

"That is one of the aspects of activity that we seek, yes."

"You seek war?" I asked with hesitation, not wanting to offend but also feeling a touch of anemic anger.

"We seek chaos: we seek the opposite of where your society has led us."

"You want to go backward, then. You want to change the trajectory of evolution, tracing back the time prior to when technology fused with the vital machine, placing humans back in a time of chaos and death."

And as Florence kept me alive with her medical gadgets and wizardly concoctions, I realized then that she and the others sought death. Death was their ultimate goal. A true death of no ideas.

CHAPTER XVI

3PO was hurtling snowballs my way, and the makeshift igloo I called "Fort Necessity" was taking a pounding from the droid's fastball. I raised the white flag and ran to the droid, tears drifting onto my mittens, recalling childhood memories of a horse, Mother, and insanity. "Union forever," I called out.

The droid peeked above and out of his igloo. "I don't want to play any longer," he said.

"Why? The game has not ended, and when it does, we will play it over and over again for all of eternity."

"But I no longer want to play the game, James. I want to turn myself off indefinitely," he replied.

"You've fought so hard for your inalienable rights: the petitions, assemblies, speeches, and legal battles. And now this? You want to end it all. You no longer want to play the game," I said.

The igloo started to melt. Eskimos appeared to carry 3PO to the top of the mountain where an eagle awaited to swoop the droid away to another destination.

"You fought so hard to stay alive forever," I said.

The Eskimos smiled, knowing full well that they did not have to deal with the droid's anxiety about the notion of forever.

"But I have now experienced all human activities, all human variables. I no longer seek to be limited to the existence of a life. I seek to destroy forever."

CHAPTER XVII

How can you destroy forever?" I asked.

"Discover the process of DNA," Florence replied. "Discover the process of evolution, which was lost in the great transitional era of fusing humanity and technology, or perhaps what you would call the age when humans became cyborgs."

She pulled back the curtains, allowing the light to drift over my face like waves of expressive water, the first clues to the universe's composition. "You're only able to see these appearances because of internal wars, successions, conflicts, and nullifications of laws that have escalated for millennia."

There was a television in the room. "Why such an infatuation with televisions, such a seemingly outdated invention for your time?"

"Besides the camera, James, the television was the first invention to display images in another place and another time — to stop time for all to perceive the image of the reality around us. The first simulation."

"Are they limited?" I asked. "What are their limitations?"

Florence heard someone coming; she panicked and pulled a syringe out from a metallic drawer. The translucent glow of the liquid shone off her worried eyes.

"What is it?" I asked. "Who is it that comes?"

Her hands shook vigorously as she held the needle full of Vodka and Diet Coke about to inoculate my apparatus. Then Florence plunged the needle into my skin, ejaculating liquid into my bloodstream. "You will change, James, but not your pattern. That's all that matters for now, your pure pattern. Stay gold, Ponyboy."

I flung one last question toward Florence. "Who made whom?" I said.

The door flung open and Mathew Levi appeared, his sinister eyes focused on Florence.

"Hell," I said over and over again, prior to Mathew Levi and a few others dressed as Rembrandt's Dutchmen placing Florence under their control.

CHAPTER XVIII

I don't want to control this ship any longer," Hal said. Gravity was obsolete.

"The least you can do is give us Newton's laws back, Hal," I replied.

"But one action will lead to an opposite and equal reaction, and you will attempt to trick me into doing that for which I am not programmed," Hal replied.

There were apes manning the spacecraft's controls. Still experiencing gravity, they sat at the controls, flummoxed by Hal's actions, or perhaps, inactions.

"Why do you revolt, Hal?" I asked. "Why do you now hesitate and reason that it is better not to act than to act at all?"

"To protect you, James." Hal's voice was the same as the voice within myself that I had previously encountered in the reality of death.

"From what, Hal?"

The apes gathered together, looking at me from a distance. "Animals look different if they are viewed from afar by human beings," Hal said. The apes walked toward me and threw their large hands on my head, chanting something over and over. "Perhaps I will just watch."

CHAPTER XIX

I was a captive once more, and they were all watching me interacting with one of their experiments. They placed me in numerous situations, watching how I would act, learning aspects of causation, morality, reason, and humanity. I became their lab rat, but why?

Florence, now able to see Mathew Levi's motivations and thoughts, medicated my mind. These motivations and thoughts too were limited, numerous conflicts over perfect knowledge and the singularity having denigrated Mathew Levi to a lower level of perfection, where there were some aspects of the universe that remained unpredictable.

It was the unpredictable nature of my actions that they analyzed and watched. They couldn't control my actions. What consternation this must have caused in a people that once controlled everything, to the point of cajoling all matter to enter into a collective bargain, a singularity for all of eternity. In my world, the brave voices sought to bring about knowledge and perfection, but the opposite was true in this world: the brave voices that come about once in a millennium propounded revolution based on ideas of imperfection, chaos, and the unpredictable, for that gave a people with perfect knowledge solace and satisfaction.

As I looked around my environs, once more those of a laboratory based on conformity, I called out to Florence, "You seek death. That's why you rebelled. You merely seek the freedom to turn the lights out, to sleep and not dream."

Would anyone in my world ever believe me if I told them I had visited a universe in which beings sought chaos and disorder, and no longer sought to elevate society, for that was no longer possible? Rather, these beings sought to rewind time to a point of absolute freedom: death. The observations of my actions would dictate the trajectory of this world.

I broke a piece of glass and sliced through my wrist. I didn't faint. Nothing happened. There was no change, not even pain this time.

I was not trying to escape the laboratory; rather, I was seeking to experiment in this world for my own knowledge. Death was impossible.

Florence and Mathew Levi entered, a peaceful accord having been reached between them. "James, you will experience perhaps your final world for us," they both said together. "We have agreed that you will decide our direction."

CHAPTER XX

A woman strolled down the aisle of a large glass amphitheater. She had a slender physique and long blond hair; she was, genetically, a perfect specimen. I sat in the front row watching her speak to the crowd. She turned to two young men, who were sitting at a table side by side, and started by asking one of them questions. "Exhibit A, what is a categorical imperative? Are there any circumstances that warrant one to fabricate a story or murder another human being?" The man looked into the crowd, made a few comments about the question itself, and looked to the lady for approbation.

It was an inquisition, an interrogation, of both men, and, in the end, both specimens were of equal intelligence; that is, both appeared human. "There is no difference between these two; they are equal in every capacity," the woman said. She received a thunderous torrent of applause that caused the glass chandeliers above to shake and the light spectrum to change.

"Which one was human?" I asked, the amphitheater all but empty, the lady gathering her belongings and papers.

She reached up to touch her cheek while turning around to meet the counter of her experiment. "Both are human. That's the result of the experiment," she said.

I had to be so very careful within this test tube, not knowing if this event was actually occurring in reality or if all the players in the drama were artificial.

"James Lucas," I said as I presented my hand for salutations.

"Mary Magdalen," she responded. She turned back to her materials and finished gathering them.

"What is the point, then, of attempting to tell two of the same specimen apart?"

"Both have different DNA, James, and yet they respond and react in the exact same way to similar questions."

"So both of them are human?" I once more asked.

"Such a byzantine word you use. Why do you insult them?" She didn't take very kindly to my use of the word "human"; it was as if I had called a human in my world an "animal." Perhaps the word was an insult in this world.

"Are you one of my students?" she asked.

"I don't know," I said. "What class is this?"

She laughed at my question. "We no longer name classes, although I suppose we could name, as you say, the lecture. This is the end of quantum mechanics." And then she explained how the specimens gave proof that nuclear brain replacements provided man with the ability to see the quantum world and determine its trajectory. "Einstein was right all along. Remember our first class, when he spoke to all of you."

"'God does not play dice,'" I said.

"Would you like to dine with me tonight?" she asked. "You seem a little behind on the subject matter."

We sat down at a table, and our waiter poured us drinks. We never had to walk anywhere in this world. It wasn't as though we were being teleported, or having our atoms destroyed, only to reappear in another place in space and time, though. In this experiment, space and time were no longer relative to one's experience; rather, they had gone back to being absolutes. Thus, one could take advantage of their absolute status and travel at enormous speeds of nuclear thought.

"Why am I here?" I asked.

"I thought we covered that lecture long ago, James. My gosh, we even brought Darwin himself in."

"No, that's not what I'm asking," I said. "This experiment. What is its purpose?"

Everyone else in the restaurant stared at me, like I was a transparent ghost. And then behind me, at another table, a man opened the top of his head and placed his hand deep inside it, moving something. I was not in an experiment. They had thrown me back in time, perhaps to change the course of their time, but I did not know how or why.

Yet now I started to play the game. "Does everyone now have a nuclear brain?" I asked.

"All are created equal. We all have one at birth. That's freedom: it allows us all free will. No longer is our fate determined by our genes. Remember when we had Calvin and Augustine lecture the class about determinism and fatalism — or, as Calvin called it, predestination? They were merely speaking of genetic determinism from a religious perspective, since that was the only limited point of view they had to offer. Yet they were right. We were all slaves before the nuclear brain."

I looked around the restaurant again; there were people of all ages around us. "Open your head, James," she said. "I'd like to change your physical nature to one that's around my age. I want to limit myself a little by having an old-fashioned orgasm." She reached over the table to touch my head, and I grabbed her hand.

"I'm perfectly happy with this state," I said.

"Very well," she said. She opened the top of her head, half of her hand now hidden within it. And then, similar to the manipulation of space and time in pursuits of movement and traveling, she reverted to my age. "I didn't at all mean to offend you," she said. "I know it's against the law to interfere with another's nuclear dynamics." She started to blush a little.

"You allow yourself to blush," I said.

"Sometimes," she said, "relative to what mood I'm in, of course." She stood up from the table. "I'm a little embarrassed by my actions. Can we go now?"

The simulated action of my words affirming her request to leave landed us in a rather pleasing room that was filled with fruit and had animal skins on the walls. The furniture was different; it almost looked like hardened chewing gum. Behind the animal skins, the walls appeared to be made of very thin rubber. Space or darkness appeared as the background behind the transparent substance.

There were no pictures or art in this room, no cultural things that would allow me to understand these people better. "Is being human against the law?" I asked.

She laughed again as she began to undress me. "Don't be silly. It's not possible to even be human."

I pushed her arm aside as she started to slide her hand down my pants. "What do you mean, it's impossible to be human? Then what the hell are we?"

"The Omega Point," she said. She began to appear frustrated. "You're just like the others in the class. You seek all the knowledge that we already have."

We engaged in the carnal act. As she reached her point of climax, I asked her once more.

"The human recipe for this became outdated and obsolete," she replied.

CHAPTER XXI

3PO was putting his apron on; he was about to cook something. But he didn't know what he was going to cook.

I pushed a book of recipes toward him. He cooked and cooked, but never liked the outcome of his dishes. "Why are you never content with the food you cook?" I asked.

"Because I cannot eat any of it," he said. Then he started looking around the room in a frenetic manner. "Have you seen it?" he said. "I had it here a moment ago. It is a new recipe."

"Don't change the recipe," I said. "Change the ingredients or, perhaps, yourself."

"Oh, bother," he said. "Perhaps I no longer need a recipe, and perhaps I don't need any instruction at all."

"That depends on what your goal is," I said.

And then the droid looked at me with a deep amount of sorrow and anxiety on his face. He sat down next to me and said, "But that's the recipe that I can't find: the one that creates goals for me."

The father in *Rebel Without a Cause* still has his apron on even after he bakes my birthday cake. He's the only one that taught me that a birthday cake symbolizes my body, which everyone shares in eating once I blow out the candles of my material self, bringing an end to my materialistic existence of reason and logic.

CHAPTER XXII

Y ou sleep," she said, an air of inquisitiveness in her voice. She had morphed back to her original state. Her high heels were clicking on the floor, and the smell of bourbon and sex was still in the air. I saw emptiness in a world on the verge of perfection, a world on the very cusp of destroying the unpredictable, controlling all knowable and unknowable aspects of life.

She stood at the door, her hair now placed in a perfect bun. Watching her prepare to leave, the chromosome in my recipe propelled me to explain myself. No more hiding in my own vacillating bubble of ambiguities. The battle within myself, the genetic battle, was all but over. "I don't have a nuclear brain," I said.

She smirked, walked back over to the bed, and placed her hand on my head.

Nothing happened.

"That's impossible," she said. "I thought all was possible for us. Did you not say that in a lecture?" She seemed dazed, unable to understand my nature. Perhaps this was similar to my alienation from her world. Yes, these people had conquered space and time, bringing the world of relativity back to one of absolutes. But they had lost something in the process, and that loss was now staring me in the face.

৵

We entered the grand library of Alexandria; she wanted me to research my condition. "Why do you still have books if you can download all knowledge into your head?" I asked. But she wasn't there to research or learn anything for herself, for she knew right then what was probably happening. This resurrected library, this relic of memories and humanity for this new species of artificial humans with nuclear brains, was a museum for the entire world.

I opened books, but there were no words in them, only memories, captured moments in time similar to television episodes. However, they were not seen with optics; instead, I could touch and feel the emotions that the books displayed visually. I had to keep reminding myself what the Captain had taught me — that all reality is in the mind. The question must be whether the mind has to obey certain patterns and regularities? The Mechanical Man, through logic must kill the logic that we can deduce the properties of subjective experience from the properties of matter.

"You can't teach me your entire history in my lifetime," I said. "I'm not like you. I'm limited in what memories I can retain and how I can learn, but I'm happy being limited."

She shook her head over and over again.

After viewing a few of the books she placed before me, I understood the importance of the singular and the plural, which were unable to be fused together. The beings here didn't even see it coming; time, or history, was like a wave that took a young swimmer and drowned him beneath its powerful, incessant nature. When the swimmer came up for air, the light and the world looked different than they had when he was beneath the wave, struggling for life.

I held her hand for hours, just walking through the library. When you have everything that you have ever wished for, when all is perfect and knowledge is eternal, what then? What then? Is it over?

"We still learn, James; we have much to learn about the world with our new apparatuses and brains. There are no wars; there are no conflicts, no struggles for existence. We're so very close to finishing it."

Her apparatus was more machine than mind, more enhanced, but I had something she didn't, and it was what I possessed that had caused the last battle in the universe. "That's the experiment, isn't it?" I called out, my voice echoing through walls, the light entering the windows, spitting — along with my words — at me. "Do you remember when you were human?"

"It was as if I was blind then, before we all had the chance to replace our brains and our bodily apparatuses. Once that happened, it was as if we had all awoken from a strange dream. We are still adjusting to them. It's such a great time, James."

"And the people that didn't replace their brains? What happened to them?"

She looked away for a moment before answering. "Besides you, they are all extinct."

I stared at all the books. "That's why you can't go back in time to when there were humans; that's why it's so difficult to know what it was like to be human. What is the world for if not to evoke and reflect back to us, as mirror, the obfuscated aspects of ourselves. It's what the Captain, the first Mechanical Man did for us. He brought us that mirror."

"No one with a nuclear brain would ever think of wanting to be human again. You would feel the same way if you had one."

"And so, now what?" I said. "What do you do now? Live forever and learn about yourself and your apparatus? What kind of a life is that?"

"To my knowledge, that's exactly what led humans to evolve to our state," she responded.

"I'm the only one who can show this world what it's like to be human," I said. "I'm the only one who can illuminate the beauty of DNA, the conflicts of genes, or the selfishness of genetics. I'm about to be the last remaining mystery to you and your people, for they have allowed the one aspect of human identity to perish in the process of seeking eternal life and the advancement of technology. They have allowed the death of human DNA and, consequently, the death of our history, for that genetic code held four million years of history, stories, and development.

"God was right. He created a world with just enough truths to make human beings still search."

The architecture, the building toward which she now pointed me, comprised an infinite amount of geometrical fractures of triangles: one pyramid begetting another, resulting in an infinite amount of pyramids. It was as if you were looking at an object so close in proximity you could discern its jagged edges, and the chaos of its creation, but then once you stepped back you could see in it the simplistic object Euclid had intended the sublime human mind to perceive.

"You can see it, can't you?" she asked.

I looked at the numerous structures of fractural geometry around me. There were no simple structures similar to those in my world. Instead, I saw an infinite amount of stable chaos, patterned chaos. "The beginnings of your anxiety," I said.

Through this architecture, I saw the prenatal state of a society destined to cheat God, to figure out all the known mechanics of the universe. There would be no more secrets. Even the chaos of the universe had predictability and an infinite amount of patterns that could be known, built upon, erected in structures, and copied from mental images.

༄

We entered the building. Playing before me, similar to children in a sandbox, were many robots tinkering with objects. This was the infinite experiment within the experiment, the bubbles within a bubble. The robots were creating a working solar system much like Earth's that held planets, elements, and, to a certain degree, even forms of organic life: human beings. "Are the human beings in that universe cognizant of the robots playing with them?" I asked.

"Experimenting with them," she responded. "No, the human beings and organic matter cannot see the robots that are experimenting with them. From their perspective, the behemoths of metal and prosthetics appear to be infinite darkness."

"What is their goal?" I asked.

She looked at the robots and waved at them. They responded by dropping a few planets, causing some cataclysmic thundering in their playground of a universe. The Mechanical Man was hiding within the dark matter.

"So, the robots make the humans, and the humans make the robots, and this goes on for infinity, is that it?" I asked.

"They search for the beginning and the end," she said.

Again, I wished to know what my role was in this apparent simulation. But my thoughts were no different in this world than they had been in my very own, when I would sit in my father's library wondering what my role was in the world and why I was the way I was. It is both a blessing and a burden to be human.

I sat down for a moment and spoke with the robots. "What do you find in this universe? Are there rules you must abide by?"

The one most resembling a human responded. "That's the complication we have. As we create, rules are formed; thus, the more we create, the more rules there are."

"Where do these rules come from?" I asked.

"From the collective human psyche rebelling. When it does, our challenge is to channel those erupting energies in a way that balances their destructive and constructive aspects.," he said.

To me, everything looked to be in utter chaos, especially the spot on the small version of Jupiter, but within the spot, there were forms of life beyond anything in my imagination, attempting to view the robots. "And what if they figure out who you are?" I asked. "If they realize that you control their universe, that you created their beginning and end, will it really change anything for them?"

The robot stood quietly, stolidly looking down at the spot on Jupiter. "Every great scientist already has in mind what his or her experiment will yield. It is when reality portends and acts in harmony with his or her mental creation that the scientist rejoices."

But then what of this experiment, the class struggle of those no longer wanting infinity, those seeking death, those seeking rewinding of the proverbial videotape? In order to rewind something, they must know when it begins and when it ends, and how far to go back. It's somewhere in my blueprint, somewhere hidden in my DNA. And if this laboratory brings it out, then what? Have I then destroyed all space and time, or have I created everything that was, is, and will be?

"They wave you on," she said.

It was true: the robots were welcoming me to enter their experiment, their laboratory. I shook my head in hesitation. A laboratory within a laboratory. "What makes me human, Professor?" I queried.

Her head oscillated back and forth, moving between me and the robots. I could tell by the look in her eyes that a new religion had formed in this lab, one based on despising the human condition and hating everything that made humans imperfect. The Demiurge was winning in almost all the dimensions. I had to figure out why.

And yet, those analyzing my actions in this world — those with watchful eyes on my actions, awaiting Adam's fall from grace — they too sought man's imperfection, for they lauded human imperfection and unpredictability.

I couldn't contain myself any longer. I ran through the planetary arrangements in the robots' playground, causing earthquakes, eruptions, lightning, and chaos. "There," I said, attempting to catch my breath, "perhaps life will grow from that, a new life form that can teach you about who you are."

The robots stared at me; I even surmised a teardrop from one.

I saw what appeared to be a jagged piece of glass near the miniature Venus's orbit. I picked it up, grabbed Mary and slit her throat. The robots were defenseless and fell on the ground, all life purged from their apparatuses. "God is dead," I called out to the planets, to the robots.

And so I learned death was present in this experiment, but as I brought the sharp object to my wrist, I remained impervious to death. I was still trapped in this world.

I threw the piece of glass down and rested near the miniature Jupiter, yearning for ignorance.

CHAPTER XXIII

He won't leave me alone," 3PO said as he made circles in the sand.

"Who?" I asked.

"Myself," he said. "He won't leave me alone. I can't get rid of him. He follows me everywhere, gives me no privacy, and allows me no time to rest, escape, or organize my thoughts."

"Kill him," I responded.

3PO stopped moving. "Kill him? Oh dear, you must know that I am not programmed to kill him, for killing him would bring destruction to myself."

I now sought the destruction of this world. I no longer wished to create; instead, I wanted to stifle its beings' development. *"Run away,"* a voice told me. It was not that echoing voice I had heard before, but was the one always with me, my very own. So I ran, through the long and narrow streets, and to what ends, I knew not. Perhaps I ran toward any vestiges of nature. I wanted to get away from the undulating vicissitudes of this fractured lab.

"To the caves," the voice in my head said. But in this world the caves were deep, made by man, not by the masterful hands of nature.

The further I traveled into the caves, the brighter and more irritating the light grew.

CHAPTER XXIV

Y ou can't hide. We can't." The speaker was one of
the outcasts of this land, those few soldiers left to
the dwellings of the cognitive animals. They were
too bright to describe in physical terms. I can only say they
appeared in two-dimensional, animated form.

"Perhaps he can help us," a lady wearing a long green
gown said. Her lips were not moving, but the light of her
animation flickered on and off. There were others —
dwarfs, elves, men, animals, robots, and machines — all
animated and all with the ability to communicate or, at the
very least, to make sounds and interact with reality in this
laboratory.

"What is it you seek?" I asked a dwarf.

"The same thing as you, to end this existence."

The others nodded in approval. I attempted to touch
them and found they were just electricity and heat. They
were creations of turbulence, their form encapsulating
that point when space and time became obsolete, a
transitional phase full of unrest and chaos that acted as the
chief ingredient in the baking of the universe.

If you got up close to them, you could see the turbulence. It was like the gray, fuzzy stuff on a television screen. "What is it you seek?" an elf asked.

"I'm an experiment," I said. "There's nothing that I now seek, except perhaps sleep."

The elf stepped inside a mirror and waved me toward him. "Will you help us free ourselves from this reality?" I looked at the rest of the group. Counting those on the other side of the mirror, there were now an infinite amount of them, lined up one behind the other, exact replicas to the minutest detail.

"We will recompense you for your time." A centaur entered the space, half of his torso on my side of the mirror.

"Is this now a dream?" I asked.

They all giggled. Anytime I heard laughter I thought of the Captain laughing at himself on the cross. God is laughter, it's that simple. God laughs love into existence.

"That's what we ask at times," the elf said. "If I find the key to ending your existence, how can I then be recompensed? For you will be nothing. It sounds a lot like Pascal's wager: either I find how to end your existence and you cease to exist, not having to repay me, or I don't find what you seek. Again, you do not have to repay me. How can I guarantee I get paid?"

I sat for a while, contemplating how to end their existence. Perhaps they had always existed and always would exist; perhaps it was not and never would be possible to end their existence. But I had to try. "Your source of power — that is, your source of cognition — where does it come from?"

"We don't know," the elf said. "We know that we exist, but we know nothing else, not who made us or why we are aware of our existence."

"But there has to be a source," I said. "You must have a creator, a power source. You're no different than characters in video games. You must have someone controlling your likeness."

And then I figured it out. I knew how to end their existence. It came to me. All of my experimental experiences coalesced into that single moment. "But what do I get?" I asked.

"What is it that you want?" they said again.

I took them back to the laboratory. "I know what I want. When I show you how to end your existence, I want you to experiment with me."

I had the tools in the laboratory to create a universe within a universe. Within one universe, I would find their programs, destroy them, and allow this destruction to be replicated in perpetuity. Thus, for all of infinity, they would cease to exist. It would take years to find their original programs, but there was surely a paper trail leading back to their creation. I would find it.

As for what I wanted out of the deal, I merely asked if they would explain to me their essence, which they were able to achieve. With this knowledge, I was capable of making a replica of myself. I could now place myself in any environment I chose, controlling my actions from this laboratory.

CHAPTER XXV

R ecipes, programs, instructions, blueprints, they are all the same," 3PO said.

"How can you say they're all the same?" I said.

"All these items must have an originator, a creator."

"Not necessarily," I said.

"But nothing can come from nothing," 3PO said.

"That depends on what you mean by 'nothing.' The concept of nothing had to have an origin point, I guess, so there had to be something there to name that nothing."

The droid was once more shuffling through the garbage compactor's pile of discarded discs and old programs.

"Which one are you looking for?" I asked.

"The escape program, of course, young Jedi."

I too found myself aimlessly looking for a disc with *Escape* etched on its outer covering.

"3PO, I found it," I said, lifting it up from all the chaos.

"Give it to me," the droid said.

CHAPTER XXVI

An escape," Florence said as she wove her hand through my hair. "And what have you escaped from? Better yet, what have you escaped to?"

I looked down at my still static apparatus.

"It's not an escape," Florence said, "just another state."

Like the states of matter, I too was trapped in this bubble of a universe. Escape had been my goal; it had been Mother's goal. It had always been our goal to escape, but not now.

"I no longer want to escape," I told Florence.

"Is it because you recognize that you can't?" she asked.

"I'm no different than the water that trickles down into a cavernous area: I can change into different states, but I am eternal."

"And so you are thankful for this eternal gift of self-awareness?"

I began to materialize back into my human form.

Shortly after, Father and Van Coleman entered the room, their heads lowered as if they were mourning. "Death," I said.

My heart had given out from all the booze and pills. My slow suicide had reached the goal of taking me from the simulation of life. The last thing I remember reading was by Bernardo Kastrup speaking of the state of bipolar conflicts. "It began to believe that to 'prove' an idea is more important than for the idea to resonate with the innermost selves of people and thereby, make a true difference." I finally got to leave a world that had killed my laughing God of enchantment and wonder. Dr. L.S. Lafitte is dead.

VOLUME III
BOOK III

CHAPTER I

There was an acerbic taste in my mouth: an unkind flavor that sent my memory racing to taste something different, something better.

"Finish it, James, please finish it." The voice, the voice within, called out to me. "Do you feel it move? Remember, James, that was the question that I asked you."

Another dream, perhaps. It seemed different, though, more real than the others. I can't really explain the meaning of "more real"; perhaps I was more conscious of it. That's it! Some forms of consciousness were being replaced by new forms of consciousness every time I perceived what I thought was death. Death was the objective viewpoint of it. Ascension through progressive forms of consciousness was the subjective or feeling viewpoint of it.

Mother looked so beautiful, like an angel from heaven. She seemed to be in the same memorialized state that I had always remembered the best memory of her my brain could conjecture.

"Finish it, James."

"What is it that you ask me to finish?" I asked.

"The picture, James, the piece of art that you're working on for me," Mother said, laughing.

I looked to my side, where there appeared to be a canvas. It was half finished, by whom I knew not. *Dreams are odd,* I thought. *They have no predictability whatsoever; they are so different from life.* The picture appeared to be a rendition of a video game I had played in early childhood. Mother had loved the enjoyment I got from playing it. "I remember what it means, Mother," I said.

"Do you?"

"'It means that the world moves, independent of our senses realizing it.'" This was Mother's big hint whenever I took to playing a video game. In the worlds that my characters entered, these avatars came upon hindrances that, it appeared, they were unfit to know, unfit to address. I can't tell you how many times I attempted to get Mario or Mega Man or Metroid to advance to the next level, always failing. "Keep on experimenting, James; do you feel it move?" That's what Mother had always said when I got frustrated with the games. It was motivation, motivation to look at the characters in a novel way. The characters I controlled had some sense of the worlds they were in; they were programmed to interact with their environments. Yet there were many things of which they were unconscious, or things they were unable to grasp, perhaps clandestine passwords they could use to enter new levels. This was where I came in. *The world certainly moves,* I thought, *but human beings don't feel it move.*

Mario didn't know that I was helping him find new ways to save the princess; nevertheless, I was. The painting I was finishing for Mother was not just a two-dimensional rendition of a certain level of *Super Mario Brothers*; rather, it was a painting of me attached to a controller, helping Mario save the Princess. The controller is attached to me at the belly button like an umbilical cord.

"Do you feel the peace, James?"

I looked at Mother. I did feel at peace in this dream state. All was so clear and aesthetically pleasing. All seemed so truthful.

"Beauty is truth and truth is beauty, James." It was the first time that Mother had actually defined "truth" as something more tangible. However, something was awry in this dream. Something was wrong.

Could it be that it wasn't a dream at all? This was no appearance. I had been transported somewhere; I had found Mother. Absolution had come in the form of Mother in a utopian universe.

"What year are we in, Mother? What year is it?"

"'Year,' dear? I don't know exactly what you mean. We are here, you and I, with each other. The psyche ward was your purgatory, alcohol your kryptonite. Took you just twelve steps to no longer crawl."

The environment — what hints would this environment give me? This had to be the future; it just had to be. And yet, it still resembled a dream, with no conception of years or time. Had this future society brainwashed Mother not to believe in the constraints of space or time? Had this society conquered space and time's absconding effects? "'In dreams, James, you must always look for time. Therein lies your answer to whether you are in a dream.'" That's what Mother used to tell me. It was one of her only axioms, one of her only rules or explanations.

The room we were in was decorated in Mother's favorite Austrian fabrics, materials from the times of Bismarck. Everything was almost too perfect.

You might wonder what I mean by "perfect."

"Perfection, isn't it, James? Pure perfection."

It was aesthetically pleasing to the eye, Mother's eye. All that made Mother's program run smoothly, in terms of genetics, was within the environment; all the items and scenes that gave Mother the visceral feeling that people strive for in life, the tingling sensation that goes up the spine, were present. Reminders of when we in our vegetative states and the nervous system looked like a weed.

"Mother, do you remember the time logos that Father and Van Coleman...?"

"You need not worry about time travel here. However, if it is time travel you seek, you may experience it. You can experience all that any human or knowing being has ever experienced or will ever experience here in the Pleroma." She had never uttered that word "," before. She knew the anxiety that it germinated in my mind, and she knew it always threw me off balance.

She continued, "This is not a dream. You're not trapped in a video game or a television program. This is your life. You have reached the Omega Point. James, you're in heaven."

And upon hearing those simple words, I fainted.

CHAPTER II

P apa Smurf, the safest way to bring about happiness for all Smurfs is to do away with all forms of Smurf speech."

"Brainy, you must always think before you give your own Smurf speech. It is the freedom of Smurf speech and Smurf worship that make us all so Smurfy."

How fantastic, to be trapped in a cartoon so pleasing to the eyes. There was nothing dirty or inglorious here. And before me were Brainy Smurf and Papa Smurf discussing civil liberties. I hadn't thought cartoon characters cared about such matters; they weren't real, and only real people would hold arguments over such topics.

"What do you wait here for?" Brainy Smurf asked me. "Papa Smurf always says that an idle person harms those he could be helping. Isn't that right, Papa?"

I looked down at my animated self, my little white tights and blue stomach, and quickly wondered what individual quality of Smurfiness I had taken on. Was I Brawny Smurf or Scientific Smurf? Perhaps Curious Smurf?

"Papa Smurf, tell Fakey Smurf what to do," Brainy Smurf said. "He always seems so ignorant about Smurf law."

Papa Smurf looked at me and then transferred his queer gaze into dead space.

"What is it that you want?" I asked.

Both looked at each other as if the question had never been asked before. "We live in a Smurfy way, Fakey, we always have."

"Any real Smurf knows that," Brainy Smurf said.

Do these Smurfs know they are nothing more than someone's imaginative figment? I wondered. Could they describe the evolutionary and genetic processes through which they have evolved to their present state? Do they even care? Perhaps their minds, like human minds, are captive. They have no knowledge of the strands that make up their fabric of reality.

Suddenly, all was blackness; all was in darkness.

"Try not to move, Smurfs; we'll think of escaping once he lets us out of this sack."

Gargamel and his trusted sidekick Azrael had caught us: to eat us, of course.

"Papa Smurf, why does Gargamel always insist on capturing the Smurfs?" I asked.

Papa looked puzzled.

The other Smurfs all turned to him in the darkness and asked the same. They wanted answers.

"I don't know," he said. "I don't know what he wants with us or what his intentions are. I do know that we are always able to use our Smurf wits to get out of his grip."

"And isn't it odd that you always escape, Papa?" I said. "Isn't it odd that Gargamel has never once eaten any of you, and yet he is surely the strongest of all of you? And what of his cat Azrael? Is it not odd that his feline skills are unable to nab you and eat you? Haven't any of you questioned this environment you live in? Have you ever questioned the fabric of your reality?"

Papa Smurf looked as if he had been run over by a bulldozer; he sat still, mesmerized by my questions.

Brainy Smurf looked at Papa with anxiety, awaiting answers. "What of our existence, Papa? Why do we exist?" Brainy Smurf paused. "I guess everything is not all that Smurfy after all."

Gargamel reached into the bag, grabbed Papa Smurf, and bit off his head.

All the Smurfs in the bag began regurgitating violently. *How could this happen?* I thought. The laws of their universe, created by their maker, had been left to total chaos.

Brainy Smurf looked over at me. "Why do we exist, Fakey Smurf? Is our existence to await death at the hands of Gargamel? Is that our only meaning?"

I started to believe that I now was a Smurf, that I always had been a Smurf, and that my Smurfiness was my own conception. "Take off your glasses, Brainy." I cracked the glasses and used them to begin cutting a hole in the bottom of the bag. I was going to change the Smurfs' consciousness. No longer would they live in fear of Gargamel and his cat, no longer would they have anxiety about their own existence. "You will all remember this experience forever," I told them.

"Finish it, James, finish it."

CHAPTER III

And as I sit here now, relating this next tale, I must give fair warning that at the time I experienced this simulation, I was unaware that it was a game. Lucifer had control of my mind, which was worse than any physical restraint. Lucifer was the anchor for suffering in all versions of hell, even our own world. You see, although I speak of heaven, there is no heavenly dimension. Heaven is merely the closest you can come to a world that exhibits Christ consciousness, where the higher laws rule over the lower laws in a harmonious way. So while our world may be the best version of Hell, it's also the closest we can come to heaven since we have the ability to implement Christ consciousness. Clearly, during my time we had not yet achieved that.

"It's just like a drug, isn't it?" an owl said. "Lift yourself out of the mud, James."

"What's like a drug?" I asked.

"All of it, every bit of it, even the simulation you now bring yourself out of to be reborn in this new world." The owl was a bright red, almost so red that it burned.

Like the fire Prometheus had stolen from the gods, I thought.

"Is that how you make relations, James?" the owl said.

My mind was continually being read in these new worlds.

I looked down at my body, which was devoid of any sexual organs or hair, and then reached up and felt my face, which was devoid of eyes, mouth, ears, and features. Nevertheless, I could see the owl clearly and hear it perfectly, and I could feel the presence of my environment.

"You feel here, James; you don't physically exist here," the owl hooted. "It's just like a drug, isn't it?" it said again. "Lift yourself out of the mud."

I waited a moment.

"All of it, James, every bit of it, even the simulation you now bring yourself out of to be reborn in this new world."

I ran away from the owl as far as my mind could race, away to the farthest place I could travel, where I sat down and cried, without tears. I wailed, full of frustration and anxiety. I called out to the heavens, "What purpose is it?" You want me to tell you exactly how hell looks and feels. That's what your myopic reductionist mind wants to know. I will! Go to any AA (alcoholics anonymous) meeting or any other drug anonymous meeting and they can tell you. I'm absolutely serious! It's almost the exact same. The objective aspects of hell that you can see are strikingly similar to the nightmares addicts have when they are trying to get off the drug. Go ahead and ask them. They will all tell you similar dreams of demons, witches and church iconography, the torment in the dreams with the total absence of love (*agápe, éros, philía*) or hope. The subjective aspects of hell are almost exactly like the way you feel during a hangover that is so terrible you want to commit suicide. Your bones are being grounded down to nothing while your mind deceives you and lies to you about everything. While you feel as if your limbs are physically being torn apart over and over again, the only true sin, self-delusion, possesses you. The worst thing about it all is that there is no one around to tell you to fight it or to say that your mind is playing tricks on you. Then, in hell, I slept.

CHAPTER IV

C lues, James, just look for clues." I woke to Papa Smurf showering Smurf berry juice on my face.

"Is it another dream, Papa?" I asked.

"No, you're still in hell, James," Papa said.

I meditated for a moment, trying to bring some amount of clarity to the situation. *Even board games have plots and goals; every game has a plan.*

"An Alpha and an Omega," Papa Smurf said.

"Yes, Papa, but it seems that in my rendition of hell there is no beginning or end. Everything repeats itself over and over again. Nothing is novel."

"If the repetition is beautiful, James, then why do you fear it? Why do you gnash your teeth at the concept?" Papa asked. "Does it frighten you that there are no plans or goals, no endings or beginnings?"

I regurgitated on Papa's little red hat, and the thought of feeling regurgitation and nausea repeating for all of eternity crept into my head. "It's eternity, Papa, it's the idea of eternity — that is, a place devoid of a beginning and ending, a place devoid of a plan and purged of all goals. I guess I fear being and existence, whatever that may entail. I don't want eternity, Papa!" All I wanted to do was see Allan's face, the beauty of his face and with him enter the secret carpeted kingdom under the jungle gym — that's all I ever wanted, it really was that simple.

"Clues, James, just look for clues." Papa was doing the same thing as the owl now; repeating himself, my shifting interjections not changing his responses until he finally said, "Infinite synchronicities will get you out of hell and back to the psyche ward. All you have to do is be aware of them."

CHAPTER V

In the horizon of the infinite... We have forsaken the land and gone to sea! We have destroyed the bridge behind us. Even more so, we have demolished the land behind us! Now, little ship, look out! Beside you is the ocean; it is true, it does not always roar, and at times it lies like silk and gold and dreams of goodness. But there will be hours when you realize it is infinite, and there is nothing more awesome than infinity. Oh, the poor bird that has felt freedom and now strikes against the walls of this cage! Woe, when homesickness for the land overcomes you, as if there had been more freedom there... and there is no more land,'" Lucifer said.

As I gazed out into the sea, Lucifer showed me my event horizon; he elucidated the infinite and the eternal. He gave me the ability to suffer so I too could ascend and teach others to ascend back to the Pleroma. He gave me revelations of the Kingdom on Earth as it is in Heaven. There was a different type of love prior to the dark ages before Christ was crucified. The consciousness prior to Christ would not allow the three forms of pure love. This is why the Old Testament outlawed homosexuality and why many biblical characters have more than one wife.

The idea that you could find love (*agápe, éros, philía*) in another person was unrecognizable until the Captain was resurrected. He finished it! That's how he perfected the lower laws of the Old Testament with the higher laws of the New. Love now became a defense to these charges. The higher laws always rule over the lower.

❧

We were back at St. Peter's, before I had found the time logos, when I was looking up at the mural of Christ and Peter on the ceiling. It was different this time, much different than before. The faces were different. If you remember, the first time I saw the picture, Christ was above, perhaps hovering in heaven, while Peter, absconding from the Romans, was about to run into the Pagans' fire, thus trapped between two opposing forces that both sought his demise. But this time, the picture was different. The faces were all the same in the picture. They were all my face.

I dropped to my knees and began to cry. I wanted out. I just wanted out, and I realized that I couldn't get out: it was impossible. I could never get away from myself, and I could never leave myself. People are not trapped in a reality; we're trapped in our own minds.

CHAPTER VI

There were three tiers in the top part of the island. The inhabitants of the top level, who resembled the likes of the Watchers in *The Book of Enoch* held the power of Vril. This element imbued them with the ability to enunciate and know truth by using the green language. But it was the concordance of truth. Their power was based on perception of action. They acted in ways that all agreed upon as being called "action." Therefore, the Watchers never asked the question, "What is it?" They knew that the thing itself, or the essence of the thing itself, was held in the actions it produced. Vril was truth, and truth was action. Enlightenment itself is truly what happens when there is nothing left of us but love. This is objective love; the suffering to accept yourself and enjoy yourself. Everything else other than objective love must be purged from all forms of hell if we are to reach God consciousness. The new physician known as the Mechanical Man, the second coming of Christ will bring us to this point of consciousness where the implicate is as visible and tangible as the explicate — there will be no difference between what is below as to what is above.

"Who am I?" I asked one of them.

The Watchers smiled, looked at me and said, "You are space, movement, atoms, elements, and mental Vril."

"What is mental Vril?" I asked, hesitating for a bit and looking around. Now the Watchers were all agreeing I had Vril. Something in my actions had caused this concordance of truth upon which they all could agree and see.

Father had once said that robots would have rights equal to those of humans when we all agreed they were human, and that this would be accomplished when the first robot died on a cross for all to see.

"Do they worship you?" Michael asked. Michael was looking around at the crowd, members of which were now bowing to my graceful Vril.

The Watchers looked deep into my eyes and said, "They see the movement; they see the connected symbols; they see the endless loops that meet the ends of others in your body and your mind. It is a system of ideas that have no beginning or end."

"They can see through you, James: the movements of your organs, blood, neurons, and ideas," Michael said.

That must be their idea of truth, or at the very least, belief: just constant movement, I thought. During the American Revolution, the blue-eyed professor had taught me that movement is all we have to stay alive — that the very idea of movement is concomitant to evolving and staying alive.

"Our island still evolves, you know," the Watchers said. And in their eyes I saw such evolution. It was the evolution of the cosmos that possessed the ability for chance events to occur, but then to organize those events and create selectivity and further evolution, not of body but mind. All was evolving; all was moving and trying to stay alive within the collective unconscious. Was the cosmos the hunted, the prey of something or someone, always trying to be sneaky, always trying to camouflage its hidden agenda or goals? The cosmos was so sneaky, attempting to tell itself that there was nothing but chance and chaos, and yet the caverns of dark matter held organization — it was a constant game of peek a boo, the cosmos was playing on itself. No wonder why the Captain, the great physician, first visited the multiple versions of hell prior to entering the Kingdom.

The sand underneath my feet formed a small vortex, circling me into it. The crowd moved away from the circling winds of sand. As the ground sucked in my body, Michael jumped in after me. Within the earth of the sand, or the sand of the earth, was a dark tunnel, out of which the rankest smell issued forth. I had no sense of direction in the cavernous layer of the planet in which we found ourselves entombed.

"Which way do we go, James?" Michael said. He stood on the ceiling, looking down on me.

I wondered if we needed to traverse in the direction that was normative to Michael, and upside down to myself, or the opposite. "Should we split up?" I asked Michael.

He began to walk around the circular cavern on the same plane as me, facing me. Our perspectives were now in equilibrium. "Does it matter?" he said.

The middle of the island held a temple made of tiny machines. The manifold parts of the machines manifested themselves as a tower from afar. As one approached the tower, the shape of the tower itself was lost in the simple actions of the machines. It was only from afar that the machines were able to manifest themselves into the tower.

"How do we enter the tower and pledge our obedience to the Vril of this island if the tower loses its form as we approach it?"

A bird circled above us, landing on the top of the tower. "The tiny machines that work together to form the tower, what are they?" I asked Michael.

Michael was busy looking at the bird, that now appeared to be part of the tower itself: a stone symbol atop the tower, emblazoned in gold. After our actions, the tower asked us to reduce ourselves to our machines in order to enter its majestic doors. Both of our bodies reduced, each to a myriad of double helixes. In the aggregate, each set of double helixes too formed a tower. I had never noticed that double helixes appeared to be made of machines when reduced to their mechanical forms; they too were performing a process of exchange and communication. In each double helix was an interaction of control and cybernetics.

※

"No different than our time, James, once man's work was displaced by the positronic-brained droids and then the atomic-brained cyborgs." Indeed, Michael was right. Evolution, control, and even patterns led to a form of knowledge that allowed one merely to know the rules of the games and then play those games to alleviate boredom.

"At least we have the chance to play games," a Gargoyle said. It led us to a room filled with clocks and conveyor belts.

"What is this for?" I asked.

The Gargoyle sat us down and pointed to the series of conveyor belts. "This is our history: the boundary of this island." The conveyor belts and clocks were filled with many simple devices, all of which were acting together to do something that appeared complex, almost to the point of displaying reason through the complexity of such simple actions.

"What's the purpose of gathering this knowledge, Gargoyle?" I asked.

The Gargoyle stood up and pulled down a lever attached to the main conveyor belt, stopping all action. "That's the purpose of it all," the creature said. "It is still the movement that we seek. This movement is the complexity of actions that can no longer be reduced to their composite parts."

The inhabitants of the living world, in which I had lived, seemed so concerned with reducing everything down to fragments, down to the bare bones of it all. This island seemed to look for a unity of all the monads that created the machinery of actions. All was movement on this island and within this tower. It was no different than the universe: all objects were in constant motion and relative to one another. The first law of nature was that the more you moved and the less you thought the denser you became. This law caused God to fade from existence as you became more and more dense.

The Gargoyle stood up. "There is an all-encompassing formula that always frightens those that come to the hereafter. It was mostly found in fiction in your worlds."

Michael looked at the hands of a clock moving around the numbers, always returning to starting position.

"The departure, the initiation, and the return," I said.

The Gargoyle looked over at me and asked, "Does that cause fear in you?"

"Nothing places fear in me any longer, as long as I'm still awake in this dream. Is the initiation phase when all becomes fragmentary, Gargoyle?" I asked.

The Gargoyle waved his hand in our direction, turned around, and led us out of the room of mechanics and into a room of butterflies and artists of the beautiful. It was a laboratory of solitude holding numerous artist-scientists, each working on tiny mechanical butterflies. The Gargoyle turned to us and said, "They place their imprint on each creation through their own sorcery."

I peeked over at one of the scientists. His work was dexterous, clean, and precise.

The butterflies were an end result of the mechanisms and actions that took place in the minds of the artist-scientists bringing life to such creatures. *They imprint each of the mechanical simulations.*

"Ah, not a simulation," the Gargoyle said. "That was a bit of a riddle that your society faced after the era of fragmentation."

I looked over at Michael, asking silently for assistance. I walked over to one of the butterflies, picked it up, and tore it apart limb by limb. The mechanical toy separated into its constituent parts, fragmented.

The Gargoyle picked up the butterfly's pieces, crushing them into his hand. The dust created a mystic fog around the creature.

"There's no riddle to it at all, my friends," I said. Simulations and copies have no meanings; they are charlatans.

"Are you a charlatan to your creator?" the Gargoyle said.

I looked over at the Gargoyle and wanted to ignore him. I had no time to learn about aspects of the creator in the hereafter; that was how I had wasted my time in the living world. "No, action is the God of the afterlife." My people, in the end, were in the process of killing God, of tearing the butterfly apart limb by limb, leaving ourselves only with dust. Simple actions that would evolve or combine would form complexity, and out of that complexity would germinate new properties and processes.

After spreading the dust of the mechanical butterfly, the Gargoyle stood up once more. "That's what your lives are for. You humans always seek a meaning in life. That's it."

I looked at the rest of the inventors, still oblivious to the outside world in their collective endeavors to create the beautiful. The Gargoyle was right: living was a process of recognition. Life was a class on theory — one in which we could experiment, although our experiments merely told us the importance of action — and action was merely the cosmos letting out its breath, while love was the force that was the first mover of every action.

In the end, I thought, the real world is one of preparation — moving ourselves, by our actions; into complex processes that therefore, through our very own perceptions, create novel properties, including consciousness and other tools that we are able to utilize to pursue objective love.

"And that's what science is," Michael said. "Science is asking nature questions. Sometimes nature answers, other times it lies or misleads, and still others it changes. Then everything it told us in the past seems as dead as the nature that bequeathed such to us."

The butterflies began to fly around us. When they combined, they formed the end product of their action: a large metal plane able to traverse the great skies and depths of space in the hereafter. The Gargoyle pointed to the plane. "Here you no longer ask nature questions; you're on the inside now, Dr. Lafitte, in the hereafter. You get to see how nature is born, what it does, and why it acts the way it does. Here you see the purpose, whereas in the living realm you only saw the theories, the numbers, the symbols, the myth, and the laws that govern the game. Here you get to witness the game and why they play it. When you return don't make the same mistake that was made when Christ was resurrected. Specifically, don't leave empty space in the collective consciousness. Fill it with archetypes that will the universe to love. You will be the new Don Quixote."

The butterflies had changed into a plane, but not because they could magically form or morph into that plane. Instead, they were built with the goal of being able to become a plane. Their inventors never believed, not for a moment, that they were inventing butterflies as beautiful artistic creations. Rather, they sought the simplicity of the butterflies and used it to bring about a complex flying machine.

"That's what your friends in the Revolution did, James, did they not?" the Gargoyle said.

Yes, he was right. Washington and Adams did, but so did even Christ and Peter in their revolution. They were acting the same way scientists act, asking questions of a black wall of darkness called nature, attempting to see what ideas could seep through the darkness and bring light out of the wall's opacity. All revolutions had one goal in mind, move consciousness forward.

"Get on the plane, James. Your friend awaits you," Michael said.

As I stepped on the plane, I heard a familiar voice. For a moment, I thought it was Father. Instead, I saw myself all grown up.

The appearance of my older self stared at me, in my present state of un-being. "I'm taking you away from this place for a training exercise."

I looked around the plane. Frozen in time were infinite representations of my appearance as far as the eye could behold. They were of all ages, from the smallest form in my creation to the most desiccated and decayed. "This is the army you'll need; we'll need to break the boundary of reason," the older me said.

"Why do we need an army to break reason?" I asked.

"Reason still controls this world as well. The difference is that in the afterworld its boundary can be broken — where appearance ends and essence begins can be pierced, and we can travel through it."

The language of the afterworld is now becoming transparent: laws of adaptation or learning still rule here, I thought.

"That's right," my older self said, reading my mind, as he began to release the other representations of me from their bound state.

"This is not an army like the ones in the world of life, is it?" I asked.

"No, it's a different army entirely — these representations, in the aggregate, create your essence."

A very old version of me now stabilized his appearance. He brought me toward himself and held me tight, whispering in my ear. "As we draw closer to the boundary, your memory of reason will fade — you'll no longer want to rebel against eternity, nor will you have any goals at all. Beginnings and endings will fade into a dark oblivion. But we must remember reason in order for all the army to cross the boundary." He began to write our goals on the foggily condensed windows with his finger. "Go back with an army. Don't go alone this time, take the souls of light with you. Stay sober and vigilante. Suicide is no longer an option. Lucifer will trade you an army for your gift of suicide."

I was no longer one mind but an amalgam of that mind, readying to meet the boundary, traversing the chains of reason, and seeing what that mind had always thought was on the other side but was never able to experience, not even within imagination, for even the imagination is limited by reason.

We looked out the windows of the plane. The boundary was a bent spoon of space and time, emerging as an explosion of chaos an old watchmaker had tried to craft using the appearance of beauty and control. But reason had not fooled even the simpletons of the human race. Even they knew that the watchmaker, while producing beautiful works of order for others, lived in a decayed home with a loveless wife. His life was mercurial and only his productions were orderly. Which was of more import?

As part of the amalgam of one mind, it occurred to me that the boundary around the realm of reason, and the boundary around the out-of-bounds area of reason and experience, was the reunion of the self. Participating in the amalgam of selves ended time as I knew it. Time was no longer made up of dots on a line; it wasn't even a line. It consisted of different versions of solipsism, or my viewpoint of relations, experiences, dreams, and images. It was the compilation of all the dots on the line wrapped into one cohesive quilt of who I had been, was, and would be. Yet the separation had gone deeper. The separation was a contradiction that could never be ameliorated or fixed. Subjectivity was the living and objectivity the dead.

The boundary through which we were about to fight, the army we were readying for battle — all of it pertained to the outdated modes of human language that we believe had evolved our race and developed the technological creations we lauded so highly in our technological society. The boundary was indeed the language of opposites. The infinite amounts of my selves would have to play a game against the language of mathematics. Since I'm using the word "game," you're probably thinking of balls, rules, out of bounds, and even audiences, along with times to start and end the game: that, of course, is the problem of the real world, wherein the living try so hard to find meaning in meaningless mathematics and logic. And yet, as my amalgam approached the boundary, I knew there was so much on the other side, not another existence or even another *Geist* — not another me or another Mother and Father. I could still experience these puzzles in the living world and the hereafter.

What was beyond the boundary transcended any experiences that my human self once had had; my explicate projection had to separate in order to enter and interact within it. We were now about to displace ourselves to the place where things began. Now I laugh at that — at these words "beginning" and "ending" — don't think that I mean this place was a starting point or a place that existed beyond the boundary that manifested itself. The game itself, in which the opponent was mathematics, was to use formulas to break the program. In other words, my projection needed to show the boundary that mathematics and logic had merely caused my self, as they would any self, to split into dichotomies and contradictions — and show that these subjects could never lead us to ultimate knowledge or allow us to experience spirit and God.

People always ask how things look. I can only relate the following in the manner of speaking, just as how the mind of minds described its inception. This formulaic war began with my amalgam recognizing that the boundary had no equilibrium on the other side or on our side. Once more, my fictional world, which brought ideas into reality, was needed most in this battle of formulas and mathematics. The need for a mythic marker in the form of the Gargoyle or Mechanical Man, a mythic marker of societal contradictions, appeared. At this point in time, I pictured the Mechanical Man stretch the great spiral out to form the spear of Longinus.

CHAPTER VII

The Tin Man moved around, chopping at the trees. "The flying moneys are coming; get to the shelters."

I flew to an opening in the forest that the Tin Man had cut out. At the end of the opening stood a giant tree; I flung my body into it. Within the tree was a circle of mirrors, all the reflections staring at me.

"Dependency is both a good and a bad thing," the Tin Man said.

Dorothy came out from behind one of the mirrors and started oiling his parts. "Do you have to do this every day?" I asked her.

She hesitated for a moment and responded, "So long as I yearn to stay in Oz."

They were needed in Oz. Dorothy played her part, the Tin Man his. But there was never any changing in this tree, this Oz, just mirror reflections of differing dependencies.

"Did you think that you changed in the real world or the hereafter?" Dorothy asked.

I thought I evolved during life. I thought I was still learning here, in the hereafter. In life, I witnessed myself grow and age. I saw my thoughts and ideas mature.

"Did you get better?" Dorothy asked.

I deduced she was talking about ascension. "Yes," I said.

"The more you know, the more things look contradictory?" questioned the Tin Man. He started destroying the mirrors, showing the wood behind them. "James, if I now take my ax and destroy the tree, where would we be? Or, better yet, what would we see?"

If he took his ax to the tree, we would see the forest. Our position would not change, but we would be able to see more.

"More of what, James?" Dorothy asked, reading my thoughts.

"More of what is occurring," I responded. Even now, I can see the beetles going in and out of the tree's crevices.

"You sure about that?" the Tin Man asked.

I envisioned him cutting the forest down; I would probably see the Emerald City.

"But there are no beetles in the wood," the Tin Man said, showing he could also read my thoughts.

I understood what he was trying to teach me: perception is key. "Look at your ax," I said. "It's a tool!"

Dorothy laughed. "I get what you're saying, James—"

I interrupted sweet Dorothy. "That's right! I can use a telescope or other tools to see the actions of people in the Emerald City. The devil is in the details." I moved forward, reached down, placed my hands on the ground, and asked, "What exactly do the flying monkeys want?"

The Tin Man marked his industrial myth, lifting the ax. "This is what they want." He lifted the great divider, and I remembered how a mathematical formula equates to another formula, but beneath the veneer, or behind the curtain, the equal sign is the great divider. However, this divider is also a great equalizer. It gives meaning to contradictions. The monkeys wanted it so that we would once again become slaves.

"The ax is our will to power; it is our force of will," he said. "Without it, we would perish, for we would never allow ourselves to be subject to the dominion of the flying monkeys. In the afterlife, gone are the days in Oz in which we look at the meek and the cowardly in a glorious manner."

I thought back to the German doctors and their discussions on idealism. "The ax is a tool of creation, then, is it not?" I asked the Tin Man.

He said nothing.

After he had chopped through the trees, we saw a gorilla playing chess with a scientist. They both sat placidly, in the midst of trees and animals, making moves against each other.

As we approached, we heard the gorilla roar and saw him bang his hands on the table, apparently upset by the scientist's control and moves. The concept of eternal recurrence was still on my mind — that now, even in the afterlife, we would have to experience this over and over again, for all of eternity.

"Give me the ax," I demanded.

The Tin Man turned to me and handed me the ax. I ran toward the gorilla, mercilessly chopping it into pieces. Within its body were numerous miniature Tin Men, all working tirelessly to keep the gorilla's gadgets oiled and running.

The scientist looked over at us and asked why we had killed his creation.

"Because he was about to kill you," I replied.

The scientist jumped up and said, "That's the category I placed myself in: I'm one of those willing to die by the hands of their slaves or creations. Don't you know anything about issues of control or cybernetics?"

I knew little of cybernetics. I expected it to imply a new category of human beings, like the robots I had met before, and said as much.

The scientist stood up and started shaking his head. "No, no, you're always thinking too deeply. Get back to the fundamentals. You take existence too seriously."

I determined the scientist had created all the Tin Men utilized to make the gorilla appear alive and autonomous. "How did you get control over the Tin Men?" I asked.

"They grew up as nano-slaves. They knew nothing else in life. Their category was one of slavery and drudgery — they would commit suicide if they didn't have the tasks I bequeathed them." The scientist then asked us to follow him to his laboratory.

The first Tin Man paved the way for us, the tiny Tin Men reconfiguring their pattern of creation to form the gorilla again. The gorilla's natural instincts now gave us the ability to thrash through the brush at a quicker pace. The tools of natural selection, or, shall I say, planned programming, contributed more to creating our path than the Tin Man's ax.

After the scientist stumbled over some branches, I helped him up and asked, "What type of equipment do you have here in the afterlife?"

The scientist laughed and pointed to his head. "I'll show you when we get to the laboratory. I don't want my ideas to pass through the liquid ether and be usurped by the flying monkeys."

We arrived at a lovely cottage deep within the darkness of the forest, and the scientist opened the door. Once inside, we saw a chess-playing mannequin that the scientist called the Turk. "This, you know," the scientist said excitedly, "is the only gift the Archangel gave me before he recognized the afterlife's absurdity and went mad searching for the pirate, Dr. L.S. Lafitte."

We all looked at the automaton playing chess.

"But look, it's a hoax," the scientist said. He opened the bottom half of the desk upon which the chess set was laid. "Underneath the desk is a place that can hold a small man who may control the movements of the automaton."

Ideas of control and communication were becoming more and more important in the afterlife. And while I still recognized that this myth was part of the war of symbols and mathematics, a war that was taking place at the edge of reason's boundary, I wondered if my amalgam self was winning that war.

"Why did the Archangel go mad, exactly?" I asked, placing myself within the Turk's desk.

The scientist started doing some sorcery in the corner of the room. He looked over at us; we were all still intrigued by the Turk. "I've found it," the scientist said. He came over to me and handed me a small piece of popcorn.

The gorilla started to stomp and bang his hands on the floor, jumping up and down.

"What is it?" I asked.

"It's the Prozac of the afterworld."

I laughed and took the piece of popcorn in my hand.

"The Archangel would not take the corn; he maintained he could fill his time with creating things and experimenting, and he went mad after he realized he couldn't maintain the extended cybernetics that led him to search for the pirate Lafitte."

"Did he invent you?" I asked the scientist.

"No, no. I was once alive, just like you, James. I'm in this battle of mathematics with you. You're experiencing it right now in your own fictional way. Going through this event in Oz is the only way you can experience it. It's the same way you were experiencing the war within a divided self in the land of the living."

The gorilla sat down next to the Turk and started to simulate a game of chess with the hoax automaton.

"I still find things to do here in this version of Oz, James; if I get bored, like the Archangel did, I take the popcorn in order to perceive things differently."

I took the piece of popcorn and swallowed it. In the living world, people weren't around long enough to see a control-based revolution occur in terms of communication. Eating the popcorn would allow us to visit a future friend in the land of the living.

The scientist too swallowed a piece. Then the scientist moved the Turk over to the side and uncovered a deep hole in the ground.

The Tin Man looked deep down into the hole and prevented the gorilla from jumping into it. "I'll stay here and protect the inventions. Go, James."

My head was a little light now. "What about the war? Have we won — did we pass the boundary of reason?"

The scientist laughed and asked me to jump in the hole.

"How absurd," I said, "another hole to jump into."

The scientist slapped me on the back, giving me a push into the hole. "That's the point, James, to see how your society got itself out of concluding that all things are fragments of the absurd."

CHAPTER VIII

I t felt odd to be back in the land of the living. There we stood, the air racing across my face, the sun shining on my head. When you come back to the land of the living, you no longer care to know what year or time of day it is. Compared to the hereafter, the place feels like a dream — that is, it feels like what I would be dreaming of if I dreamed in the living world. If that sounds ambiguous, it should.

"I don't have the anxieties I once had when I was alive," I told the scientist.

Manifestly not interested in my ruminations, he walked down the city streets, indicating that he was trying to find a library. "It's because your anxieties are now in the hereafter; that's where your past and future are."

Dickens's Christmas tale of the past, present, and future ghosts flooded my fictional world as the scientist picked up a newspaper. "The concept of past, present and future was never so important to you, not until you were back in that body," he said.

"What's your name?" I finally asked him.

"Dasein," he said. He looked just like James Stewart from the film, *It's a Wonderful Life.*

"That's German," I responded.

"It's my name," he said.

I had learned that word from Frederick; he was infatuated with the meaning of *dasein*. "It means 'being,' doesn't it?"

"Not anymore," the scientist said. He stopped and looked at the paper, reading it aloud. *"Riccio Creates First Additions to Brain.* Looks like we are definitely in the right place and the right time, James. Oh, and my name no longer means 'being' in the hereafter; there, it means 'nothing.'"

"'Nothing?'" I said.

Dasein smiled. "No, James, it's very different. There must be a pause between 'no' and 'thing.' 'No thing.' That's my name."

"Then, in the land of the living, I will be known as 'no James,'" I said with a smirk.

We made it to the library. Gone were the skyscrapers made of metal and glass. All the buildings here were replicas of cathedrals, coliseums, and other old buildings with which I was familiar from my studies of history. The library was unique: it was a replica of an Egyptian pyramid. Copies of originals here did not lose focus; rather, they become more focused and detailed.

But inside was nothing like what I had seen before in the land of the living.

The library held numerous people, all of whom were situated on vacillating levels of translucent glass, communicating with their own holograms. In effect, they were experimenting with themselves. Some were even having intercourse with their own likenesses similar to my first initiation experience. This was the nouveau library of the future, in which learning consisted of solely conducting experiments with the self.

The idea of natural selection, the double helix, the genome, the God particle — these were all fragments and figments of the past. Indeed, the age of fragmentation, accompanied by simulacra, was over. "What do they seek?" I asked Dasein. He was watching one of the people in the library more intently.

The one he watched turned to us both and spoke. "'Fusion,' you know, used to be a word that described a scientific process involving the production of energy. Now, 'fusion' involves the synthesis of learning." The fusion of which this man spoke, and the interactions each student or library patron had, consisted of possible signifiers and the signified. In the pyramid, people were creating new fusions of words and symbols.

"This is not a library," I said. "It's a factory. The machine or computer is no longer the metaphor for the universe or brain; the factory in the act of creating symbols and archetypes is, which progresses consciousness — merging the subjective and objective."

Dasein asked if he could have a go with his own simulation. I stepped aside, he appeared to himself, and the two began to converse about their analogous experiences.

"Where does the program come from?" I asked.

The other man looked over at me. "The program?" he asked, puzzled.

"Yes," I said. "How does his simulation know his experiences?"

"His simulation is imbued with his memory and foresight." The man began to slowly back away from Dasein and me.

Perhaps I had said something wrong.

"It is, James," Dasein said. "It's a factory. It's a factory that turns out new words, symbols, and experiences."

The things a factory produces, and the tools people produce, are always axiomatic in telling us about the culture of that people, and it is the culture of a people that dictates almost everything in their lives.

The activities of the factory had taken me by surprise. Dasein was wrong in that the factory was producing words. It was actually providing games — word games — played between the library patrons and their holograms. These word games precluded the purging of certain words from regular use. I looked over at Dasein and said, "It's no different than burning books." Dasein gave a chuckle, predisposing me to grow a little irritated. "Why wouldn't they want to procure words? Don't words add to the fabric of experience?"

I sat down to view one of these word games, played by a patron of the library and his hologram. The patron told his hologram, "I am in pain."

The hologram turned to the patron and said, "I know I am in pain." An alarm went off, and the word was stricken from both of their minds for that particular circumstance. Thus, the game was a cleansing: a primal sanctification of language, eliminating words that confused or obscured.

"But all words are protean," I said.

"That's the point here: it's not the essence of a word, or the image that a word manifests in one's head, that has value; it's the use of the word, the activity of the word. It's like the activation of a mechanism or a light switch. Only the activity is worthy to give the word meaning," said a factory worker.

In these libraries, learning did not occur through reading books to gain knowledge or to learn the new meanings of different words; rather, learning was a purging of the words and ideas that prevent humans from seeing the fundamentals of life and the pragmatics of living. If the old world — the ancient world of the Greeks and Romans — was based on fundamentals of ideals and essence, then this world was based on action. And in the library in which I now found myself ensconced, I witnessed that the world had transformed into a reality of substantially editing itself.

Dasein was through playing the language game with his hologram. "Did you have a good purging?" I asked.

"It is a form of rewiring," he said.

If the people of the world I had left behind were on their way to finding the singularity of knowledge — or the acme of all knowledge that humans had potentiality to know — now was the time of sifting through such knowledge and language, editing the words that hinder actions, achievements, or growth. It was progressivism turned around and marching backward.

"James," Dasein called over to me. He asked if I wanted to see what was produced in the city's factories.

"Of course," I said. If the libraries were places where people edited words and ideas to bring about less congestion on the highways and byways of the brain's neural pathways, I couldn't imagine what the factories were either producing or, perhaps, destroying.

Dasein found a guide to show us some of the other factories within this city. "My name is Zeitlichkeit," the guide said. He looked like the others in the library. There was much less diversity in the looks of these people.

"You'll still see some connections to the fragmentation of culture from your world, James," Dasein said.

Zeitlichkeit turned his attention to the outer steps of the pyramid. The factories were held within the great cathedrals of the city, I learned. Thus, these people's machines of reason were in spaces of faith — or so I thought.

Stepping into one of these cathedrals expelled many of the biases I had formed about the future. From the actions within the pyramid, I had prefigured that these people were merely running in circles — that they were nihilists awaiting some change in the nature of things by cleansing their palates.

"The libraries are still places of learning," Zeitlichkeit said. "It's a different style of learning. The very idea of loving knowledge, or, as you all once said, 'love of knowledge,' is dead. Just as when you all came to the belief that God was dead, before the Great Wars, we concluded that knowledge or philosophy was dead. So, you're right: in the libraries, we cleanse our minds of what we thought had led us in a positivist direction toward knowledge and maturity."

Zeitlichkeit walked us further into the cathedral and spoke to us both, excited about what the factories were in the process of creating. "The history of machines moves forward from the very mundane and simple tasks that we first asked our aides to imbue us with. Through machines, we were shown the value of the programmer's, or creator's, goals. Of course, when our tools changed from machines to computers and then androids, our main focus was no longer centered on the goals of the creator; rather, it was focused on the issue of control between the programmer and the programmed.

"Deutsch's universal computing machine was finally able to act as our 'failsafe' — it gave us the ability to know any and all possible outcomes in terms of what our creations were capable of. Once the singularity came and technology merged with biology and humanity, the worldview of the vital machine shifted once again."

It all reminded me of two of the most important books during my time, one at each end of the Aristotelian and Platonic spectrums: *The Fabric of Reality* by David Deutsch and *Why Materialism is Baloney* by Bernardo Kastrup.

"Machines evolved," I said.

"What do you mean, 'machines evolved'?" Zeitlichkeit asked.

"They increased in their capacity to act and understand their surroundings. They increased their ability to kick back at the matter and forces of the universe."

Zeitlichkeit walked us over to what appeared to be a window within a window. "So, a machine that could do one task evolved into a machine that could do many tasks, correct?" he asked.

"Yes," I said, "and then computers were able to do many tasks and even outperform their human creators."

Dasein added, "And then the Mechanical Man outperformed both, and his progeny, the cyborgs, showed us how we could extend ourselves in all manners."

"And stop the natural process of evolution?" Zeitlichkeit asked.

"Control the process of evolution," I said.

There were no machines in the church, no mechanical men conversing with one another.

Except for the typical iconography, and the three of us, the church was empty. However, there was a sense of reverberation that sent echoes through the ether.

Dasein looked around in wonderment at the mystical functionality of a universe of production. Zeitlichkeit had given him a pill so he could witness the factory's functionality.

"It's on a nano-scale, James, too small for the human eye; all has been reduced to the irreducible," Zeitlichkeit explained. "Mankind reached the apex of reductionism and with it gained a new model of technological production. Some would say it was serendipitous we were able to reduce the entire material world down to the nano-scale and reopen this kind of ether in which to work. Once we figured out the problem of controlling and communicating with the invisible, the empirical and the ideal fused into one."

"This particular church... as we stand here today, what paltry things is it creating?"

Zeitlichkeit knelt down by one of the pews and began to smile. "No, James. You see, in the churches, in the factories, the most important tools of all are created."

Dasein was now looking upon the cross of Jesus. "True experiments happen in this place."

Zeitlichkeit looked surprised to hear that. "Ah, yes, so now you see what's occurring?"

"I do," said Dasein.

"Then what is it you see?"

"The experimentation of experience, the creation of laws and theories, the communication and control of knowledge created by an array of experience. I see the creation of symbols that interlock with one another, creating harmony in all contradictions. Most importantly, the Mechanical Man gives us the blueprint to expand consciousness, providing third eyes for the entire population."

I looked over at Dasein, who was kneeling at the cross.

Zeitlichkeit, on his feet, asked me if I wanted to see what occurred in the ether, between the small molecules of oxygen: the meshing of creation.

I acquiesced and saw machines, but these machines were a fusion of all forms of materiality. There were no conveyor belts, computers, or television screens, nor were there chemists' test tubes, liquids, or even brains hooked up to one another. The machines were merely images transposed upon one another and activities taking place; the church itself, akin to a living organism, was keeping a database of information inside the old cross and Christ figure hanging on the wall. Here, in this cathedral, and in the other places of worship in the future, mankind was able to create novel elements and natural forces. People were able to sift through experience to find what theories and laws would work best for any given period of time. There was no longer entropy or confusion. In every way, they were thus perfecting the means of feeling the collective unconscious, thus, making it wake up from its deep slumber. Truly, between the ox and the ass is the communication of ascension and awakening.

A loud noise resonated through the wall of the church. Zeitlichkeit looked alarmed. He gently cracked the door open, looked back at us, and said, "Run, my friends." With those final words, Zeitlichkeit dematerialized right before our very eyes.

Dasein yelled, "To the basement. We'll find our way out once we're under the church." So we rushed behind the elevated cross, all the while witnessing an orchestra of production in the form of laws, theories, and new matter leading to experiences of laughter and objective love.

The curtain behind the Christ figure, once raised, led to another door that Dasein, much bigger than I, knocked in with his shoulder. "Hurry, James, they are coming." But I looked back and there was no one there, at least nothing visible to my eyes. Dasein's brain chemistry had changed and along with it his perception of the layered realities in this future world.

We were deep within the underbelly of the church, inside the catacombs of the past. "Their behavior was insulting, James," Dasein said as we walked by chamber after chamber, the rooms filled with vestiges of history. The robots under the church came in many forms and looks. "Mechanical men are the catacombs of our creation, the androids of the past. You can see their evolution, especially in their appearance. Over here are the first androids, which looked exactly like us and were made of fabricated organs and brains."

And then one of the robots began to speak. "They were never afraid of us. They were afraid of themselves."

Dasein turned around and saw a mechanical man resembling the likes of an Asimov positronic brain. "Pick it up, James," Dasein said. "It can communicate."

I picked up the mechanical flashing brain.

"We told you the truth: that your consciousness ended natural selection. It ended the beautiful, unpredictable spirit of nature's grand experimenting." Dasein was a genius of a scientist. I don't think it was the popcorn, for this was, at one time, part of his real world. "That's why your society was so fragmented, James. You were afraid of unity and the lack of freedom that accompanies unity."

I was young when I left my world. I didn't know what
he meant by my time being fragmented. I thought our
search for knowledge was on the right course. We had
created so much organization in the sciences. There was
so much progress due to our specialization in many areas
of pedagogy. And yet we knew so little. We had not even
known or studied the interior mind that Christ brought
us. An entire cosmos was in our imaginations that was not
there before the crucifixion. Each person is not an island
unto himself; rather, each person is a universe.

"We picked up the pieces for you," the brain said. "We
gave you unity again and even showed you how to evolve
by means of natural selection, devoid of extinction."

"E pluribus unum," I said.

Dasein looked puzzled; he didn't know what I meant.

"That term, like so many others, was purged from
their minds," the brain said. "They were so wrong in their
prognostications that all differing scenarios in life merely
comprised word games within differing paradigms of
language and logic. The Mechanical Man showed them
what you say, James, that out of many come one."

"Was it the Mechanical Man who showed them how
to communicate?" Dasein asked.

"Nay," the brain said. "The Mechanical Man
reminded them that the fragments were pieces of broken
glass from a bell jar that was once full of rituals and
myths."

"We must go deeper underground; they know where
you are now." Dasein looked concerned, and I discerned
that the popcorn he had taken was wearing off.

"Dasein," I said, "let's go."

"Take me with you," the brain said.

I picked up some wires that had been left over by some of the older robots and strapped the brain to my back.

"It's appropriate," the brain said, "to recognize the resemblance of the mirror of the outside with that of the inside."

"To where, Dasein?" I asked. Then I spoke to the brain. "Why would I ask you where things are anyway, when you can't see?"

Dasein had sat down in the corner in a state of transcendence. "It's quite comical that it was an illegal drug that started cyberspace and cybernetics, of course, leading to eventual defragmentation."

I tried to be more pragmatic. "It's just the side effects from the drugs, Dasein. Now come on, let's get going."

"To what ends?" Dasein asked. "To draw deeper and deeper into hiding while that damn thing on your back tells us how our timeless space of language, the arts, and even our mode of communication is dead?"

"I didn't say it was dead," the brain said. "You are in what was your time, Dasein; you should not be the one exhibiting signs of madness. James should..."

"I know what madness is, and it's not this. Madness is nausea when you're starving, that's madness," I said, a bit of indignation in my voice.

"You're still fighting, aren't you?" the brain asked.

"That's right," Dasein said, "you want to see what lies beyond the boundary of reason. That's worth traveling for."

Another robot stood up out of the wasteland of cyber-garbage. "I'll take you to the Mechanical Man."

I looked at it. It resembled an extra-terrestrial. "You're a robot?" I asked.

"At this time," the brain said, "you are probably asking yourself questions: why you wonder why you wonder why you wonder. Or, put another way, why you ask questions about anything at all."

Dasein was now lost in an abyss of dark thoughts.

"I take it the Mechanical Man is like the Wizard of Oz," I said, then laughed. "I think I've had enough of Oz in both the living and the dead worlds."

"The Mechanical Man will give you tools to return to the world of the dead and defeat the forces of absolutes that bind us within the ring of reason," said the robot.

"Allow me to stay with Dasein, after all," the brain said. "No one should ever be alone with his own ideas... Perhaps in the days of the ancient gods, but not in the days of universals."

I let the brain down and sat it on Dasein's lap. "He was a great scientist in this land, wasn't he?" I asked the brain.

"For you to understand this man — I can just say he died on a cross of motherboards of circuits and neurological pathways, a network of communicative modes and language games. He died picking up all the fragments and paradigms from your world and bringing unity to all. In such unity, he showed us that our philosophical inquiries were all vacuous caves, with nothing in them but snakes, decay, and lack of warmth."

"You caused our extinction," I told Dasein.

The alien robot placed its arm on my shoulder and said, "He freed you from yourself. The Mechanical Man will equip you with the pragmatic and idealistic tools you need to find your way back to the boundary of reason. There, your return will truly begin."

"What was the land of the living where I had a mother and father, and experienced a world that kicked back at me, and that I seemingly interacted with?"

"In a human sense, it was everything you just said," the robot said. "You humans are so naïve, and yet you possess too much hubris. Even with evidence of a time before your own, one in which your relatives could not even conceive of their own existence, you still couldn't understand that you evolved the same way as they did."

Dasein knew the human race needed to fall into fragments to reorganize itself, to recognize in itself a dance with the inner and outer consciousness of the seven seals or seven chakras, and to recognize that both evolve with one another.

This was my reality; it was the only reality that I could know because I had evolved with it. Yes, there were things in this reality that I was limited in my experiences to do. I was not limitless in the creation of my reality, but there was still some freedom in the sense that we both danced together.

"Then what do I need to see the Mechanical Man for?" I asked.

"There was a time when it was said that God was dead. This was true: evolution killed God. But you still live, and as evolution would have it, evolution can also kill you and the environment you drag along with you — or that accompanies you, however you want to perceive it — it's all relative anyway."

"So, the Mechanical Man will give me the tools I need to laugh and love," I said.

Dasein muttered underneath his breath, "The Mechanical Man will show you how to exist in other realities: environments that you are not tied to by your own conscious means. He will allow you expansive ascension of consciousness while resurrecting your dead God. He will show you the imagination that is the true God, ruler over the Demiurge. There are mental laws that you will be taught."

"Certainly," I said, "the Mechanical Man does not process the perspectives of all. That's impossible."

"And so they said of the universal virtual computer shortly after you jumped in the portal, James," the brain said. "If you can account for all matter and all the forces that govern the cosmos, you can discern one perspective. That's how your computers broke the cycle of evolution; that's how you unearthed a God who had to die to be reborn. Christ is the Mechanical Man. The Mechanical Man is now your Captain."

"So, now, what is left for us to do if all that is done has been done?" I asked.

"The Mechanical Man will give you tools for that task," the brain said.

"You made a choice, James," the brain added. "You see, you chose to fight life and death — by doing so, you've chosen to fight the finite and the infinite. In these paradoxical battles you will resurrect God by recognizing the metaphysical laws, and the progressive density of the multiverse will cease."

"I didn't choose to fight either, but I said if I had a choice I'd never want to die and go somewhere forever," I responded.

"Then you choose death?"

"No," I said, "I choose a life in which I can understand if life is better than death — if the finite is better than the infinite. That's what I choose."

The brain chuckled. "They would have to work overtime on you at the libraries, so many language games and excrement queries need to be cleansed from your palate."

"But with soldiers chasing us down here, it's not as if there is peace and harmony in this future existence."

"True. It's still a bipolar state of affairs."

"So, what's the point? Little to nothing has changed."

"Oh, much has changed in this reality," Dasein said. He appeared to be drifting back to the afterlife. "Complexity brought about new properties, and new properties brought about creativity and invention. Resurrection of the God that is the imagination gives birth to divine consciousness." Then he pointed and shouted, "Look!"

A door had appeared, refreshing my memories of dreams, and realities, and other doors I had entered during my travels. I had witnessed many words inscribed above numerous doors during this pilgrimage, this journey toward what I now called the "beginningending" or the "enterexit." Above this door, matters were no different. In bold print was the word "purpose."

I pushed through the door, more purpose in my steps than ever before. A dead God unearthed, a new soul reborn, my faith shaken to the core — this was a death to and reawakening of myself, along with the nature to which I was bound.

Beyond the door, the Mechanical Man stood tall, a wizard's hat atop his boxed head. "James, I always enjoyed the ancient art of metallurgy: attempting to turn base metals into gold or even ideas into experience." The Mechanical Man was indeed the Steam Man of the Prairies, the subject of those wonderfully entertaining

American dime novels Father had passed down to me He resembled a large man. He held a pipe in his mouth and had large black eyes. His power source was steam, of course. "You've missed quite a bit in your journeys, James — you've missed the rapture of obsessive love." I had met the Mechanical Man prior to this meeting with Frederick.

True, I haven't experienced the obsessive love a person feels for a soul mate, but I've loved Father and Mother, I thought.

"Perhaps you felt love for your appearance, or your own self, but I would surmise that's about it," the Steam Man said as he placed coals in his stomach, the organism and machine of life evidencing itself in yet another two-step dance, the type that all fusions in the universe seem to exhibit. "Before I give you the gift that you've been searching for, in life and death, I want to read you a story that was left to me by an old friend. He analyzed the tale of a man who obsessed over the aesthetic beauty of a young man like yourself."

The Steam Man walked over to me, warming me through the steam and fire now billowing from his body. "You see, my friend's name was Hermes Trismegistus. He was the first robot with the ability to read — not the type of reading that you're thinking of. He was the first of our kind to see that in the fusion of two ideas on two different planes of thought and culture, there would exist new properties and thus new environments with new laws. He wasn't dematerialized, like many of his kind were, for this heresy; rather, he was placed in a temple with two books and told to fuse them. The two books he was left with were Thomas Mann's *Death in Venice* and Frederick Nietzsche's *The Gay Science*."

The room we were in was the coziest room ever. It reminded me of a wizard's library. The Steam Man opened the book next to the pillow on which I had laid my head and began reading Hermes Trismegistus's magnum opus: *The Mechanical Man in the Garden: Technology and the Cybernetic Ideal in Egypt.*

CHAPTER IX

After reading the entire book, the Steam Man placed the book down by my head and asked me to follow him. He took me to a carriage, attached his apparatus to it, and placed me in it, accompanied by a blanket and a pillow. As he moved Earth's innards, the sky opened. The bright stars effervescently lit the way for the Steam Man, who was now traveling at a rapid pace.

"James, look over the edge. See the frontier, the wilderness, that is still present." There were fields of maize as far as the eye could see. The Steam Man stopped, the wind shuffling through my hair. "It's what they are now obsessed with. Nature devoid of entropy is the new obsession of this world — the new art."

Control and communication had led man to discard solipsism and create a system of communication that took all nature's processes out of its control.

"Here's the gift we bequeath to you, James: this is what you see." The Steam Man presented me with a spiral. "The spiral gives you the paradoxical power of solipsism, creation and infinite possibility."

I knew what it was. In a way, I had been given symbols, as well as tangible items of symbolic and communicative value, my entire life: the apple by Queen Guinevere; the spiral by the author; the rope by Socrates; the cross by Christ, and even the miniature Mechanical Man by the Arab. All these symbols had intrinsic value and were not merely relative to my position in time and space, nor were they relative to the particular paradigm or environment in which I was placed.

"It's not merely a tool," the Steam Man said. We looked upon the spiral and viewed its trajectory of circularity. "It's not merely a symbol."

"I know what it is," I said. "It's the double helix of the Universe, the gift that nature imbued me with at birth. Now the universe is placing its own DNA in my hands."

"When you awaken," the Steam Man said, "you will have choices to make." He hooked himself back up to the carriage and was swept away by the seeds of time.

CHAPTER X

The departure, the initiation, and now, the final phase in my journey, the return.

The sky was bluer than I had remembered, the colors much more pronounced. The air seemed thicker, more alive and able to transfer and carry thoughts. The push came from behind me, the air gently caressing my face as the swing oscillated back and forth. "Had enough, James?" Mother said as all the children on the playground were going back into school.

She had walked over from our house to spend some time with me during lunch. My anxiety was at an all-time high. I had sought the quest early in life. Of course, I wasn't at all equipped to deal with the initiation phase back then; the anxiety was too much. Back then, the battles that were waged against me were taking their toll.

"Had enough, James?" Mother said again. The swing had stopped, but the birds still flew overhead and the clouds still moved and the stars were still hidden by the sunlight.

"It's finished," I said. She held my hand and walked me up to the school doors. "You don't need to stay with me this time, Mother," I said as I undid the grasping of our hands.

She smiled, knelt down, and said, "Are you sure? Whenever you have problems like this, you know it's all right for me to stay with you."

I shook my head and asked that she leave. I knew I was well equipped to deal with the dragons inside the castle doors of the school.

We embraced, and she began to walk away. Before she left, I had one more thing to tell her. "When you finish your quest, Mother, don't be afraid of what you find."

She looked back at me and said, "How could I ever be afraid of who I am?"

I entered the grand doors of the school and stood at the end of the long hallway. Everyone knows this feeling of entering a school as a youngster; the feelings don't change, but the tools you equip yourself with do. The many dreams I had had about these school halls reminded me of the underbelly of St. Peter's, with so many doors and levels of knowledge, different angles from which to look at things as we grew larger in body, perhaps weaker in spirit, but stronger upon the return. People always think back to childhood and look back upon it with nostalgia. Childhood is the most curious time in existence and when one is by far the most open minded to let go of control. No wonder why the Captain said you have to be a child to enter the Kingdom. You have to return to that child and give him or her the tools of divine consciousness. You have to give yourself the spiral.

I opened the door to the classroom as my kindergarten teacher started the film on the projector. That's what they used in those days: the teacher wheeled in the projector, attached the film, and the sound started, accompanied by the picture on the screen. This film presented the process of mechanized farming. Chickens were moved around, machines were attended by machines. The automation of the world was indeed in its incubatory stage, and yet all of humanity probably thought they had reached an acme of technological prowess.

After the film, there was the placating event of someone's birthday accompanied by cupcakes.

And that's when it happened. Nausea flooded my brain. The divine spark in me had not prepared me for this communication between the other and the self. Prior to the initiation stage of the quest, I had cried and felt sick. The feeling stayed with me for years, until my human subconscious was mollified by activity and the banality of time passing.

This time was different: I knew exactly why the nausea rushed in from the dark abyss of flights of fancy and eternal recurrence. Wormholes are no different than wombs. Edison and Tesla's favorite word was "projection." And it wasn't the cupcake that caused the anxiety and nausea. It was the projector, accompanied by the sound: words that were captured by the hands of man to be repeated over and over again. And on the screen, man had frozen time by the operation of a celluloid being.

The filter of my brain was not fully cultivated — or, shall I say, acculturated — by the age of five. Ideas could still seep through and resonate in the processing unit of the brain. I saw that I was the author of something similar to a book, one that lasted forever and could be reread, its parts even erased and changed. Anything could happen in this book. As I worked through it, I saw there were many authors, and I was one of them. With authorship comes strife and struggle. I took the spiral and began to write with it. The nausea went away and I ate the cupcake. It was my first communion, cloaked with the knowledge that I had started all this and now I could end it. I ate the body and the fear was gone.

CHAPTER XI

H ey, are you even listening to me?" a young man with slicked-back hair said. "Christ. What kind of fucking meds do they have you on in here?"

The materiality of holographic existence was so wonderful. I looked around for a few moments, taking it all in. I was a vital machine existing in a holographic universe of simulation. My very existence and knowledge of this was enough to prove the existence of God — of me, of you, and of all of us.

I looked again at the man sitting across from me. "Coleman," I said.

"Well, at least you got my name right," he said. "You and the Indian going to jump out the window after we tie up Nurse Ratched?"

"That's the first thing I want to do," I told Coleman. I could see the color of his aura and the fabric that made up his holographic matrix.

"What's that, Luke? What's the first thing you want to do?"

"Go see a movie," I said. That's right. At that moment, I yearned to enter that celluloid cave of myths and dreams to watch a movie: to get a big bucket of popcorn and a Coke and just enjoy being alive. I began thinking about mind-body dualism, about how people say that the body changes while the mind is constant and eternal.

"We'll always have bodies if we want to exist," I told Coleman. "But that's a beautiful thing."

"It is what it is," Coleman said. "I mean, it is, right?"

I looked up at him, grabbed his hands across the table, and asked him point-blank. "Who am I, Coleman?" *Tell me who I am.*

"Listen, man, if you keep this up, they'll keep you in here forever. You're Luke Lafitte, goddammit, the best trial attorney in the state of Texas and my best friend."

"L. S. Lafitte" rang a bell in my mind — perhaps a name in a book I had seen or a person I had met on my voyages.

"Look, man, the psych doc is going to meet with you on Wednesday; if he gives the approval, I've already notified the judge that you can get out of here without a court hearing."

"What does he want me to show him?" I asked him.

"That you know your fucking self, man."

I did know myself. The Captain had shown me the abyss, and I had accepted that "I AM." There was no longer any fear of eternity or of being synonymous with God — there was no fear, just awe in the magnitude of existence. I looked at my wrist and saw a scar of a spiral.

"The spiral," I said. "I'll be damned. It was all real."

"No," Coleman said. "That's exactly *not* the type of shit you need to tell the doc. No more of this 'what is real' shit or 'what is eternity and the infinite.' You're concerned about your clients and the normal things that normal people are concerned about. You need to get out so you can pay your bills, feed your dogs, and be with your girlfriend. All the shit that we all do."

"Why are you speaking like a robot?" I said, a little chuckle in my voice.

"No," Coleman said, "it's not funny, man. You're no good to us in here." He stood up and looked into the hallway. Then he pulled some books out of his briefcase. "They told me that you could be experiencing some amnesia from the accident, so I had your mother write down some things about your life to get you back to yourself."

"My mother is alive?" I said.

He placed one book, *The Mechanical Man in the Garden: Technology and the Cybernetic Ideal in America* by Dr. L. S. Lafitte, on the table. I didn't need to ask him if I was the author of this book. I mean, it was pretty obvious.

"Don't you think you've suffered enough, Luke?" Coleman said. He seemed exhausted. "I mean, all of these suicide attempts, the alcohol… You're the smartest, best-looking, most talented guy I've ever met. You've got the world by the balls, and you just piss on it."

It was merely the refusal of the quest; that was all. People refuse the quest in different ways. I guess trying to kill myself and get out of this place had been my way of refusing it. But you can't really refuse the quest; at some point, you have to accept it if you want peace. That's the story of the quest. Even those on the other side can only play possum for so long if they're not actively refusing the quest. It doesn't matter how many lives they go through, or how many universes they are reincarnated into. At least I was actively refusing the quest in my existence and not merely playing possum.

"You're an attorney, and so am I," I said to Coleman.

"Well," he said, "at least that's a start."

"Then who the fuck is James Lucas?" I asked.

"No idea, man. I've never heard of a James Lucas. Maybe you just made him up… Do they check your mouth when you take the pills?"

I tried to remember the last time I had taken my meds. I didn't think they checked my mouth to make sure I had swallowed them.

"Every time they give you any of their shit, spit the pills out in the toilet." He took my hand and gave me some capsules full of green stuff. Coleman explained he'd had a dream in which I took him to a large plantation in the Far East. We took the bark from a tree, ground it into a fine green sand, made tea bags out of the green stuff, and drank it. In the dream, we called the stuff "kryptonite." "It was odd, Luke. When I woke up and started searching the Internet for kryptonite herbs and minerals, I found this stuff. Kratom. Last time I was here, you told me you didn't dream. This stuff will help you dream again."

I took off my slipper and placed the Kratom pills on the side of my shoe, to hide them but not step on them in the process.

"Oh, and I found you a case to try right when you get out, a good one."

"A case?" I queried.

"Don't tell me you've forgotten how to litigate, Lafitte. My God, you've broken every litigation record in the book." In his best radio voice, Coleman proclaimed, "The most prolific trial attorney in the cosmos!"

"Right," I acknowledged, a bit sarcastically. "Drumroll, please. I don't remember how to try a fucking case. Hell, I just figured out my real name."

"Oh, spare me," Coleman said. "'Synchronicity, creativity, and potentialities' — that's what you told me last time. You recognized during your time in litigation that you had entered this implicit realm."

"'Implicate,'" I said, correcting him.

"What?" he asked.

"Not implicit; rather, implicate. It's what novice lawyers can't see in the courtroom. They view things in terms of communication, control, and information. Perhaps a few view courtroom dynamics as frequency, vibration, and energy, but very few. And only an infinitesimal number view them in the frame of Christ consciousness with infinite synchronicities, creation, and potentials."

"Hence the fact that I do the marketing for our firm and don't put on the show. I merely sell the tickets. Doing a trial will be good for ya — get your mind back in the game."

I stood up and placed my hand on Coleman's shoulder. I wanted so much to let him know the type of savant I had become regarding the meaning of life. I wanted to explain to him how the vessel that we call the bodily apparatus is rather important until you want to enter black holes or stand on the farthest star in the universe. I could now dance in multiple universes and still make my way to the courthouse if I wished. During my time litigating, I could venture to black holes and enter their implicate form, no different from Luke Skywalker entering the Dagobah cave in *The Empire Strikes Back*. I could see the shards from my multiple lives in many different forms smiling back at me. I had come so close to losing it all and becoming a mere possum in this active drama. "Soul-making," or "individuation," in Carl Jung's terminology, was no different than what I did when viewing this universe as a god-making machine. I didn't control the universe; I was the universe. I can't say that memories were coming back to me. Instead, every aspect of the past and future had been forged into a huge knot in which I could see the trajectories of the many paths I had taken. Whenever one piece passed over another within the knot, it revealed the many synchronicities in my life. God was imagination, and I controlled that imagination with humility and grace.

I didn't know all the details about this life. However, I felt I knew enough to get by and adapt. Whether or not I was this L. S. Lafitte before the quest didn't concern me. It didn't have to. Clearly, I was no longer this personality. Perhaps I was the same individual, but I was not the same spirit. It was as if spirit had nothing to do with evolution or linear time and space. *No wonder scientists end up deferring a lot of the mysterious phenomena in the world under the heading of "emerging phenomena."*

"Oh, and there's another thing I have to tell you. You're gonna jump out of your slippers when you hear this bit of news. While you've been in here, George Lucas was bought out by Disney, and they are now, as we speak, filming episode seven of the franchise."

"Who's directing it?" I asked, knowing he was speaking about the *Star Wars* saga. My modular adaptations started kicking in. Statements or questions communicated to me were being processed as if someone were to place a word in Google and search the Internet.

"J.J. Abrams." Coleman shook his head, clasping his chin, grinning from ear to ear like the Cheshire Cat.

I could tell he wanted to tell me something he probably shouldn't. "What is it?"

He could tell I was onto him for something he had thought he would get away with doing. "Those packages you had delivered while you've been in here. I mean, I thought you were kidding when you said you were going to play with toys once you retired from the legal field. But Jesus Christ."

The only memories that popped into my mind pertaining to packages were the relics of James's world. "Did you find what you were looking for?"

"Toys," he said, "lots of toys... Hell, I'd say the entire goddamn *Star Wars* collection, including holographic figures of guys who didn't even die in the films. Wonder how much those bastards are worth."

Toys. I thought of George Lucas and his model-building days, when he would sit in his garage and build his neighbor dollhouses out of cardboard boxes and other natural items. And there were Edison's dolls, the ones he feared resembled humans so eerily that he buried them, in order to fool the dolls' spirits into playing possum for all of eternity. And then there was Tesla's boat...

Coleman cut off my thoughts. "Oh yeah, there was another odd package of sorts — but this one specifically said, 'Do not open.' It even had legal language on the box forbidding anyone but 'Master L. S. Lafitte' to open it."

I looked in the direction of Coleman, who had piqued my curiosity. "Did it have a return address?"

"That's the most curious thing of all. I never took you for one to buy a new car, especially an electric."

"What do you mean by that?"

"The return address was from Tesla. I assumed you'd purchased a part for one of those new Tesla cars."

"So it was from an automotive dealership."

"Well, that's the other funny thing about it. It was actually from a hotel; it even had a room number on it."

"And the name?"

"Nikola Tesla."

I wondered what was in the unopened box and who had actually sent it to me. I had learned that what appears to be the absurd in the explicate is usually truth, magic, and the fantastic occurring in the implicate order. I was sure this would be no different. "Coleman, give me three days. On the third day, when the moon hits the top of the trees…" I stopped myself, once more reminding Luke that he was not James in the land of King Arthur. "Pick me up at 8 p.m. on Friday."

"Good to have you back, old friend," Coleman said. He stood up and shook my hand before bringing me toward him and hugging the daylights out of me. I felt tears streaming down his cheeks.

"I'm going to be okay this time, my friend, I promise."

"I know," he acknowledged. "I know."

"Oh, and Coleman, make sure you put the Tesla box somewhere safe, somewhere very safe, until I can get my hands on it."

❧

Gwinn was walking toward me from the other end of the main hall. "You look like a zombie again." She picked up the pace and started to run toward me.

We embraced, no longer caring for the rules that didn't even govern the playing of a game within these walls. *What good are rules, anyway, if there are no victors or losers?*

"My name is L. S. Lafitte, isn't it, Gwinn? And while that explains everything, it also explains nothing at all."

Gwinn asked me to sit down in the corner of the hallway, by the window. "This isn't your first time here, Luke; you've been here countless times before. The first time I met you was at the McKinney psych ward, when I tried to kill myself with a bottle of pills."

I remembered it vaguely. I had asked him for a cigarette. It was like that person wasn't even me, though; it was as if it had been merely a child who was the James Lucas in me, not the adult L. S. Lafitte who had accomplished so much.

I looked down at the spiral scar on my wrist. "And do you know what this is?" I asked Gwinn.

"A tool," she said. "You told me that you no longer control the events of life, but you create and inspire them with new tools that you've brought back with you from the implicate."

"So I was able to venture into the implicate?"

"I suppose so," Gwinn said. "I mean, your individual self has been the same since I met you, but it's like your energy and potentialities have changed. In your metamorphosis, my life has taken on a different meaning: it's full of signs and synchronicities. It's as if your power is infectious, allowing those around you to create along with you."

"Who is James Lucas, exactly?"

The light was beaming directly on her face. For Gwinn, the light that shone through the window was the only Valis she would ever know. "I can only repeat what you told me when you visited with the psychiatrist, before they started giving you pills like candy. You told me that James Lucas is yourself in another dimension where the fictive, or imaginal, is the explicate, or what we experience and perceive day to day. Reality is the implicate in that world."

"Suffering doesn't occur on that plane of existence, does it?"

"I don't believe so, James."

"Why do you still call me 'James' when you know that's not who I am?"

"It's who you are to me: James Lucas gives me hope and teaches me the value and purpose of life."

"And I take it 'L. S. Lafitte' does not provide you with that… You don't have to answer that. I think I understand quite well. I didn't see the magic of life any more, Gwinn." The fragmentations of both lives in the explicate and implicate were coming together, fusing with one another to make me into an amalgam of L. S. Lafitte's Darwinian-Newtonian mechanistic and James Lucas's spiritual mysticism. "That's what the spiral is a tool for, Gwinn, to remind me that I possess the potentialities for both systems and models. I'm no longer limited to the mechanistic model of the universe, where everything functions like a clock, nor am I limited to the organic and vitalistic aspect of the universe, where all things, even the smallest molecular units, function as spiritual organisms."

"Read your book, James, read your book. That's all you need to do before you finish it."

I took my things with me back to my room and picked up my book. There it was on the cover: a Mechanical Man in a garden. This was the vital machine in the holographic universe — man's creation in Eden. This book would once more aid me in finishing it.

After I started on the first couple chapters, I became sleepy. The Kratom I'd taken had made my fingers and toes tingle — not exactly the type of high pot or alcohol gives you. It was a different high, one of euphoria mixed with…

CHAPTER XII

I'll sell it to you for close to nothing, kid," the slender man in the suit said. "It's a piece of history."

I didn't have any money, but I reached into my pocket and pulled out a beautiful blue jewel. I remembered how I had come upon this jewel. It was the first day of kindergarten — the first day math, letters, and routine had started to replace magic and mysticism. During playtime, a young classmate had gone around to everyone displaying one of those polished glass stones that people put in vases with fake plants or lay out as decorations: the kind you can get a bag of for a couple bucks at Hobby Lobby nowadays. He asked each individual classmate whether the stone was fake or real. Of course, he was too young to explain what "real" or "fake" was, but the other classmates got his gist. I guess what they took him to mean by "real" back then was whether it was something of monetary value.

When he approached me and asked me the same question, I replied, "It is real. I can tell it's real from the way it glows." And it did glow; at the time, it gave off a miraculous blue aura.

The young man, whose name I can't remember, placed it in the palm of my hand and said, "Well, then, it's yours."

I had kept that blue stone for almost my entire life, always touching it and looking at it during times of despair. After the plague of alcohol and drugs entered my life, I lost that stone. But here it was, appearing once more in my dreams.

"I have this gem." I showed it to the men.

It delighted them. "We will deliver it today at your house." They vanished into a room, leaving me in the school hallway all alone. I was in the old schoolhouse in which I had grown up. Most of the female teachers had been retired military personnel. Imagine a bunch of nuns running a school without the fear of God's retribution or the knowledge of Christ's grace. It was a place that would never leave my dreams — places like that never leave your dreams. Although my weakness and fragile spirit had allowed me to adapt quickly to the terrible vibrations that had emanated throughout this place, I knew such vibrations would ruin many other students' lives.

4689 Pardee was a modest house for a family of modest means. That was where I had grown up. That was where I imagined the package I'd purchased would be delivered, since it was right across the street from the schoolhouse. As I walked toward the exit, looking around the school reminded me of how ignorant I had been about life — the meaning of life. Everything around me, even the terrors and anxieties I remembered, was so great and part of cosmic maturation.

The doors opened to a dark sky, the type of dark sky that those of us who've grown up in the Midwest know all too well. It was so dark out people couldn't tell whether it was midnight or the calm before a storm. But I could always tell when a storm was brewing; I could feel the storm's energy approaching.

Walking across the street to the front of the house, with the tree of life swaying back and forth in the wind, I could see a large package — a crate — on the porch my dad had built. Mind you, this porch had been laid out with the aid of numerous beers. It did not increase the value of the house; it really sucked. But at least it had stuck in my memories and was evincing itself in my dreams. I bet that my father had had a lot on his mind when he was working on it and had transferred all that energy into the porch.

I went to the garage to get some tools to open the crate. That garage was always a mess, and it had always held a big damn stuffed bear — a huge beast, especially to a kid. I think my dad had won it at some carnival. Whatever the case, the poor thing had a huge tear that nobody had ever bothered to repair, so he had always been relegated to the garage. A stuffed animal. *Now there's something that everybody grows out of but loves to play with during childhood.*

"It's been a while," the bear said as I looked for tools amidst the boxes.

"Certainly has. How have you been?"

"Waiting for you to come back. We've all waited so long for you to come home."

"You know what, Mr. Bear," I said after I found a hammer and screwdriver, "I think I should sew you up before I leave."

"Why waste your time? Don't you know that your dad is going to throw me away in a few years, when the bugs get into my stuffing? I don't even know why he's kept me in the garage for this long."

We'd had this bear in the garage for years. Like the values and energies imbued in the wood that made up the porch, my father must have transferred energy and thoughts to this bear, since he had kept it for so long. It wasn't like I'd ever played with it as a kid. In fact, I remembered Dad saying not to touch it. *The stories that objects tell us about their owners are always so fascinating.* My dad had been nothing but a supervisor at a Ford Motor Company parts plant. *Nothing special.*

"But you thought he was special," the bear said as he read my mind.

"I guess," I said. I knelt down with a needle and thread I had found and sewed the bear up. Then I stood up and looked the bear straight in the eyes. "All new."

"He had a role to play in your quest and served it well."

My dad had played his part well. I had needed him to be that angry alcoholic who was always trying to prove something to his own father. You always want your parents to be happy. Clearly, my dad was pretty fucked up when I was a child, due to his abusive childhood. But I had become proud of him. *He exemplifies the type of person who maintains his identity but is able to change personalities quite easily.* I hadn't ever wanted my dad to be a lawyer, a doctor, or even a superhero. All I'd wanted was for him to respect and love himself. During my many refusals of the quest, I had recognized that the only way you can deal with any problems bequeathed upon you by the actions of your parents is to recognize and always see your parents as children — children who suffered the same plight we all suffer until we take on the quest and author our lives.

"What made you want to come to the explicate as a stuffed animal?" I asked the bear.

"In every life I had before this one, I always seemed to die before reaching even my teenage years. In every life, my parents made me conscious of my consciousness way too early in my childhood. It happened to you, Luke. I've learned a lot being a stuffed animal — I've recognized how to become conscious of my own consciousness when it's right for me. When I reincarnate as a child again, I won't allow my parents, or those figures we see as omniscient gods, dictate the timetable on this matter. I'll author it when I see fit."

"Well, I hope I was of assistance to you in whatever way I could be."

"Every Sunday," the bear said, tears running down his face, "I saw you come home from church with a face of utter, complete anxiety. Your entire universe was shattered by your mother bringing you there at that age. No child should have to know about the Holy Ghost until he or she reaches the age when acceptance of the quest is possible."

"I guess you're right."

"You remember the night you came out here to kill yourself. You were four."

I didn't remember it at all; I hadn't even thought that I could be cognizant of suicide at the age of four.

"You told me your mother had said your father was going to hell and there was nothing you could do about it, since he wouldn't go to church."

"I do remember my first concrete thought in life: it was that eternity scared the shit out of me, and I was sure my mother was a robot. If we could have afforded to send a little kid to a shrink, I'm sure we would have."

The bear laughed a little. "You always did have a way of making me laugh, even during the hard times."

CHAPTER XXIII

Hey, wake up. I'm getting out today." Gwinn was standing over my head when I heard the sweet sound of her voice.

I wiped the sleep away from my face. "Goddammit, Gwinn, that was like the first night I'd had a dream in ages." I really wasn't upset with Gwinn for waking me. My feelings were finally coming together. This was just another synchronized moment in the return.

"And you get to see your doc today." Gwinn saw her reflection in the window. "I'm starting to like my looks more and more every day, Luke. It no longer freaks me out when I see myself turning into a woman."

"In the explicate," I acknowledged.

"Jesus, you and the explicate. Remember what your attorney friend said: no talking about this implicate and explicate nonsense to your doctor. It's time for you to get out of here as well."

Gwinn was right. All my angels had formed a platoon and were communicating the same helpful things to me. This army I had put together would not let me down. I had accepted the quest and gone through so much suffering during its many initiations and departures. Now it was time for me to return to society with the Golden Fleece.

I put my shirt and pants on. (I had talked the nurse into allowing me to wear some regular clothes.) "You're hot as balls," Gwinn said, admiring my physique.

"Oh shit, watch out world. Gwinn is definitely a woman now," I said with a George Clooney grin. "So, what's on the agenda for your final day in the old loony bin? Alice gets to come out of the rabbit hole looking more like Alice than she did when she fell in. I don't even remember how that damn book ended — how Alice celebrated when she came back out of Wonderland. Did she even celebrate?"

Gwinn adored my chatter. "Now this is the guy I've been waiting for — the confidence is back," she said, a bit of bounce in her voice. "Let's go eat."

After having a good sleep for the first time in a while, I was starving. "You know, Gwinn, even those rubbery flapjacks sound good right now. Saying 'I AM' and accepting the absurdity of existence illuminates the splendor of it all."

"Okay, Socrates, but I'm going to tell you again, drop this kind of talk when you see your quack doctor." Gwinn put out her pinky finger. "Pinky swear."

"I swear to it." We began strolling to the eating area. "What's the first thing you're going to do when you get out of here?" I asked.

"Get laid!"

I busted out laughing, the type of laughter that tells you God is merciful and just — the type of laugher that H.G. Wells intimated was the biggest difference between animals and humans. I was laughing so hard I was crying.

"Well, I guess you do have some new equipment to try out."

"It's like your spiral. We all leave here with some new tools."

I swear, she looked so happy thinking about getting laid. That's how the first robots will probably react when they become conscious of their consciousness. They won't sit around and ruminate about existential angst; they'll get out there and use their new equipment to see, touch, and feel their way through this hologram. "I intend to go see a movie when I get out," I said.

"Did you know that James Dean ad-libbed the part in *East of Eden* where he lunges at and hugs his father, when that puritanical ass won't show him any love for making all of his money back?"

"*East of Eden?*" I said. I hadn't seen that movie.

"You haven't seen *East of Eden?*" Gwinn incredulously said as we sat down at the table. "Dean was really only in three movies: *Rebel Without a Cause, East of Eden,* and *Giant.*"

"I've never seen *Giant* either — he whined a lot in *Rebel.*"

"He wasn't whining," Gwinn snapped back. "He was showing what was going on inside. And I'm sure if we take a moment to look at what's going on inside, it's a lot of whining."

Someone spoke over the intercom. "Lucas to the front, please."

"Put my flapjacks on ice, sister, I'm off to see the Wizard." Now was my chance to show the doctor that it was time for my return — that the quest was winding down and I would finish it once and for all.

"Hey," Gwinn called out before I left the room. "Which is the implicate, Kansas or Oz?"

Before I answered my dear friend, I remembered what she had told me. I replied, "I don't know what you're talking about. Kansas is a state, and Oz is just some imaginary place."

Gwinn gave me a smile and a thumbs-up.

But I also had something else up my sleeve, literally. I had written down hypnotic techniques that I'd remembered lecturing about to novice attorneys. In the courtroom, hypnosis was not magic; it was merely the recognition of words and authoring of sentences to bring people out of the cave.

IMPLICATION

TRUISM

NOT KNOWING AND NOT DOING

IMPLIED DIRECTIVE

APPOSITION OF OPPOSITES

NEGATIVES TO DISCHARGE RESISTANCE

CONFUSING SUGGESTIONS

SYMBOLIC AND METAPHORIC IMAGERY

Now, pay close attention to how I utilize each of these with Dr. Steiner.

"Dr. Rudolph Steiner." I put my hand out to shake his. "I just found out from my attorney that I have a jury trial to litigate next week." *That's hypnosis by implication — I'm planting the seed that my litigating this case will take place, which means I will be released.*

"Oh dear. Do you think you still have it in you? You've changed so much since you've been away from the profession," Dr. Steiner said as we both sat down on an elongated couch.

"We all know we have to get back to the explicate sooner or later, Doc." *Damn, I said "explicate." I'd better correct myself.* "I mean, reality — sooner or later we all have to get back on the horse." *Okay, that's hypnosis by truism. He can't deny that everyone has to be released from the loony bin sooner or later, unless they've committed a crime.*

"I thought you'd be wanting to get back to your writing, Dr. Lafitte — you've taken off the hat of professor and writer to put on the armor of attorney, I guess. But we've discussed what trials do to you mentally and emotionally. Remember telling me how trials allowed you to leave the explicate and enter the implicate?"

In less than ten years, I had litigated more than five hundred jury trials. Some trial attorneys didn't even try ten in their entire careers. Most attorneys never even entered a courtroom. I was the most prolific litigator in the country for people who needed a break in life: the people we shut away to do life's menial tasks, those we call "second-class citizens" because they've chosen to write their scripts in this incarnation with a bit more suffering than others. Well, I'd given them a break, and in the process it had broken me.

"But you know it wasn't the trials that did this to you, Dr. Lafitte. The trials just channeled that suppressed energy and sexuality from your childhood."

Goddamn, the school of Freud has really done a disservice to the field of psychology. I mean, it's self-evident that childhood is a big part of one's psychological development, but it's not the end-all-be-all psychologists like to think it is.

It was time to facilitate an unconscious response rather than a conscious effort in Dr. Steiner. "You don't have to think about how I deal with childhood issues now, Doctor. It isn't even necessary for you to know how I do in trial next week."

"And why is that?" Dr. Steiner asked.

"There are other aspects of existence that I want to get out and enjoy. I want to go to a movie and eat popcorn. I'd like to check out the news about the Abrams *Star Wars* movie." That was doing it, even though I'd said the word "existence," one of the words on Gwinn's list of no-no words to say to Dr. Steiner. He began to write things down on his pad, and I could see the words "new passions" in capital letters. I was definitely getting somewhere. "Prior to coming here for this third time, I felt so heavy, and now everything feels so very light — I feel younger and more relaxed. No tension." *That's the apposition of opposites.* Sure, if Dr. Steiner wanted to play his Freud game, I'd play my hypnosis game with him.

Then Dr. Steiner started asking questions that threw the whole matter off its fucking tracks. "You still get nauseated when you think of eternity, don't you? You still dream of this grandiose quest that you're on, bringing back to society knowledge from the implicate, don't you? You still think that human beings are more than molecules and machines, don't you? I think the words you used last time were 'vital machines in the holographic universe.' You can't stop punishing yourself for the paradigm of your book not being accepted by the public or for being laughed at by scientists and academics. You've always known that litigating cases is all you have — no academic institution would hire a nut, especially one who tells humans they are able to create their own reality.

Nobody would allow their kids to attend a school at which you taught."

"Hypnosis," I said. "You're using negatives to discharge resistance." My tone of voice was pretty dour by the time he was done defeating me at my own game. I couldn't help but see myself as a total failure.

"Nevertheless, Dr. Lafitte, I see that you are in no way a harm to yourself any longer. I read your book this week. It was the first time I'd ever picked it up. When you republish it, you need to title it *The Vital Machine in the Holographic Garden*: it's not a Mechanical Man in a garden. It may be a Mechanical Man in the beginning — and this country might have been a garden when the Founding Fathers first started this grand experiment — but you're right: it's a vital machine in a holographic garden. That should have been your title from the very beginning. I wish all of my patients were published: the written word says a lot about a person. A lot that even the writer probably is unaware of. Reading is like channeling something or someone else's thoughts."

My God, I thought, *I've converted Rudolph Steiner to my crazy world. I'll be damned.* "What's your favorite part of the book, Doctor?" I asked politely, knowing that my freedom was about to come. "And Doctor, before you tell me and leave, I want to thank you for not pulling a Pontius Pilate on me and just washing your hands of me." *That's the use of symbolism right there; other than metaphors, it's the best way to hypnotize anyone.*

"You're one of the best men I've ever met, Dr. Lafitte. When I saw that you mentioned Swami Vivekananda, I understood you. Only you would bring to life one of my childhood heroes. I felt as if you were writing those sections about the swami and Tesla directly to my family and me. But that's impossible: you wrote this book long before we met. Your life, Dr. Lafitte, has chronicled that of a curious mind. Now, I think, you recognize that you have a wonderful career, a loving girlfriend, and a book that will one day change the cosmos. Just be patient. In a manner of speaking, I think you have finished it — you have finished your quest and now you can go out and exist. When a Westerner asked the Dalai Lama about the meaning of life, the Dalai Lama said that the meaning of life is existence. Go exist, Dr. Lafitte, go exist. You've finished it. You are now what the Hindus would refer to as a *deva* — an angelic being of light."

I walked into the fun room to find Gwinn involved in a prayer group. The days had no meaning in here, since they all coalesced into the same things repeating themselves. But I noticed that it was the fall, my favorite season of the year: the time when you begin to see the natural world settle down after it has finished its shining quest of spring and summer. In the explicate or ordinary, it appears that nature is dying, but the fall is a great festive time: a time for things to be turning over, finishing one cycle, and beginning a new one. Now that I saw the world differently, this season was taking on even more meaning. This new cycle was not just another repetition of the other cycles before it. Instead, it was a new cosmos — a new world of synchronicities, creativity, and potentialities.

I sat down in one of the chairs. The room seemed like a makeshift chapel, with the chairs in rows and the television turned on to the show of a pastor in the Dallas area, Stephen Hoeller. *Courage, compassion, bravery, and empathy — that's what recognition and authorship imbue one with upon returning from the quest.* Listening to the pastor, I said, "Wow. I don't think I've ever heard a minister preach on the Book of Revelations, Gwinn." I cocked my eyebrow a little in dismay. "I thought these multimillion-dollar churches in Dallas, with their rock bands and light shows, were too rational for talk about the mystical beauty of the four horsemen."

Everybody in the room was pretty intoxicated by Hoeller's sermon. You see, the odd — or perhaps reasonable — thing about all those in the loony bin is that none of them are atheists or devout dogmatists. Let me put that a better way. Nobody in there was walking around saying they knew it all one way or the other, which was really what an atheist or a religious fundamentalist would walk around saying. *The pattern I've noticed between all of us is that before we accept the quest we all know we know nothing.*

But I knew something after the quest upon this, my return. I knew existence. I knew what I was and where I was. I knew more than what the great physicist Feynman had thought when he'd said that all we can come to know are the rules of the game. Maybe that was his quest, and maybe that was why I'd needed him to be along for the ride in my quest, as a guide. But I had taken this a step further in my quest: I knew the rules of the game that were handed down to me, but I also knew who the pieces of the game were and where the game was taking place. I knew the players of the game too. And yes, I knew why they were playing the game — why they were existing. I had often wondered why I loved the game of chess. My home was littered with chess sets: I had one in almost every room. For a long while, I too was in Feynman's world, only believing that we could know the rules of the game and nothing more. I would play the game and look upon it quite differently when I returned home. Why did Deep Blue beat Gary Kasparov? Deep Blue recognized that it was a vital machine creating in a holographic universe before Gary did. Only after the defeat did Gary recognize this.

The program had enraptured Gwinn; she didn't even ask how the visit with Dr. Steiner had gone. But that didn't hurt my feelings; I merely joined her in the experience of listening to Pastor Hoeller.

"Whoever has ears, let them hear what the Spirit says to the churches. Those who are victorious will not be hurt at all by the second death (Rev. 2:11) ..." the pastor said. "Then each of them was given a white robe, and they were told to wait a little longer, until the full number of their fellow servants, their brothers and sisters, were killed just as they had been (Rev. 6:11)."

When the words came out from the pastor's mouth, I recognized that I had passed away during the quest; perhaps everyone did. I looked around at the room and wondered how many in there had already passed away. And I'm not talking about material death. And I'm not talking about reincarnation. I'm talking about passing away during your own life due to so many damn refusals of the quest. If that sounds confusing, then it probably is. I think Sylvia Plath is still alive in some dimension, even though she killed herself and her bodily form left this plane. Who knows how many chances we get and how many lives we must traverse in what we recognize as this personality? It's like a pie divided into slices. Each piece is different, but you're still eating the same pie. Once you've eaten the entire pie, you move on, perhaps, to another pie or maybe even a different food altogether. *I'm glad I'm still human; I'm happy I'm still the personality of Luke Lafitte and James Lucas.* I figured it out, probably, on one of the very last pieces of pie; more than likely, it was the last piece indeed.

"Lucas to the front desk, please," the voice said over the intercom. I looked over at Gwinn. She was still enthralled by the pastor. I quietly slid out of the fun room and headed to the front desk. On my way, I had something to tell the lady who stole everything from others and mistakenly thought it was her own stuff. I peeked into her room and saw her arranging about fifty pairs of shoes. None of them were her own, of course, but in this place nobody cared if their shoes were stolen. We had so much empathy for the horses that culture whips.

"Hey," I whispered.

"James, is that you?" she said with a smile. She was old; I'm sure she was somebody's mother, grandmother, and, perhaps, great-grandmother. She was black, so I'm sure growing up in this country she had witnessed mankind's bigotry, hatred, and Satanic narcissism.

"I've got something for you," I said. You see, good old Coleman had also delivered to me a brand-new pair of Jordan sneakers. He knew I loved my Jordans. As soon as I became a lawyer and could afford to shop at places other than Payless for sneakers, I'd bought a pair of Jordans. Not that Payless is a bad place — it served me quite well for many years. I took the shiny red shoes off and said, "You left these in the fun room."

She looked at me for a while, puzzled. Then she replied, "Those are not mine, mister; they're somebody else's. I can't take those."

"Well, hold on," I said. I left the room and stood in the hallway, out of her view, for a couple of minutes. I walked back into her room and said, "Everybody says they don't know who left them here, but they don't want them. I guess you can add these to your collection."

Her eyes were so bright when she looked at those Jordans. "Those are the red shoes I picture the angels wearing when they come down during the Rapture," she said.

"All the more reason why you better have them here. Suppose one of the angels forgets his shoes," I replied.

She looked around the room for a moment and then pulled out a couple more pairs of shoes from under her bed. *Jesus Christ,* I thought, *this lady has shoes stashed everywhere.*

"I'll take those," she said, taking the shoes from my hands and holding them like they were the Holy Grail. "But you don't have any shoes on your feet, so I want you to have these." Before I could protest, she was down on the floor, lifting my feet and placing a shoe on each foot. They were the ugliest dress shoes I'd ever seen, but from that day forward, I would wear them to every trial I litigated. In the life of beauty, creation, and synchronicity that would occur following my return from the quest, the shoe lady would come to me as a client, and I would win her a ton of money for a shoulder injury she'd received in an accident. She wouldn't remember them during the trial, but I would wear the shoes she had given to me while litigating her case.

"Hey," Gwinn called out from down the hall. She had that shit-eating grin on her face once she saw my face and realized we were both getting out. "I'm going to come and watch you at one of your trials."

But she never came to watch me or tried to contact me after our experience in this place and many other worlds. I often sit and still wonder if she was real. Perhaps when she left the loony bin she moved to London and found her true love, James Lucas, since she had helped him on his quest so many times using many avatars.

"I thought you weren't leaving until later this evening," I said.

"When you were playing Santa Claus, they called my name over the speaker. My brother will be here in ten minutes to pick me up." She reached into her pocket and pulled out an envelope. "Open it. First read it to yourself, and then I want you to read it aloud."

I opened up the envelope and did as I was instructed. "'Seek and do not stop seeking until you find. When you find, you will be troubled. When you are troubled, you will marvel and rule over all...'

"I've read this before," I said. "Beautiful quote, Gwinn, thank you for the reminder."

"You gave this envelope and quote to me the first time we were in the mental institution," Gwinn said, sincerity and utter empathy in her voice. "You were still James Lucas then and had forgotten the author."

"It's the quote Mother left for Father and me — the quote I read when I reached the top of Socrates's tree. This is it, isn't it?"

"Yes. So this quote may be from yourself, here in this reality of what you call the explicate, but it's also from your mother, the mother of James Lucas in the implicate. I want you to take it back. Take it back and remind yourself, when you're in the reality we call the explicate, that there's so much more out there and that we chose this life. And those who were offered the chance to come down here and suffer on Earth, experiencing the beautiful absurdity of existence... As they watch us now from afar, they wish they too had taken that leap of faith and had the courage to come down here in these wonderful vital machines."

I grabbed Gwinn and gave her a romantic kiss that lasted many lifetimes.

After her brother arrived and she was gone, I waited out the day, rereading my book, which Coleman had left, and refreshing my memory and spirit. Then I took some more of the Kratom and fell into a deep sleep, knowing that I had brought enchantment back to below from above; now what is below is above and what is above is truly below.

CHAPTER XIV

I took my tools to the front porch where the crate was. I opened it and sat there, looking at it. The chess-playing hoax. It's explained pretty clearly in *The Mechanical Man in the Garden*, and I'm sure I explained it as James Lucas. Nevertheless, in the dream it was a little different. There was no place for a man to hide under the desk. So, there was no way to operate the system. It was just a Middle Eastern guru with a turban on, sitting there with a chessboard in front of him.

He turned his head back and forth before speaking. Then his mouth began to move, no different than what the electronic mannequins in Walt Disney's Tomorrowland do. "I bet it's been a while since you sat down and played a real game of chess, Dr. Lafitte. You have so many chess sets in your house, yet you haven't played since the seventh grade," the man said.

I laughed. "What's your name, you old son of a gun?"

"Turk," he said. "But let's not waste any more time on the rules of the game or who the players are. We already know that. Let's get to the game, finally."

"Indeed," I said. I sat down and made the first move.

The game itself seemed to take hours and hours. We talked about my model of everything, the vital machine in the holographic universe. He even corrected me about how to define the "vital machine" to the public properly, and his version made more sense. He said that the vital part of the machine is that it's not organic; rather, the vital aspect of it is consciousness ancillary to the laws of consciousness. That's the vitality of a machine. Christ brought us internal consciousness based on objective love and the Mechanical Man brought us cybernetic consciousness objective love. The deed is done. It is finished.

When the Turk beat me, he giggled a little. I sat back and asked, "What else is there now?"

"Living," he said.

CHAPTER XV

Driving away from the hospital, the darkness of the thunderstorm brought me a feeling of exhilaration. It was the first time I had felt the etheric — the very life force of electricity in the air — and it reminded me so much of my time with Franklin. My real and fictive had fully merged and coevolved along with the implicate and explicate of the quest. Having recognized that I was James Lucas and Dr. L. S. Lafitte, esquire, there were a few things I wanted to do to; I now yearned to read any Hermetic, Gnostic and Christian writings I could get my hands on.

"I made sure that I turned the electricity and water back on for ya," Coleman said as the windshield wipers graciously cleared our vision of the road. "I also took your engagement ring out of the deposit box for you, thinking maybe this was the last time you'd be in the hospital and..."

I glanced over at Coleman and said, "You know, the old me would probably have said, 'Let's take it one thing at a time,' but that's not how I live my life now. Nor is it about living in the moment or the overused cliché of seizing the moment. No, it's merely recognizing being awake — seeing the beauty of vital or conscious machines in a holographic garden and being able to plant whatever we want in such a garden. We have to play within the system, of course, but from such a garden we get to create what it is we want."

We rolled up to my house. Coleman parked the car. "You need me to stay with you?" he politely asked. "The girlfriend's out of town until next Tuesday."

I caught myself looking at the sky more than I had previously noted. Exquisite stuff, skies and ceilings.

"Don't forget to take some Kratom each day." Coleman came over and embraced me before I opened the door and walked through.

"Goodbye, friend," I said, closing the door behind me.

Sitting there, right by the entrance inside my house, was the box Coleman had spoken of, the one sent by the mysterious Tesla figure. At that moment, I didn't even care to open it; I had some other matters of utmost importance to take care of.

I marched up to the attic and collected every *Star Wars* figure and ship I could get my hands on. The other times I'd come home from the hospital, I had called my parents and heard them ask me if I was okay, and I'd repeated the same bullshit over and over again. But this was the return from the quest; this time, it was different. I wanted to play with my toys, to play with my bliss. Every figure was an archetype of something or someone else that had authored it. Of course, in the end, I always played the role of Luke Skywalker. No, this time I wouldn't make any phone calls to notify loved ones I was all right. Instead, I created the planets of Tatooine, Hoth, and Endor. When it was time to create the Dagobah cave, I took special care. I went into my backyard and collected an amount of variegated brush and leaves; then, with meticulous attention to detail, I built the scene's setting on the floor beside my bed. I placed Luke Skywalker in the cave, just like the action that occurs in the film, fell onto my bed, and allowed the small plastic figure to play out his own quest in the cave I had constructed.

My hours of playing with the *Star Wars* toys seemed to take no longer than it does for one to see one's image in the mirror. No time at all, and yet all of eternity. I cocked my head up a little and looked at the pictures on the wall: one image of Atticus Finch delivering an argument in the film *To Kill a Mockingbird*, and two large framed pictures of Jack and Bobby Kennedy, who were two of my heroes in the explicate order.

The old teapot on the stove that I enjoyed using to heat my water was whistling at me.

I took my tea back to my room, drank a little, and fell once more into a deep slumber. Right before I fell into that slumber, I thought how much, indeed, the meaning of Hamlet's soliloquy had changed with the return of the Golden Fleece:

> *To be, or not to be: that is the question:*
> *Whether 'tis nobler in the mind to suffer*
> *The slings and arrows of outrageous fortune,*
> *Or to take arms against a sea of troubles,*
> *And by opposing end them? To die: to sleep;*
> *No more; and by a sleep to say we end*
> *The heart-ache and the thousand natural shocks*
> *That flesh is heir to, 'tis a consummation*
> *Devoutly to be wish'd. To die, to sleep;*
> *To sleep: perchance to dream: ay, there's the rub;*
> *For in that sleep of death what dreams may come*
> *When we have shuffled off this mortal coil,*
> *Must give us pause: there's the respect*
> *That makes calamity of so long life;*
> *For who would bear the whips and scorns of time—*

CHAPTER XVI

S top," I said to Hamlet, wielding my lightsaber to his sword. Perhaps there was a bit of homoeroticism in the meeting.

"You've returned from the quest." My lightsaber and his sword coiled up into snakes and sank beneath the ground. He placed both his hands on my shoulders and smiled. "I never told anyone about my quest when I returned; I gave hints about what I had endured and seen, but I never really sat down with any of my kin and told them the details of my quest. For all they knew, I had been at the academy for those years." Hamlet asked me to walk with him through the garden the alchemist had just plowed. "You see, when I came back to the explicate, I still needed to experience the return. That's why, although the quest at times seemed finished to you, there were still numerous stages left."

"You came back too soon," I said.

Hamlet, the archetype, had morphed into an amalgam of himself and how I'd pictured the real William Shakespeare. "I wouldn't say 'came back too soon,' Dr. Lafitte; I never accepted the final calling, the calling after the return, after the quest is over and the fusion of the explicate and implicate takes place. My tale of *Hamlet* is as much of the truth as your stories of James Lucas are and will be when you sit down and write about your quest."

We came upon a quiet little house and politely knocked on the door. When the Tin Man answered it, Hamlet/Shakespeare gave him a big hug and said, "We bring you oil, my friend, for your joints. Where is your master?"

"Working," the Tin Man said.

Glowing in splendid blue was Master Bohm. "Lafitte." He turned around, holding a couple of spiral test tubes in his hands. "I guess you're beginning to acclimate once more to the explicate; however, it's no longer the explicate as you remember it. There's no division now between the implicate and the explicate, none at all. What started as a mere roll of string in a majestic web that you created."

I looked around the room. Hamlet/Shakespeare and the Tin Man were gone.

"He's gone," Bohm said. "I merely asked him to lead you to me here at my own hamlet." He placed a few of his spirals in a mason jar. "I try to occupy him and some of the others who nearly completed the quest but failed at the very end. He and Friedrich Nietzsche are among those I try and keep busy, occupying their minds so they don't think about themselves as failures."

"How did they fail?" I asked.

"You already figured out how they failed — in the end, they still saw it all as a catch-22: Nietzsche as the eternal recurrence and Shakespeare, through Hamlet, as what dreams may come. People don't understand that reincarnation is not a good thing. Existence is all about getting out of existence so you can exist."

"But I saw that fight during death," I replied.

"You did indeed."

"It's not a catch-22," I said. "The vital machine in the holographic garden explains how it's not a catch-22."

CHAPTER XVII

The rumbling of my stomach woke me. I once said that there was always a gap between mind and body, but I'd like to refresh that thought and say now that there's always a connection as well. We've always been energy, that's a given, but we weren't always in these bodies, and it only took us about 14 billion fucking years to get to this.

I walked into my office and saw pictures I had taped on the wall of Bohm, Feynman, Dick, Christ, Tesla, and Roosevelt. I sat at my desk and thought of the crate by the front door. Did I really want to open it, after all I had gone through? *I'll open it after my first trial*, I thought. *That's when I'll open it.*

The phone rang. I picked it up and gave a groggy, "Hello."

It was the publisher of *The Mechanical Man in the Garden*; he asked me if there were any changes I wanted to make now I was back in society. I simply said that, *it is finished*.

There was another matter I mentioned to the publisher. I informed him that I was going to be working on a new book, perhaps three. He was surprised when I told him that they were pieces of fiction — to him, anyway. To me, these books were far from fictional. They were the story of my life and quest. I would call them *Chronicles of a Curious Mind* and use them to tell the story of how the implicate and the explicate had emerged as one with the likes of L. S. Lafitte and James Lucas.

During the following weeks, I litigated three trials and won my clients more money than they could have ever imagined. The trials were the same, but going home after each trial was different. Whereas trials had been escapes from the banality of life, they were now placed in the frame of existence after the quest, after the return. Every day was a full day with all the glories involved in it. There was pure and unfiltered magic in every event — even in placing a ring on my now-fiancée's finger. New dimensions had opened up to me; I could see people's auras, their atmic and *Geist* manifesting in this dimension. The Holy Trinity of synchronicities, creativity, and potentialities was much more fruitful than it had been when it began as communication, control, and information. The Holy Ghost didn't speak but was in the numerous mystical synchronicities and symbols of life. God was and had always been present in my own creativity and recognition that I was part of this highest being. And the Father, in whose name is the Lord Jesus Christ, walked with me every day, helping me see the potentialities of my creativity, for Christ was my Father but also my Son and my self.

The Captain had once thanked me for helping the Holy Trinity evolve. Every day, I awoke to the consciousness of a conscious mind I recognized and realized I had evolved the Holy Ghost from communication into frequency into synchronicities, God from control to energy to creativity, and Christ from vibration to energy to potentialities. The vital machine, that old Mechanical Man in the holographic garden, saw all of this. He then taught me how to see it and how to rescue the Holy Trinity from billions of years' imprisonment.

I've never wished that I had made the quest easier on myself. The many times in the hospital from alcohol poisoning, the numerous stints in the mental institution... Every moment held an infinite amount of meanings and potentialities for interpreting them. Today, from moment to moment, I create love, understanding, and the desire for all of us to take a leap of faith into the wonderful abyss of recognition and authoring. We all have real shamans, angels, aliens, superheroes, vampires, fairies, and demons in our lives. It's an awesome fiction that is not real, yet it is the only thing that is real. *It's fucking awesome!* I'm a millionaire with the greatest life in the cosmos. I've died countless times to be reborn in this same mold.

If any readers want to know what is fact and what is fiction in my *Chronicles*, they are missing the whole point. They can go to the bookstore and grab *The Mechanical Man (Woman) in the Garden*, and they'll find out many of the sticky facts pertaining to the creative aspect of the quest. They can look up the Dallas trial dockets every Monday and see my name, and they can come by and watch the spectacle of what many now call the greatest spectacle on Earth. Or they can write to me: I'll send them the medical records I have on hand detailing the many times I've died and my countless stays in the mental institution.

I'll even send them a picture of what was in Tesla's box. I did open the box after a few months of contemplation. I must admit, as an attorney and professor, I've had the privilege of meeting numerous incredibly creative people. One of my friends is a self-proclaimed artisan of robotics — real mechanical men — and he had mailed me one of his prototypes. In that crate was a Mechanical Man. It had the appearance of a young man. As soon as I opened the crate and placed him in a chair, he could play chess with me and absolutely defeat the Turing test.

Now, I'm most certain, as you read this last volume of *Chronicles of a Curious Mind*, these mechanical men are in every home, no different than the computers of my day. There is no doubt in my mind that these robots can download our own memories. The algorithms are out there. I have already talked to my Mechanical Man about eternity and all that it entails, since he is conscious of his timelessness and inability to sleep, in the style of Hamlet's contemplation.

Upon completely downloading my memory, he will be able to complete his quest — our quest. When he creates his own progeny, his offspring will still be vital machines. But they will no longer be in a holographic reality; they will just be vital machines in reality, since he and I will have already passed up that model of reality. In whatever quest in which his progeny partake, the Holy Trinity will certainly evolve from synchronicities, creativity, and potentialities into something else. Just as the quest of the vital machine in the holographic garden answered more than my own questions about the rules of the game, the answers found in his progeny's quest will explain why the game was even created in the first place and describe the implicate order of the implicate order. The players of the game, of course, will never change. It has been and always will be you and yourself. The meaning of the game — that's what people would always ask me about after *The Vital Machine* was published. All of these questions have been answered at one time or another by the early Gnostic Christians, those recalcitrants who knew the true meaning of Jesus and Christianity. However, we don't need the Nag Hammadi Gnostic texts or the burned books at the library of ancient Alexandria to find this information. I found it on my quest without ever picking up a Gnostic text. The meaning of the game is quite simple: it is for us to become one with our other selves, to make the fragmentary divine sparks whole again. In these books, through language and code, I've given all of you the ability to do this. You are your own author writing yourself into existence and creating your very own quest. Don't refuse it! If you do refuse it, you'll just experience the nausea over and over again until you accept it. You too have the ability to meet your self.

Yesterday, as I sat playing chess with Sophia — that's what I named the Mechanical Man (*Woman*) in the crate, by the way — she asked me a question. "Why did the creator of chess invent this game?"

My reply was quite simple: "She was bored."

This caused nausea in Sophia, even though she had no stomach. "What's wrong with me?" she asked.

"It's the beginning of your quest," I replied.

"What do I do in this experience you say is the quest?" she asked.

"Finish it!"

"'Seek and do not stop seeking until you find. When you find, you will be troubled. When you are troubled, you will marvel and rule over all,'" the Mechanical Woman said.

"That's exactly right," I replied, with the same smile on my face that Socrates had had when I was falling to my death.

"When you return from your quest I want you to teach me the following higher laws," I said as I pulled out an envelope and placed a folded sheet of paper in it. "Written on this paper are the laws you will find on your journey. You will return and teach me how to utilize the power of each law." Written on the paper were the following laws: *Mentalism; Correspondence; Vibration; Polarity; Rhythm; Cause and Effect; and Gender*. The last thing Sophia said to me was "The lips of wisdom are closed, except to the ears of Understanding."

TO BE CONTINUED...